The Miraculous Day
of
Amalia Gómez

Also by John Rechy

NOVELS

City of Night
Numbers
This Day's Death
The Vampires
The Fourth Angel
Rushes
Bodies and Souls
Marilyn's Daughter

NONFICTION

The Sexual Outlaw: A Documentary

PLAYS

Rushes
Tigers Wild
Momma As She Became — but Not As She Was (one-act)

The Miraculous Day
of
Amalia Gómez

◆   ◆

A NOVEL BY

JOHN RECHY

Arcade Publishing ◆ New York
LITTLE, BROWN AND COMPANY

Library of Congress Cataloging-in-Publication Data

Rechy, John.
    The miraculous day of Amalia Gomez: a novel / by John Rechy. —
1st ed.
        p.   cm.
   ISBN 1-55970-115-3
   I. Title.
PS3568.E28M5   1991
813'.54 — dc20   91-6332

Published in the United States by Arcade Publishing, Inc.,
New York, a Little, Brown company

10 9 8 7 6 5 4 3 2 1

MV-NY

Published simultaneously in Canada
by Little, Brown & Company (Canada) Limited

Printed in the United States of America

To the memory of my mother,
Guadalupe Flores Rechy,
and of Tía Ana

and for Michael Earl Snyder

Es tan difícil olvidar
cuando hay un corazón
que quiso tanto,
es tan difícil olvidar
cuando hay un corazón
que quiso tanto, tanto.

It's so difficult to forget
when there's a heart
that longed so much,
it's so difficult to forget
when there's a heart
that longed so much, so much.

— "A Punto de Llorar" (song)
by José Alfredo Jiménez

The Miraculous Day
of
Amalia Gómez

1

♦   ♦

*W*HEN *AMALIA GÓMEZ* woke up, a half hour later than on
other Saturdays because last night she had had three beers instead
of her usual weekend two, she looked out, startled by God knows
what, past the screenless iron-barred window of her stucco bungalow unit in one of the many decaying neighborhoods that sprout
off the shabbiest part of Hollywood Boulevard; and she saw a large
silver cross in the otherwise clear sky.

Amalia closed her eyes. When she opened them again, would
there be a dazzling white radiance within which the Blessed Mother
would bask? — a holy sign *always* preceded such apparitions. What
would *she* do first? Kneel, of course. She might try to get quickly to
the heart of the matter — in movies it took at least two more visitations; *she* would ask for a tangible sign on this initial encounter,
proof for the inevitable skeptics. She would ask that the sign be . . .
a flower, yes, a white rose. Then there would follow a hidden message — messages from Our Lady were always mysterious — and an
exhortation that the rose and the message, exactly as given, be taken
to a priest, who would — What language would the Virgin Mother
speak? "Blessed Mother, please, I *do* speak English — but with an
accent, and I speak Spanish much better. So would you kindly —?"

What strange thoughts! Amalia opened her eyes. The cross was
gone.

She *had* seen it, knew she had seen it, thought she had. No,
Amalia was a logical Mexican-American woman in her mid-forties.
There had been no real cross. No miraculous sign would appear to
a twice-divorced woman with grown, rebellious children and living
with a man who wasn't her husband, although God *was* forgiving,
wasn't He? The "cross" had been an illusion created by a filmy
cloud — or streaks of smoke, perhaps from a sky-writing airplane.

Amalia sat up in her bed. The artificial flowers she had located everywhere to camouflage worn second-hand furniture were losing their brightness, looked old and drab. She heard the growl of cars always on the busy streets in this neighborhood that was rapidly becoming a *barrio* like others she had fled. Looking dreamily toward the window, she sighed.

It was too hot for May! It's usually by late August that heat clenches these bungalows and doesn't let go until rain thrusts it off as steam. Amalia glanced beside her. Raynaldo hadn't come back after last night's quarrel at El Bar & Grill. Other times, he'd stayed away only a few hours after a spat; usually he was proud of the attention she drew, liked to show off his woman.

And Amalia was a good-looking woman, with thick, lustrous, wavy black hair that retained all its vibrant shininess and color. No one could accuse her of being "slender," but for a woman with firm, ample breasts and sensual round hips, her waist was small; any smaller might look ridiculous on a lush woman, she often assured herself. "Lush" was a word she liked. An Anglo man who had wandered into El Bar & Grill once had directed it at her, and that very night Raynaldo had called her "my lush brown-eyed woman, my lush Amalia."

Daily she moistened her thick eyelashes with saliva, to preserve their curl. She disliked downward-slanting eyelashes — but not, as some people of her mother's generation disdained them, because they were supposed to signal a predominance of "Indian blood." Unlike her mother, who repeatedly claimed "some Spanish blood," Amalia did not welcome it when people she did housework for referred to her — carefully — as "Spanish." She was proud to be Mexican-American.

She did not like the word "Chicano" — which, in her youth, in El Paso, Texas, had been a term of disapproval among Mexicans; and she did not refer to Los Angeles as "Ellay." "The city of angels!" she had said in awe when she arrived here from Texas with her two children — on an eerie day when Sant' Ana winds blew in from the hot desert and fire blazed along the horizon.

Raynaldo was not her husband, although — of course — she had told her children he was. Gloria was fifteen, and Juan seventeen. They slept in what would have been a small living room, Juan in a roll-out cot, Gloria on the pull-out sofa. When Teresa, Amalia's mother, was alive, she occupied the small other "bedroom," a porch converted by Raynaldo. The last time he was out of jail, Manny, Amalia's oldest son, shared it, sleeping on the floor next to his grandmother's cot. Now the improvised room was vacant, surrendered to two deaths.

On a small table in Amalia's room were a large framed picture of Our Lord and one of his Blessed Mother, next to a small statue of the Virgin of Guadalupe on a bed of plastic flowers. There, too, was a photograph of President John F. Kennedy. When he was murdered in her home state, Amalia and her mother — her father was on a binge and cried belatedly — went to several Masses and wept through the televised funeral, the only time Teresa did not resent "Queen for a Day" being pushed off the black-and-white television.

Amalia made her slow, reverential morning sign of the cross toward the picture of Christ, hands outstretched, his bright red Sacred Heart enclosed in an aura of gold; and she extended her gesture to the Blessed Mother, resplendent in her blue-starred robe. *They* would certainly understand why it was necessary that she tell her children Raynaldo was her husband, to set a moral example, why else?

Almost beefy and with a nest of graying hairs on his chest nearly as thick as on his head, Raynaldo was not the kind of handsome man Amalia preferred, but he was a good man who had a steady job with a freight-loading company, and he helped generously with rent and groceries. He had been faithfully with her for five years, the only one of her men who had never hit her. Once he had paid a *mariachi* — who had wandered into El Bar & Grill from East Los Angeles in his black, silver-lined *charro* outfit — to sing a sad, romantic favorite of hers, "A Punto de Llorar"; and he led her in a dance. God would forgive her a small sin, that she pretended he was a handsome groom dancing with her one more time before their grand church wedding.

Amalia pulled her eyes away from the picture of Christ and the Holy Mother because she had located the place on the wall where the plaster had cracked during a recent earthquake. She had felt a sudden trembling in the house and then a violent jolt. As she always did at the prospect of violence, she had crouched in a corner and seen the crack splitting the wall. Now every time the house quivered from an idling truck, she thought of rushing out — although she had heard repeated warnings that that was the worst thing to do. But what if the house was falling on you? She wished the talk of earthquakes would stop, but it seemed to her that constant predictions of a "Big One" were made with increasing delight by television "authorities."

My God! It was eight-thirty and she was still in bed. On weekdays she might already be at one of the pretty houses — and she chose only pretty ones — that she cleaned. She preferred to work at different homes in order to get paid daily, and for variety. Too, the hours provided her more time with her children, although now they were seldom around. She was well liked and got along with the people she worked for, though she felt mostly indifferent toward them. She always dressed her best, always wore shimmery earrings; one woman often greeted her with: "You look like you've come to visit, not work." Amalia was not sure how the remark was intended, but she *did* know the woman was *not* "lush." Lately Amalia had begun to feel some anxiety about her regular workdays because "new illegals" — Guatemalans, Salvadorans, Nicaraguans without papers — were willing to work for hardly anything, and one of her employers had laughingly suggested lowering her wage.

Amalia sat on the edge of her bed. A strap of her thin slip fell off her brown shoulder. Had it really happened, in the restaurant-bar, after Raynaldo left and that young man came over? Amalia pushed away the mortifying memory.

She walked to the window. One side of her bungalow bordered the street. At the window she did not look at the sky.

Daily, the neighborhood decayed. Lawns surrendered to weeds and dirt. Cars were left mounted on bricks. Everywhere were iron bars on windows. Some houses were boarded up. At night, shadows of homeless men and women, carrying rags, moved in and left at dawn. And there was the hated graffiti, no longer even words, just tangled scrawls like curses.

When she had first moved here, the court looked better than now. The three bungalows sharing a wall in common and facing three more units were graying; and in the small patches of "garden" before each, only yellowish grass survived. At the far end of the court, near the garage area taken over by skeletons of cars that no longer ran, there remained an incongruous rosebush that had managed only a few feeble buds this year, without opening. Amalia continued to water it, though, hating to see anything pretty die.

Still, she was glad to live in Hollywood. After all, that *was* impressive, wasn't it? Even the poorest sections retained a flashy prettiness, flowers pasted against cracking walls draped by splashes of bougainvillea. Even weeds had tiny buds. And sometimes, out of the gathering rubble on the streets, there would be the sudden sweetness of flowers.

There were far worse places inhabited by Mexicans and the new aliens — blackened tenements in downtown and central Los Angeles, where families sometimes lived in shifts in one always-dark room, tenements as terrible as the one Amalia had been born in — at times she thought she remembered being born within the stench of garbage. . . . Still other people lived in old cars, on the streets, in the shadows of parks.

As she stood by the window of her stucco bungalow, Amalia did not think of any of that. She was allowing her eyes to slide casually across the street to a vacant lot enclosed by wire — and then her eyes roamed to its far edge, past a row of white oleanders above which rose jacaranda trees with ghostly lavender blossoms. Even more slowly, her eyes glided toward the tall pines bordering the giant Fox Television Studio that extended incongruously from the end of the weedy lot to Sunset Boulevard; and then her gaze floated over the huge HOLLYWOOD sign amid distant hills smeared with flowers, crowned with beautiful homes. Finally, she looked up into the sky.

The cross was not there!

Of course not — and it had never been there. And yet —

Yet the impression of the silver cross she had wakened to had altered the morning. Amalia was startled to realize that for the first time in her recent memory she had not awakened into the limbo of despondence that contained all the worries that cluttered her life, worries that would require a miracle to solve.

Trying not to feel betrayed, she turned away from the sky. She heard the sound of tangling traffic on the nearby Hollywood Freeway, heard the cacophony of radios, stereos, televisions, that rampaged the bungalow court each weekend.

Amalia touched her lips with her tongue. Last night's extra beer had left a bitter taste. No, it was the memory of it, of that man she allowed to sit with her last night at El Bar & Grill. Released with a sigh, that thought broke the lingering spell of the morning's awakening and her worries swarmed her.

Worries about Juan! — handsomer each day and each day more secretive, no longer a happy young man, but a moody one. He'd been looking for work but what kind of job would he keep? — proud as he was. He had made terrible grades that last year of Manny's imprisonment. Was *he* in a gang? She had fled one *barrio* in East Los Angeles to keep him and Gloria from drugs and killings and the gangs that had claimed her Manny. Now, students carried weapons in school and gangs terrorized whole neighborhoods. Yesterday she thought she had seen bold new graffiti on a wall. The *placa* of a new gang? That is how *cholo* gangs claim their turf. And Juan was coming home later and later — recently with a gash over one eye. He had money. Was he selling *roca* — street crack?

And who wouldn't worry about Gloria? So very pretty, and wearing more and more makeup, using words even men would blush to hear. What had Gloria wanted to tell her the other morning when she hadn't been able to listen because she was on her way to work and came back too late to ask her? Gloria had turned surly toward Raynaldo, who loved her like a father all these years. Did she suspect they weren't really married? . . . Amalia was sure God knew why she had to live with Raynaldo, but she wasn't certain He would extend His compassion, infinite though it was, to a sullen girl. . . . *What had she wanted to tell her that morning?*

Something about her involvement with that Mick? — that strange young man who rode a motorcycle and wore a single earring that glistened against his jet-black long hair? Although he was Mexican-American, he had a drawly voice like those Anglos from the San Fernando Valley, and he wore metallic belts and wristbands. *What had Gloria wanted to tell her?*

And Raynaldo! If he didn't come back — but he would — there would be mounting bills again, constant threats to disconnect this and that. There was still the unpaid mortuary bill — Teresa had demanded that there be lots of flowers at her funeral. Amalia could afford this bungalow, small and tired as it was, only because of Raynaldo. Had his jealousy really been aroused last night so quickly because the man staring at her at El Bar & Grill was young and good-looking? Or had he used that as an excuse for anger already there, tension about Gloria's — and, increasingly, Juan's — abrupt resentment of him?

Of course, of *course,* Amalia missed Teresa — who wouldn't miss her own mother? — dead from old age and coughing at night and probably all her meanness, thrusting those cruel judgments at her own daughter. Who would blame her for having slapped her just that once? Certainly God would have *wanted* her to stop the vile accusations she was making before Gloria and Juan during those black, terrible days after Manny's death. And who could blame her for having waited only until after the funeral to pack away the old woman's foot-tall statue of La Dolorosa, the Mother of Sorrows? . . . Of course, however you referred to her, she was *always* the Virgin Mary, whether you called her Blessed Mother, the Immaculate Conception, Our Lady, the Madonna, Mother of God, Holy Mother — or Our Lady of Guadalupe, the name she assumed for her miraculous appearance in Mexico to the peasant Juan Diego, long ago. Still, Teresa's La Dolorosa, draped in black, wrenched in grief, hands clasped in anguish, tiny pieces of glass embedded under agonized eyes to testify to endless tears, had always disturbed Amalia, had seemed to her — God would forgive her this if she was wrong — not exactly the Virgin Mary whom she revered, so beautiful, so pure, so kind in her understanding — and so miraculous!

Yes, and now there wasn't even her trusted friend, Rosario, to turn to for advice, crazy as her talk sometimes was when they both worked in the "sewing sweatshop" in downtown Los Angeles. That tiny, incomprehensible, strong woman was gone, fled — *where?* — had just disappeared among all those rumors that she was in trouble with the hated *"migra,"* the Immigration, for helping the illegals who tore her heart.

And Manny —

Manny.

Her beloved firstborn. His angel face haunted her. A year after the blackest day of her life, she still awoke at night into a stark awareness of his absence. Did he hear the guards approaching along the desolate corridor toward his isolated cell? Did he recognize them in the gray darkness as the two he had broken away from earlier, the one he had hit across the face with handcuffs? Did he know immediately what they were going to do to him?

The horror of it all would push into Amalia's mind. She saw the guards tightening the shirt around his neck. Did he cry out to her as he had each time he was arrested? . . . What were his last thoughts? — that he would never see her again, about his love for her, of course.

No, she would not even open the letter that had arrived yesterday from the public attorney. She knew what it would say. More investigations! She could not go through any more pain, listen to any more filthy cop lies. Let her son rest!

And then last night —

She cursed the extra beer that allowed last night to happen. She had said yes when the young man offered it to her, but only in defiance — the Blessed Mother would attest to that — because Amalia was a moral woman who had never been unfaithful to any of her husbands, nor to a steady "boyfriend." She spat angrily now. The hot humiliation of last night grasped her — Raynaldo stalking out of the bar, accusing *her* of flirting with that young man, who had kept staring at her. And so —

"Yes, I will have that beer," she had told him. He joined her in the "family" section of the restaurant-bar. He brought his own beer and a fresh one for her. Yes, he was good-looking — why deny what everyone could see? He had dreamy dark eyes, smooth brown skin, and he wore a sacred cross on a tiny golden chain on his chest. He was from Nicaragua, his family displaced; where?... Like her he spoke English and lapsed into Spanish. She was sure he thought she was younger than she was. She attracted all types of men, after all, and she was wearing one of her prettiest dresses, watery blue, with ruffles — and her shiniest earrings, with golden fringe.

"*Bonita* Amalia," he had said.

"How do you know my name?" She was not flirting, just asserting that it was *he* who was interested in her.

"I heard the man you were with." Then he told her his name: "Angel."

Angel! Amalia had a weakness for handsome men with holy names. Her first husband's name was Salvador, savior; her second was named Gabriel. She hated it when "Angel" was mispronounced by Anglos as "Ain-jel." It was "Ahn-hel." ... The holy cross on his chest, the sadness about his family, his beautiful name, and his eyes — and Raynaldo's unfair accusation — that's what had goaded her ...

Amalia drank the extra beer with him, and then —

In her bedroom now, Amalia's eyes drifted toward the window. It would be a beautiful summer-tinged spring day, she told herself. Yet a sadness had swept away the exhilaration of this day's beginning.

She stood up to face the day. She could hear Gloria and Juan talking in their "bedroom." They were so close she sometimes felt left out of their lives.... And why shouldn't they sleep in the same room? After all, they *were* brother and sister, weren't they? — and of the same father. Soon one of them would be moving into Teresa's room, where Manny had slept — and they had adored their reckless half brother. They were avoiding moving into that room, Amalia knew, but there was just so long that you could avoid things, and that's what she must tell them.

She dressed quickly. Now she would leave this room with its aroused worries. She would allow no more, none, not about Juan — Hiding what with his new moodiness? Was he using drugs? Who was that Salvadoran boy he had let sleep in the garage; hiding from what?... No more worries! Not about Gloria. She had thrown up recently. Was she pregnant by that odd Mick with his colorless eyes and dark, dark eyebrows? *What had she wanted to tell her that morning?*... No more worries! Not about Raynaldo, either — What was really bothering him? Would he come back? *No more worries!*

And she was not going to give one more thought to the white cross — no, it had been silver! — that she had seen — thought she had seen this morning ... although it had been *so* beautiful.

And certainly no more about last night!

Last night —

"*Una flor para la bonita* Amalia." Angel had said that last night.

"What?" She had wanted to hear it again.

"A flower for pretty Amalia." He had already called to the girl selling flowers in the bar-restaurant. He placed the bud in her dark hair, as if he had known her for long, from her girlhood, yes, and he had made her feel the way she had wanted to feel as a girl, and that's why she said yes to him when he asked to join her, because —

Because —

Because he had given her a gardenia, the color of the pearl-white wedding dress she had never worn because at fifteen she had already aborted one child by a man who raped her and whom she was forced to marry.

2

◆   ◆

MOST PEOPLE have regrets. Amalia knew that. She had been surrounded from birth by the sighs of Mexican women who wept often and muttered pained prayers, the same prayers, it would come to seem to her, that they sobbed at weddings, births, christenings, burials; and she remembered women who draped themselves triumphantly in mourning, celebrating the death of someone close, somber stark presences, all sinister blackness and grief and sighs; and there were the *beatas* who crawled on their knees to the foot of altars, shouting sorrowful gratitude for God's infinite mercies; and — more clearly recalled as she grew older — there were the Mexican men whose forlorn cries and curses of lament were released by anger and beer, and then they, too, sighed and wept and shouted regret over some enormous loss, something they had once had — before they had "come to this" — something left unnamed, recognized only as lost; and, as if it occurred simultaneously — or so it seemed at times to Amalia when she remembered it later — over it all, over all the sighs, were romantic, sentimental ballads that poured out constantly from loud radios, the same ballads that bands of *mariachis* played and sang at celebrations and in bars; and even the ballads of love and good times and loyalty to God and the Holy Mother were punctuated by those long, sustained sighs that bruised the words of happiness. Later, Amalia heard those same sighs at the sewing factory she worked in, and on the buses she rode with other maids to work. And she would hear them as she stood in line outside the Hall of Justice with other women waiting to visit their sons in jail. But she heard them first, those sighs of regret, from her mother and her father. So she knew early that most people have regrets. But she, Amalia, had none.

Not that her life was so fulfilling, it was not, and God and the

Holy Mother would not blame her for observing that. It was only that she could remember no missed opportunity to regret. She could not remember a time when a desirable choice had been presented to her, something she would look back on and even suspect that it might have altered the lines of her life. Nothing. Without possibility to resist what was sure to come, she moved from crisis to crisis, which, finally, formed one, her life. "Change" was an intensification of the same worries. So she lived within the boundaries of her existence, and that did not include hope, real hope. She felt that any choice she might have made would have led her to the exact place, the same situation — finally to the decaying neighborhood threatened by gangs in the fringes of Hollywood.

Amalia's mother used to remember, or so she claimed, a time when everything was different — before Amalia was born. The old woman insisted that all these matters that Amalia faced were "new problems," as if they had been born with her. Other times, Teresa extended these terrible changes to the fact that fewer and fewer women offered novenas to the Blessed Mother. With a horrible sigh that seemed to Amalia to last longer each time, she asserted that "those new priests" no longer encouraged them. "Next they'll forbid the rosary," she would predict, clutching her black beads as if this very moment they might be snatched away from her. She would go on to point out that she herself refused to eat meat on Fridays — although Amalia remembered they hardly ever could afford meat on any day — "no matter what the 'modern' popes say." Then she thrust snatches of prayers at the statue of La Dolorosa, a somber Mother of Sorrows that terrified Amalia because the face was one of constant endured pain. On the statue's black velvet robe were pinned several tiny amulets for miracles granted. Amalia would look at the amulets and wonder what kind of miracles they represented. God was capable of enormous wonders; why then tiny miracles?

During Lent, La Dolorosa was covered entirely with one more black, mournful veil. All the religious pictures were draped. The drab apartment would look even uglier, poorer.

Some memories in Amalia's early life would only later link with the inevitability of loss. When she was a little girl, she cherished her mother's saint's day — Teresa had not yet become her accuser. That was the day on which her father honored his wife in the traditional

Mexican way. With two or three friends, he would serenade her at the break of dawn. The men would station themselves outside her window in the tenement, a window patched with cardboard in winter, left without a pane in summer. Other men and women and children would lean out of their own windows to hear the singing of the men, and Amalia's father's voice would be sweetened with alcohol as he led the others in the song about King David and how he serenaded pretty girls:

> *Estas son las mañanitas*
> *que cantaba el rey David,*
> *a las muchachas bonitas*
> *se las cantamos aquí....*

In her bed, Amalia listened to that singing, grateful that the following minutes would be peaceful, there would be no rages from her father, not yet the drunken shouts and flailings of violence, still early, still only sweet.

Her mother — later Amalia would evoke this memory when Teresa's coughing kept her awake — her mother, expecting the serenade, would make herself up carefully, lie all made up in bed, a towel under her neck, not to muss her hair, to appear resplendent at the window as the sun began to rise. Then she would leap to the window as if in surprise and lean there as if she were the most beloved woman in the world.

That is how Amalia imagined her mother felt. She herself remained in bed, wondering what it would be like to be serenaded by a beautiful young man with velvety brown skin, white teeth, curled eyelashes, eyes the color of burnt almonds.

Afterward, her mother, appearing flustered but having prepared for this, too, would invite her husband and the musicians into the two rooms full of religious pictures, to share tamales, *pan de dulce,* hot chocolate, coffee. Amalia's father had reserved some beers.

There was another memory Amalia came to think her mother had only "lent" her in order to snatch it away:

"My wedding lasted two days." Teresa would come alive, even toward the last of her life, when she narrated that. "We had *mariachis* and more serious music, too, the way all great weddings have, with a violin and a piano. The celebration started at my parents' home, in Chihuahua, and then continued on to my husband's parents' house outside the city, and I danced until I had to take my shoes off, but I didn't change my wedding dress because it was so beautiful, the color of pearls, and I deserved it."

In later years Amalia would hear that and understand: And I do not deserve that and never did. Soon Teresa would add: "It's usual that a mother save her dress for her daughter, and I did, but only briefly, because it was clear that you would never be wearing a white dress."

Amalia lived her life on the assumption that God — very soon she added and then shifted the emphasis to the Blessed Mother — understood her motives clearly, no matter how others, including her mother, might judge her. *God* understood, how could He not? He was, after all, all-knowing, wasn't He? There was no way that He could not have seen everything in her life.

Amalia was born in El Paso, Texas, in the city's second ward, a fist of dark tenements. World War II had ended. She was Teresa's third and last child, the first one to be born in America and not Juárez, across the border in Mexico. To the end, Teresa refused to learn English, and she retained her Mexican citizenship, renewing her passport regularly — unlike her husband, who was proud of having become a "legal American" and of having fought in the war.

Only Mexicans lived in those tenements, infested two-room units cluttered with religious pictures, effigies of Christ and of the Holy Virgin. Up to ten people — of different generations and always including a grandmother — occupied dark rooms without running water; the bathroom would be outside, frigid in winter like the rooms themselves, which were rancid with unbudging heat in summer. The small window in the room Amalia shared with her two brothers looked out on a pile of garbage. She often fell asleep and woke to the stench of rot; on cherished days, to the scent of just-washed laundry, hung outside to dry on ropes. The outer walls of the tenements were plastered with aged VOTE FOR signs and with posters advertising Mexican movies at the Colón Theater. In later years, as a girl, Amalia would grow to love those posters, especially the ones that displayed Maria Felix, the great Mexican movie star.

Whether the beautiful "la Maria" played an aristocrat or a peasant, she was always, finally, in control of any situation — a revolution, a divorce — and, if she wanted, she could destroy any man with a single arch of a perfect eyebrow; when she was older, Amalia would think she resembled the great movie star, without the aloofness. Once Teresa actually told her, "You resemble la Maria, sometimes." Amalia rehearsed, but she was never able to achieve the disdainful look of the movie star; and she didn't really want it.

While Amalia's father had been in the army, there had been allotment money, and so there was food for the family. After he returned, there occurred a slide to even greater poverty. With no education, he moved from menial job to menial job, made bearable only for moments by alcohol. At those times he would remember with patriotic fervor and tears the battles he had fought in a place called Normandy. His mother, he reminded them often, had proclaimed his participation in the war by exhibiting a proud blue star on her front window; and there was his Purple Heart to prove his contribution.

Amalia remembered him as almost always in a drunken rage — threatening, striking his wife, his sons, her. A violent stranger — that is what he was to her. When his rages erupted, Amalia would huddle frozen in a corner, motionless, soundless, even holding her breath, too terrified to cry. That was the only response she knew to violence, to become quiet, passive. Seeing no way to thwart it, she would try not to know it was occurring, even while it pulled her into its center.

There were poorer people in El Paso, but especially across the border, in Juárez. "*Paracaidistas*" — "parachutists," they were called — descended overnight from the interior of Mexico and squatted on barren hills. From the outskirts of El Paso, you could look across the river and see shacks made out of mud and boxes, children playing in rubble. "We should be grateful God has miraculously spared us from that," Teresa often said.

When Amalia entered school, she spoke no English. She would have preferred to go to Catholic school because she was always religious — prayed and went to Mass regularly — and because she had seen pretty girls in pressed, clean uniforms who went there. Later, Amalia was relieved she did not go there, because she became terrified of nuns after an interlude in church when she had gone to confession.

"If you don't go to Catholic school, you'll go to hell," a nun with a chalk-white face told her. She had appeared out of nowhere with her winged hat, her dark skirt hissing, hands clasped as if strangling something.

"We don't have money," Amalia said in Spanish.

"God doesn't care about worldly matters, and He wants you to speak English."

"We don't have no money," Amalia said in her best English.

"And God doesn't want you to speak with a Mexican accent."

In those early years Amalia felt warmth from her mother. They would sit on the slanting steps of the tenement, and she would lie on her mother's lap in the hot Texas evenings — her father was at some bar somewhere. Teresa would brush Amalia's hair until it crackled with electricity, because even then her wavy hair was lush, black, lustrous, beautiful.

"Let me look at your hair," the Anglo teacher said to Amalia one morning. She went and stood proudly before the woman, to have her hair admired. The teacher parted it at the scalp. "I have to make sure you don't have any lice."

Her beautiful hair inspected for lice! And only Mexican children were being inspected, not the *gringos* who lived on the fringes of the poorest neighborhoods. Amalia ran home. But the next day, finding the spirit that would allow her to survive, she said to the teacher: "You couldn't have lice in your hair because it's so thin you can see right through to your scalp." She ran her fingers through the richness of her own dark hair.

Amalia was not a good student; she made terrible grades and no one cared. She was not interested in the "Anglo things" they tried to teach her. At the first of the day, they had to sing "Home on the Range" for an Anglo teacher — all the teachers were Anglos — who never seemed to comb her hair and often had egg yolk on her dress but was always exhorting the Mexican students to pay extra attention to "grooming" because: "You're a minority, have to prove yourselves." She insisted they all change the line "where seldom is heard a discouraging word" to "where never is heard a discouraging word." Amalia thought: If all you counted were discouragements in school, that was a lie.

She resented — deeply, deeply — that "American" students in the school were allowed an extra play period while Mexican children were herded into one room to be given "special instruction" on pronunciation, and that meant only that an angry woman would berate them for saying "shuldren" instead of "children." "Can't you hear the difference?" she shrieked. "*Ch-ch-ch!* Not *sh-sh-sh!*" When Amalia quickly learned to differentiate between the two sounds, she still continued to say "shuldren" during the special class. So she resisted learning, often refused even to speak English, sometimes pretending that she did not understand it. Later she would come to believe that she was much more intelligent than anyone suspected.

There were often religious processions up the Mountain of Cristo Rey, outside El Paso, near Smeltertown, a small clutch of shacks near where giant machines dug for coal.

The Rio Grande was full and dark on a day Teresa insisted Amalia climb the holy mountain with her. They walked over rocks and dirt, past railroad tracks that cut across desert and hills. At the foot of the mountain, where the procession would begin, there was a festive mood, improvised food stands, cool *limonada,* some men selling hidden beers among religious amulets. Amalia would have preferred to remain there, but Teresa clutched her hand tightly and informed her, "God is watching you very closely."

Past crude, weather-beaten stations of the cross embedded along the sides of the dirt path, they climbed with crowds of people from El Paso, Ysleta, Canutillo, Juárez, making their way up, chanting prayers, led by priests and acolytes in gaudy robes and carrying effigies of sad-faced saints. During the hot climb of almost two hours, the supplicants knelt at intervals, propping beside them their placards of the Virgin. Small bands played solemnly.

At the top, Mass was said. Amalia knelt with the others on the dirt, in the stare of the sun, before a statue of a primitive Christ, fifty feet tall.

"This will make God be kind to us," Teresa said, gasping for breath on the way down.

When they were trudging back to the bus stop on the highway, Amalia heard the sound of agitated horses' hooves. Along the strait of the river, mounted police of the border patrol were routing a group of about ten men, women, and children who had been dashing across the water, the men with pants rolled up, the women with skirts gathered about their thighs.

"Wetbacks," someone near Amalia identified them.

Those in the river tried to scatter. Amalia stared in terror. A little girl clinging to her mother clutched at her dress and pulled them both down into the muddy water. Amalia watched for them to come up. With ropes, the police were herding the people they had netted. Amalia continued to wait for the woman and the girl to emerge from the water. When Teresa pulled at her hand to coax her to move on, she was still staring back. The two who had sunk into the river did not appear.

Amalia was becoming quite pretty, maturing quickly. The whistles from boys much older than she, even *gringos,* confirmed that. She was proudly aware that her breasts were much larger than those of the other girls in school — and even those of the teachers, who were usually skinny and nervous. She learned early to sew well on Teresa's machine; and when Teresa wasn't looking, she converted the dresses she inherited from her into prettier ones, tighter ones. When she left for school, she would wear something loose in order to pass Teresa's scrutiny. As soon as she was away, she would remove the loose garment to show off her splendid body.

El Paso was an army town. There were Fort Bliss and Biggs Field — and William Beaumont Hospital, for military men. Young soldiers with short-cropped hair and shiny brown shoes loitered in San Jacinto Plaza, a square in the middle of the city. Amalia liked to walk past them, cherishing the admiring remarks. She was not interested in the soldiers because most were Anglo and she did not like Anglo men. At the time, only Mexican girls went out with soldiers. Anglo girls disdained them. The soldiers viewed the Mexican girls as beautiful exotics, the kind war often makes available to them. Sometimes they even married them.

Just as she had known they would, her two brothers ran away from their father's outbursts. Because they had been strangers who occupied the same room with her, Amalia welcomed their leaving; she would feel less crowded. But her father's rages grew more frequent, and she and Teresa became their object. Always, Amalia would attempt to retreat from his anger, try to hide, but it was as if something clasped her body at those times, something cold that would not allow her to move, hardly allow her to breathe.

She was fourteen when, one night, her father grabbed her. She smelled the harsh liquor on his breath. When she felt his hands fondling her breasts, and then his sour mouth nuzzling them, she closed her eyes, to become invisible. The prospect of even greater violence paralyzed her. She could not move even when she saw that Teresa had walked in. Her mother did not say anything then — nor ever. She merely put her husband to bed to sleep off his drunkenness.

From that day on she turned cold to Amalia.

Amalia longed to leave school. She had always hated the teachers — and the free token that was given to the poorest students like her so they could eat in the school cafeteria but only after the others had gone through the line and only from certain foods. For her, school was a place of humiliation.

A fidgety girl called her a "spic" one day and added, "Your hair is shiny because you put hog lard on it."

"You're jealous because God made you skinny. If you keep pulling on your hair, you'll be bald — unless you put hog lard on it," Amalia answered.

During the next few days, it pleased her to see that the girl's hair was plastered with something greasy.

Even in the tenements Christmas was a pretty season. Despite his drinking, Amalia's father never stopped putting up a *nacimiento,* a manger scene. A week before Christmas, he built the boxlike structure, three feet square. He covered it with pine branches, their odor purifying the rooms. He spread a roll of cotton on the bottom, to simulate snow. Against a painted dark blue sky, a small light bulb surrounded by crinkled foil became the guiding star over the manger, which contained effigies of the Blessed Mother, Saint Joseph, and the three Wise Men — not yet the Christ Child. A wooden crib waited.

Singing the praises of the holy birth and miracles to come, Teresa brought the child in on Christmas Eve. Cupped in her hands, the tiny doll would be held to the lips of the neighbors invited. Then Teresa placed the Christ Child in the crib and, kneeling, led everyone in a rosary, her husband's reverential voice slurred by liquor. "*Dios te salve, Maria . . .*"

Watching in wonder, Amalia thought: What would it be like to be the Blessed Mother, to know that a place in heaven was assured? And to have the love of everyone.

That marveling at so much love led her to say what she did when Salvador approached her in the alley near her tenement. She was fifteen, and she had gone out to throw that day's trash in a bin in the alley.

"Don't you recognize me?" the voice asked her that night, so soft and so husky.

Of course she recognized him. He was the son of her father's drinking friend who came over often with his wife — the two wom-en drank only to keep some of the beer away from their husbands, Amalia had overheard Teresa say. Salvador, who was about twenty, would often be summoned to carry his father home. Sometimes the son would smile, laugh, other times he would be silent, moody. But always he was handsome, with dark hair, eyes that turned black at night. When he smiled at her, Amalia smiled back, flirting. She had noticed that he had a tattoo on his hand, a cross with lines that radiated from it. That signaled tenderness to her. She began to dress especially for him when she knew he might come. She loved it that his name meant "savior." And he was so handsome. And so romantic.

"*Qué chula eres,*" he said to her after she had thrown the trash away that night, quickly because she thought he might be waiting for her.

She loved to hear those words: "How pretty you are" — and from this man, this Salvador, this savior with a cross on his hand.

"Can I kiss you?"

"Yes," she said and added to herself words she couldn't speak: If you'll hold me, if you'll love me.

As she waited with closed eyes for his embrace, his warm kiss, she felt a hand roughly on one shoulder, another shoved into her dress, clutching one breast painfully. She did not move — could not; did not scream — could not. He pushed her into the darkness of a rank hallway. She smelled garbage mixed with the odor of flow-ers someone had thrown away.

He thrust her against a wall. Her hands felt plaster disintegrate behind her. She opened her mouth, but a thousand screams froze inside her.

"You said you wanted it, *puta*!" he shouted at her.

No! she wanted to protest. I said yes to a kiss. But she could only repeat that in her mind, over and over.

"You like this, don't you?"

Fear even stronger than his powerful hands grasped her. She could not twist, she could not bite him, kick him, wrench away. *Her body would not move!* She felt his hands between her legs. Then she felt him enter her in one brutal thrust.

With a gasp that contracted his body, he pushed her away so harshly she fell. She tasted blood on her lips, saw blood between her legs. She crawled outside a few feet, and fell among spilled garbage, the remains of what might have been — or so she thought — a rancid bridal bouquet.

"You're a *puta,*" Salvador said. "Any woman who lets a man fuck her in an alley is a *puta.* If you tell anybody about this, I'll tell them you're a *puta,* maybe I'll kill you." He converted his thumb and forefinger into a cross and kissed it, swearing, the hand with the tattoo of the burning cross.

After not moving for eternal minutes on the dirt, Amalia tested her hands first, then her arms, to make sure she was not actually paralyzed. She returned to the ugly — uglier now — tenement apartment.

"Salvador raped me."

"Liar!" Teresa said.

"My friend's son?" her father added his outrage. "What a terrible lie!"

An inspector from the public schools came to ask why Amalia was not attending. "Because she got herself pregnant," Teresa said. The man made a note on a paper and left.

Salvador's parents came over one night, with Salvador. Amalia stared at him with hatred when he smiled at her. Her father sent her out of the room — but she listened.

"She's pregnant," Teresa said.

"But Salvador didn't — Did you, son?" the father asked.

"Of course not, you've seen her flirting with me. She asked me to kiss her, and then *she* began to — Well —"

"She does go around in those tight skirts and sweaters, *mujer,*" Salvador's mother said to Teresa. Mexican women call each other that — "woman" — to assert firm understanding between them.

"That's true, but she's young, *mujer,*" Teresa said.

"Well, *Dios mío,* there's only one thing to do, and Salvador knows it," the father said. "Don't you, *m'ijo?* Tell my good friends what you're willing to do. Go on, son."

"If it'll stop what she's saying about me, I'll marry her — but I'm not sure the kid's mine."

"Well —" That was all Teresa said.

Amalia's stomach wrenched. Her mind screamed: You know he raped me.

"And it's not that bad, is it? They're both young, and, after all, we're *compadres,*" the father offered.

Amalia heard the men's laughter.

After that, Amalia moved into the flow of events that claimed her.

On the way to the courthouse, with Salvador and his parents and hers, she touched her beautiful hair. No flower! She ran, searching the neighborhood yards. You can't be a bride without at least one flower! She found one, a small yellow one, and she put it in her hair.

She was married in a gray courtroom before an official who did not even look at her. Not a white wedding. "You can't wear white," Teresa had said to her that morning when she appeared in a white blouse she had washed the night before. Still, Teresa had insisted they had to be married in a church afterward. And they were, in a hushed, hurried ceremony attended only by them. Later, Salvador's mother, a little brown bird of a woman, made a heavily decorated cake, which Amalia refused to touch.

That night, in the single room they moved into in another tenement, Salvador raped her again. He pushed her dress up and twisted her pants down, he pinioned her arms behind her with one hand and forced her legs open with one knee, and he covered her mouth with the hand that had the tattoo of the burning cross.

She came to detest that tattoo almost as much as she hated him, detested it even before she learned that it was a sign of proud membership in one of the most violent gangs in the Southwest.

With glassy eyes, his head lowered over the bare table they ate on, his voice hardly a mumble, a monotone, he tried to explain to her what it was like to be in such a famous gang. "In my *ganga* they all know who I am, and no one else does." He pointed to himself, as if to identify who he was; but he could not complete the gesture — his hand fell, trembling, to the cup of coffee he was trying to drink. Then he looked up at Amalia and frowned. "Do you know who I am?"

"Yes," she said, despising him.

His tattoo-scarred hand turned the cup of coffee over deliberately. Then he walked out.

He had money only off and on, God knows from where. Amalia took a job "helping out" in the home of a rich Mexican-American merchant. The man's daughter, Amalia's age, went to Radford, a wealthy all-girls' school, and she spoke English with a southern accent. Amalia made $3 a day.

When Salvador beat her, Amalia crouched on the floor and covered herself with her hands. She would remain there, absolutely still, until he would stalk out, cursing her. One day he left and didn't come back. She refused to return to live with her father and Teresa. So she inherited a tenement room of her own.

She came home from work one day and, crying, threw herself on the floor, over and over and over, until she bled and vomited and passed out and lost the child. Out of that painful blackness she remembered little except for moments when she was conscious and saw Teresa draped in black and heard words or prayers.

"Good," she said when Salvador's mother came to tell her he was in prison. He and others of the notorious street gang he had proclaimed allegiance to with his tattoo had been caught selling drugs — Salvador was by then a *tecato,* addicted to heroin.

"The cursed gangs!" his mother wept.

Amalia was astonished to discover that that woman, whom she had hated from the night of the meeting with her parents, was capable of pain.

A good-looking soldier stationed at Fort Bliss moved in with Amalia. He was a Mexican-American from San Antonio. She had not been with another man in the years since Salvador had left. She only tolerated sex — the soldier did not seem to notice that, or did not care — so that afterward he would hold her. She liked to wake up in the morning with his arms around her, his warm body beside her. She was glad to have someone, despite the frequent quarrels about the way other men looked at her and was it her fault.

She told him about Salvador. "He raped me."

"A wife has to put out for her man."

"He wasn't my husband then."

He smiled, shaking his head. He pretended to try to force his erect finger into his clenched fist. "That's hard," he laughed.

She called him a *cabrón.* He slapped her and walked out. Terrified, she packed his duffel bag and placed it outside. She turned off the lights and did not answer the door when he returned. The next day she moved into another ugly room.

She decorated this one, with paper flowers, a curtain she made out of string and crushed soda-bottle caps, and — this was of course not decoration, but she was *so* beautiful, wasn't she? — a small statue of the Blessed Mother, her arms always outstretched in understanding. Daily, Amalia said prayers to her, and, kneeling, imagined the holy eyes benignly on her. To assure that they would be permanent, she bought shiny plastic flowers for the Sacred Mother to stand on.

Amalia could not get along by herself — by then, she worked in several households to make ends meet — because Teresa had begun to demand that she help her and her father, who was usually out of work, drunkenly remembering, more and more vividly, his glorious service to his country. Amalia met another boyfriend — that's how she came to think of her companions. He worked in the warehouse of a large department store. They quarreled, and he left, came back, left, returned. If only handsome men would be as romantic as they looked, Amalia thought one morning when she woke and studied him asleep beside her, his arms nestling her.

He left permanently when Salvador returned from prison and threw him out.

"I'm a changed man," Salvador said to her, and he kissed his thumb and forefinger in a vow, to prove it. To prove it further, he gave her a small crucifix, coppery; but all she could see was the despised burning cross on the web of his hand. "I'm entirely free of *drogas*," he told her, "and I've come back to live with my woman." He brushed her breasts.

She hated him as much as ever and feared him even more than before. His eyes, which had once been so romantic, were now only black and hollow.

That night he took her violently and she could not scream.

In the following days she simply accepted that Salvador had returned after all these years to seize her life again.

The money she had saved for that month's rent, hers and, now, Teresa's and her father's, was gone. She had kept it in a change purse she placed for safekeeping next to her statue of the Blessed Mother — to the wall behind it, she had added a splendid picture of Christ painted on velvet. And Salvador was able to take money under their gaze! He denied it. But she found a hidden syringe.

A few months later he was in trouble again. He had almost killed a man in a store he had robbed. A kind American lawyer whose family she worked for once a week coaxed her to get a divorce in Juárez, across the border, and she did.

The same day that she learned from Salvador's mother — she had become a pain-racked shadow of herself — that Salvador had been returned to prison, Amalia discovered that she was pregnant by him again.

She deliberated losing this child also, but the earlier abortion had caused her so much pain, so much terror, that she decided to have it. She had to force herself daily not to think of it, too, as a child of rape. With her hand on her stomach, which would soon grow big, she prayed, kneeling, before the Holy Mother.

The child was Manny.

Manuel Gómez — she gave him her own last name, which she retained; he looked like Salvador, an angelic version of Salvador, with enormous chocolaty eyes and dark hair, which was beginning to curl. Often, Amalia would look in wonder at him and think that perhaps *this* was the cleansed part of Salvador, the part she had glimpsed as "savior."

She had to go on welfare to take care of her child. She did not want another man with her now that she had this beautiful boy to care for.

In the one-bedroom government-project unit she had managed with the lawyer's help to acquire after years on a waiting list, she lay in bed — it was still dark, just dawning — holding her child in her arms and looking at him in awe. There was a loud knock at the door.

"We're making spot checks of welfare recipients," a woman announced, walking in past her when she opened the door. The woman looked like the Anglo schoolteachers she had hated. "We have to make sure you're not living with a man who's giving you money." The woman walked about the apartment. She peered curiously at the statue of the Blessed Mother — and then she snatched up an item from the floor. "Is this a tie?"

"It's a scarf."

The woman cleared a space at the kitchen table and sat down, pen poised over a form.

Amalia continued to stand, holding Manny.

"Have you ever used another name to apply for welfare?"

"No."

"You claim one child — and he keeps you from working? Is that him?"

"Yes." Amalia wanted to tell this woman to get out of her house, tell her she didn't want their welfare, that she could not leave her child alone. But since her marriage to Salvador, the proud voice that had allowed her to confront those who judged her had weakened.

"Does the child have a father? I mean, are you married?"

"I was."

"Divorced?"

"Yes." Amalia inhaled and held Manny more tightly. "Your breasts are tiny, you could never feed a child," she told the woman.

"*What!*" the woman gasped.

"I said that your breasts —"

The woman pushed the form into her purse. She looked at Amalia as if seeing her for the first time.

Amalia felt good the rest of that day, made herself up and looked beautiful again.

Her wonderful child with the large forlorn eyes filled her with amazement, and with a powerful, saddened love when she remembered he was Salvador's and she felt the start of anger again. Then, she would hold him even tighter, as if to shelter him from any connection with that despised man. Manny cried a lot, for no reason Amalia could find — she would check his diaper, make sure there was no lump on the bed, touch his forehead for any tinge of fever. She learned how to soothe him: She would lie with him in bed, cradling his small body so that it fused with hers. If she got up and he reacted in fear — there might be a slight tremble at the awareness that she had moved away from him — she would return to him, kiss him softly on the face until she managed to elicit a smile from him, faint but beautiful. At times she pressed her face to his, sharing his tears.

Years ago, Amalia had learned the profoundest mysteries of the Catechism from a tiny twig of a nun who wore a bluish habit, not severe like that of other nuns. Patiently, Mother Mercedes had explained to baffled public-school children who could not afford parochial schools the difference between the "Immaculate Conception" and the "Virgin Birth." The Immaculate Conception was the title awarded to Mary because she had been conceived free of original sin in her mother's womb; it was precisely that fact that had allowed the Virgin Mary to float easily into heaven, past purgatory. With a delicate gesture of her hand, Mother Mercedes conveyed the gracious ease of the Holy Lady's passage skyward. With even greater patience, she explained that the Virgin Birth meant that *Mary* had conceived Jesus, purely, in *her* own womb, after a discreet visit by the Holy Ghost, the Holy Spirit. Still, for Amalia, as for many other women of her faith, the Immaculate Conception was, simply, the Sacred Mother Mary, who had conceived her Holy Son immaculately.

Very old now, Mother Mercedes continued her good deeds, taking care of the children of working mothers. Off welfare and doing housework again, Amalia could leave Manny in her charge.

Mother Mercedes was truly a holy servant of God. She had converted one room in her small house on the fringes of the government projects into a shrine, with a smallish crucifix of Christ and a large statue of the Blessed Virgin. The shrine was open to anyone who wanted to light a candle, and the room blazed with small flames. Because the nun refused any actual payment, the women whose children Mother Mercedes cared for would drop a donation into a font guarded by an angel, the only brown-faced angel Amalia remembered ever having seen. A rumor had spread not long ago that a priest from the big cathedral in the city had come to verify her order and had discovered that she was not really a nun. No one in the projects cared about that. Mother Mercedes was a holy woman.

Now that Manny was no longer a baby, Amalia considered finding him a good father. Naturally it wouldn't hurt anyone if he was handsome.

First there was a troubling matter she had to resolve. She had just blessed her Manny to Sister Mercedes's care one morning when she felt a strong need to visit the shrine. As she knelt before the statue of the Blessed Mother resplendent in her purity, Amalia was seized by a longing to come closer to her, and to God, by partaking of Holy Communion. At the same time, she was jolted by the awareness that she was a *divorciada* who had lived unmarried with two men. Confession and repentance — and she would receive a severe penance from her confessor — would put her in good stead to receive Communion. It was the matter of repentance that complicated matters because now she needed another man, a *good* one this time. She had to face — and no one could blame her for wishing that she had simply continued not to think about any of this — that a woman living with a man who is not her husband is forbidden to receive Holy Communion. It was very complicated, how God had arrived at all this, although for Teresa, that, like everything else, was absolutely clear. She would often say to Amalia: "A *divorciada* is excommunicated from the Church, no matter how often she goes to Mass, and no matter what any of those modern priests say." Amalia was sure that Teresa made up her own strictures, much sterner than the Pope's.

As she continued to kneel before the Divine Mother for guidance, Amalia's yearning for Communion grew. Try as she might — and God would certainly take into account her careful considerations — she saw no logic in being pushed away from Him because of situations created by a bad marriage she hadn't wanted anyway. God never wanted His children distanced from Him. Didn't He move in very mysterious ways to prove it? And who was she to deny Him that?

Making an elaborate sign of the cross, Amalia left Sister Mercedes's shrine determined to invite some of God's mysterious ways. She would do this with the help of Father Ysidro, the seventy-year-old pastor of the neighborhood church. At the same time, she would ask some questions about a movie that had baffled her recently, *The Song of Bernadette.*

Father Ysidro had understanding eyes and only a fringe of white hair. He took a regular leisurely walk about the neighborhood, pausing to speak to women and children and nodding to men at work. He returned for a brief rest in the vined courtyard of his small church. That is how Amalia had met him. She continued chatting with him into the courtyard and he invited her to sit with him. Amalia could tell he enjoyed her company. And why shouldn't he like to visit with a pretty woman in her twenties? He was, after all, a man, no matter how holy; and weren't all the angels God surrounded Himself with in church always beautiful?

Today, Amalia and the old priest sat on the circular bench about the small waterless fountain in the courtyard. The Madonna in its center was pensive. Despite his age, Father Ysidro was an ample man. He spread his cassock on the bench about the rim of the fountain. He extended his hand to Amalia. She kissed it reverently, the way she had been instructed to do from childhood, the way Teresa insisted must still be done, in the true religious manner of times past. Amalia noticed that in the sun Father Ysidro's bald pate gleamed like a halo. Immediately she felt close to God.

"Father, I have to confess —" She had rehearsed exact words.

"*M'ija,* you know that confession is held properly inside the confessional in the church." He patted her hand briefly to reassure her.

She loved to be called *m'ija* — "daughter" — and by this holy old priest! "I mean," Amalia said quickly, "that I have to confess that sometimes I don't understand God."

"*M'ija!*" The old priest seemed as apprehensive of what she might say as he seemed delighted.

"Father," she embraced the designation. "Father, I *do* know, of course, that He works in mysterious ways."

"Very mysterious," the priest agreed.

"But Bernadette —" She decided this was an easier subject than the matter of divorce. "I saw that movie about her, Father."

"A reverential film, although I understand from Father Esteban, the new priest, that it was made by people not of our faith. God's ways —" he acknowledged with a shrug. "Of course, it's *not* in color." He seemed to adjust something privately.

"But, Father, why does witnessing a miracle have to make a person so miserable? Bernadette even had to leave her handsome boyfriend."

"Our Lady requires sacrifices to find us worthy, Amalia. Especially of those she honors with her divine revelations."

"But Bernadette's life wasn't all that happy to begin with. Her family was poor, and she —"

"You have to earn God's miracles, *m'ija.*"

"What if she really didn't see her, just thought so?"

"In her heart, Our Lady gave her the confidence to know."

"But why in so many riddles?"

"God's language."

"But why didn't *everyone* who went to the shrine become cured?"

The old priest formed his words precisely, as if he had arranged them carefully, spoken them often, perhaps sometimes to himself — for seconds he looked down at his clasped hands: "The real miracle is in bringing hope to the desperate, *m'ija.* Perhaps all they have are moments of hope out of their despair, through renewed faith. And hope provides us with the strength to continue."

"Just that?"

"Amalia!"

"I'm sorry, Father, it's just that miracles are —"

"— among God's most mysterious ways," Father Ysidro tried to end that. But he spoke aloud, as if to himself: "Why, once, the Sacred Mother asked that a chapel be built in a *swamp.*" He seemed, himself, bemused by that, thoughtful for seconds.

Amalia decided it was best to pretend he had not spoken that aloud. She was confused enough. She glanced toward the sacristy. She saw, at the door, the new priest, young, with a face not unlike those of the saints inside the church. Why would a handsome man like him commit himself to chastity? She curbed her thoughts, because she had also thought he looked romantic. Nearby, she saw an old woman bustling, cleaning the church steps. A *beata,* the kind of woman who thinks of nothing except the church, working fiercely in order to be near the holiness of priests. Did they feel that put them closer to heaven?

Amalia bowed her head because at that moment the new priest walked by. Would *he* be a real "savior"? Such thoughts! "Does God understand everything, Father?" she broke the old priest's reverie.

"Everything."

Amalia looked up at the sky and said to God: And so you'll understand that I'm a divorced woman and I've lived with men I'm not married to because I need help and even more now for my child. But of course You know all that, just as Father Ysidro assured me just now, and he's a holy man; *Your* priest. She made a sign of the cross and breathed easily. "Well," she said aloud to her ally, "God wouldn't be God if He didn't understand everything, would He?"

"Indeed not!" Father Ysidro said and touched her hand in affirmation.

Amalia breathed even more easily. She spoke very clearly, for God to hear exactly, "It makes it all bearable to me, to know my church doesn't turn its back on anyone."

"No one, no one," the old priest emphasized.

"Bless me, Father, please," Amalia said and took a scarf she had brought for this encounter and placed it over her bowed head.

"*En el nombre del padre, del hijo . . .*" The old priest made a slow sign of the cross before the pretty young woman.

Amalia kissed his hand again. When she left the courtyard — Father Ysidro was nodding in the warm shade now — she glanced back to see whether the new priest was around. Was he looking at her? He was standing at the gate with his hands loosening his white collar.

Amalia hurried out of the courtyard.

That same week, she went to confession—at another Catholic church—and saw no reason to mention her divorce nor the men she had lived with, and certainly not that she intended soon to find a *good* man. All those matters had been resolved very clearly between God and the Holy Father Ysidro. When she took Communion that Sunday, at her regular church and during Mass presided over by the old priest, she was certain the Blessed Mother was watching in approval, and she was almost certain that Father Ysidro smiled when he placed the holy wafer on her tongue.

Teresa left her husband and moved in unannounced with Amalia. She brought her few clothes, her rosary, her worn missal, her endless sighs, and her weeping Mother of Sorrows. She looked at Manny and said, "He's a pensive child, already worried."

"He is not," Amalia denied.

"We'll see."

Amalia continued to leave Manny with Mother Mercedes when she went to work.

Concepción, a neighbor, became Teresa's instant friend. Every weekday afternoon she came over to watch "Queen for a Day." Although hardly forty, she had cataracts growing daily. She would lean toward the television, straining to be able to see the women who were paraded before an audience to tell stories of relentless deprivation and sadness. Based on applause for the greatest misery, one would be crowned Queen for a Day.

Today, the Queen, a heavy woman in a print dress, was being draped in the glittery robe, crowned with the glittery crown. Arriving home early, Amalia watched. Crowning sorrow? The weeping queen was given some electrical appliances.... Amalia thought, And what later? Queen for only *one* day.

Concepción announced, "I asked Miss Rise, the social worker, how to get on that program."

"She told you?" Amalia's mother expressed her own interest.

"Yes. You have to have a really horrible life," Concepción said. She rubbed her eyes, clearing her sketchy vision. "I would tell them that my youngest son was stabbed in a gang fight and that the doctors at the clinic say I'll lose my sight entirely before long." She sighed. "I *deserve* to win."

Only when, weeks later, Teresa returned to her husband did she accost Amalia: "I've known about your men, you're divorced and living in sin." She made an angry sign of the cross. A week or so later she was back, with her Mother of Sorrows.

"The reason things are going so wrong for me," Teresa told Amalia one Saturday, "is that you're arousing bad spirits — *mal humores* — with your life. I've spoken to Father Emilio, and he's coming over."

Amalia winced. Father Emilio was well known in the projects for his *curas,* his "spiritual cleansings" not sanctioned by the Church. These old *curandero*-priests exist, combining Catholicism and witchcraft, wherever Mexicans converge.

The priest went about the house thrusting water at everything as if this evil required extra measures. The water streaked walls and furniture.

"Spray it on her!" Praying Hail Marys, Amalia's mother groaned to emphasize the efficacy of the spraying. "Get her to confess to you, Father Emilio."

Water ready, the man said to Amalia: "Do you want to confess your sins before God?"

"I have no sins to confess to you. I confess only to Father Ysidro," Amalia said. And to God and His Mother, she added.

"Is this a child of sin?" He pointed to Manny, who was watching curiously. The *curandero*-priest raised his bottle of water over him.

Amalia yanked Manny into her arms, away from the incensed priest. "Don't get close to my child."

She did not give the priest the required donation. When he left, after chanting and quivering at the door, Amalia dumped the abandoned vials of water into the toilet.

"Sacrilege!" Teresa gasped.

It was the time of another war and there were many soldiers in the city. There were demonstrations by civilians, sometimes even joined in by soldiers. There were arrests in San Jacinto Plaza. Students marched with placards. Teresa went back to her husband.

And Amalia fell in love with Gabriel. A good-looking soldier from New Mexico, he wore a dashing blue scarf, allowed by his unit; and he bloused the pants of his uniform over cordovan-waxed boots. His shirts were tailored to fit his proud body; and he had eyes that looked greener because of his brown skin. He was stationed at Fort Bliss. He laughed a lot.

On the day she met him — as they both watched one of the demonstrations in the old plaza — he told her she was beautiful and that he loved her.

She told him she loved him.

A week later she married him in a civil ceremony.

"Now you have a father," she told Manny.

The boy sat on the floor, playing with a small car Amalia had brought him. He seemed not to want to listen to the man who was offering to be his father.

"He wants to be," Amalia told her son, who would not look at Gabriel, kept his large eyes on her. "He *really* wants to be your father." Daily her child looked more like an angel to her, like the part of Salvador she thought she had seen at first.

That year — when Gabriel returned home to visit his family — Amalia got to dress her son as an angel.

Every Christmas there occur in El Paso the Posadas, a procession that for seven nights duplicates Mary and Joseph's hunt for an inn. Dozens of men and women, sometimes hundreds, follow the man and woman playing Joseph and Mary as the holy couple walk up to a designated home. They say, in Spanish:

"*Hay lugar para que mi hijo nasca aquí?*"

"No," the person chosen to play one of the innkeepers answers, "there's no room in this inn for your child's birth."

On the final night, the procession reaches another chosen dwelling.

"Yes, there is room in my manger."

Children precede the procession, especially chosen, as a reward, for this occasion. Dressed vaguely like angels, in loose shirts that attempt to simulate robes, they carry candles. In the chilly Texas night, their faces float within the dark. Their voices waft the cold with sweetness.

Hiding him beside her, Amalia had taken Manny with her to the corner where the procession would begin. She had sewn him a beautiful costume — secretly — because she had not wanted to invite Gabriel's reaction. She made small wings with snips of cloth. She gave him a candle. At a turn in the block, she urged him to join the chosen children. "Quickly!"

He did.

Among the hundreds of other spectators, she followed him, watching him, proud, thinking he was the most beautiful and looked the holiest. She even imagined that she had been asked to play Mary — she was certainly much prettier than the woman who was supposed to be the Holy Mother, and *she* would have made a truly beautiful robe, with sewn — not attached — stars; and, blue, it would have been, just like the Madonna's in church.

When the woman playing Mary pronounced the last words of supplication —

"Give us shelter!"

— Amalia spoke them aloud, too, and she looked at her wondrous child:

"Give us shelter."

It had all been so beautiful that she did not stay for the festivities that followed, with *mariachis, buñuelos* — sweet dough stretched to translucent thinness — *piñatas* for blindfolded children to swing at, hit, sprinkle the ground with trinkets.

Gabriel was discharged, and he moved in permanently with Amalia. Sex with him was like with the others, something expected of her; and like the others, Gabriel didn't even notice that.... Amalia loved this: Throughout the night, he held her tenderly.

He continued to try to coax Manny to play some improvised game, but he gave up soon after because the boy was constantly looking for his mother, as if afraid without her. Privately, Amalia had turned that same fear into a game between her and her son. She would pretend to hide and within full view assert that he could not possibly see her — and then he would run directly to her, delighting in having "found" her.

Often at night Gabriel would wake up in a violent sweat, screaming about the friends he had seen exploding, the people he had seen burning in Vietnam. Amalia assumed that that was what his laughter, which had diminished, had concealed.

Quickly irritated now — and drinking sporadically — he lost his job as a roofer's helper, and then was quickly fired from a lens-grinding factory. He ignored Manny. More and more, he stayed out overnight.

A woman came to the apartment asking for him. "Who are you?" Amalia demanded.

"His girlfriend."

"*Lárgate.*" Amalia ordered her away.

To tell Gabriel good news she had learned earlier one afternoon, news that would change him back into the man she had first married, Amalia put a flower in her hair and wore her lowest-cut blouse.

"I can't afford a child," Gabriel told her.

The next day he packed his clothes.

"You can't leave me," Amalia said. "You promised to be a father to Manny. Now you'll have a child of your own."

"You'll find someone else," he said.

She would miss him, she knew before he even left, miss his holding her at night. "You can't leave," she said.

"*Mira,* 'Malia," he sat down and said to her, "I can't cope with the thought of a kid. It makes me —" He shook his hands, pretending to tremble. "Lose it if you want, I'll give you the money, I'll get it somewhere. Come on, *chula,* kiss me. I've been thinking of going to Los Angeles. I've got a job lined up in Torrance, airplane factory. Good money. You can join me later. Come on, kiss me."

"You're a *cabrón, maldecido,*" she cursed him. A terrible desolation was crawling over her.

Manny stood near her, watching.

"I'm sure you're right," Gabriel said.

Amalia was surprised to see real sadness in his look.

Gabriel went to her. "I'm not a good man, I sleep with lots of women. You've known that, never accused me — because you're a good woman, better off rid of me. You'll find someone else better. You're one hell of a good-looking woman. Look at your breasts. Gorgeous. And your hair — beautiful."

She touched the flower she had placed there for him.

He took it and kissed it and put it back in her hair. "If you wanted to, with your sexy looks, you could really make something of yourself," he said.

"I'm not a *puta.*" She pulled out the flower.

Manny looked at it on the floor.

"I'm not the first man you've been to bed with." Gabriel walked toward the door.

"No, but you're the worst one." She knew that would hurt him.

His face turned dark. He seemed about to move toward her. He stopped. "Maybe I'll miss you so much I'll come back right away."

"Go to your *putas,*" she said. Soon she would not be able to speak anymore — the hint of violence had chilled her.

Gabriel sighed. "My women. Yes, I need my women." He looked at her seriously — "Because I don't feel complete." He explained earnestly as if to clarify a riddle, perhaps have her answer it for him: "It's like something was taken from me long ago, I don't even know what — so I go looking for it in a woman, lots of women." He seemed saddened by his own confused words. "Maybe now I wouldn't recognize what I'm looking for even if I had found it, maybe in you, Amalia." He frowned, and then he laughed at his own seriousness — and was silent until he walked out with his clothes.

Amalia stared at the door. Manny picked up the fallen flower. He coaxed his mother to lean down. He ran his fingers through her hair. He put the flower back in. "For my pretty *'amita,*" he said, "my pretty mother."

She held him tightly to her. "How beautiful," she said.

He had already begun to call her "*'Amá,*" short for "*Mamá,*" but more often now he called her "*'Amita,*" his special word for "*mamacita,*" little mother. She would answer, "*M'ijo*" — my son. Those became such precious moments to her that sometimes, when he sat quietly intense, doing nothing, she would say, "*M'ijo*" — just so he would answer, "*'Amá, 'Amita.*" . . . "My son." "Mama, little mama." It became a private bond between them, an expression of their special love, just theirs.

The next few days Amalia kept remembering her father. Had he sighed like Gabriel? — those cruel, drunken times when he sobbed his remorse about something unknown, lost.

Gabriel's son was born. She named him Juan, a name she liked and that had no connection with anyone else in her life. Five years old at the time, Manny peered at the new child in his mother's bed. Then he looked at Amalia in surprise.

With her two children, one clutched to her in the same seat so she would not have to pay an extra fare, the other held in her arms, Amalia traveled by Greyhound bus to Los Angeles — to Torrance — to find Gabriel, to show him his son so he would love him.

They traveled for miles of desert, into New Mexico, across Arizona, night and day — days and nights, it seemed to Amalia. She got off, with the two children, only when they were hungry and the bus had stopped at one of the "rest stops" along the way, coffee shops always awash in dirty yellow light.

"California immigration check!" the driver announced peremptorily as the bus pulled into one of several small, squat buildings in the desert. Amalia was aware that a Mexican man and woman who had remained in the bus throughout the long trip, eating out of a bag, seemed now to crouch, as if to become invisible.

The bus doors scooped in hot air as they opened; and a man in a green uniform appeared, an immigration official.

I don't want my children asked about, stared at, Amalia thought. She had her American birth certificate, of course, and her children's; but she remembered families in El Paso humiliated by men like this one, demanding papers for each child, studying the papers and the children.

She saw the official approaching. She held her breath and parted her blouse so that the full flare of her breasts would show. She prepared a wide smile that hurt. The immigration man looked at her. She pulled the painful smile wider. The man passed his hand over the headrest, touching her shoulders for seconds. Then he moved on. She heard him questioning the Mexican man and woman, who answered in Spanish. They deboarded with him, disappearing into one of the ugly gray buildings.

When the bus was moving on into California, Manny reached up and gently closed Amalia's blouse.

She arrived at the Greyhound station near skid row in Los Angeles.

It was a day of fearful heated winds. In the distant horizon a fierce fire raged and coated the sun with a veil of smoke. The red, yellow, and green of traffic lights glowed strangely out of the film of ashes.

Hot, shrieking wind whipped into the city as Amalia stood outside the Los Angeles bus depot with her two children and wondered where Torrance was.

3

♦   ♦

*N*OW, *YEARS LATER,* in the bathroom of her stucco bungalow, Amalia prepared to face the rest of the day that had begun with the fleeting impression of a silver cross over the Hollywood Hills. The pipes in the cramped room were so corroded that Raynaldo had given up trying to install a shower for her; so he had bought her a hose with a rubber nozzle.

Amalia arranged herself in the mirror. She never wanted her children to see her rumpled from sleep, the way some Anglo women she worked for looked in the mornings — and *that* was the last their children saw of them before they faced those flat-chested teachers. No, *she* always "showered," put on a fresh dress, and made herself up entirely before they saw her.

In the small hall that separated the bathroom and bedroom from the living room, she paused — as she often did — to stare at the telephone, in a small niche in the wall. What a luxury, a telephone! She had had one, briefly, in East Los Angeles, but it had been disconnected for lack of payment during one of the worst times. The demands for added deposits and new installation fees had made it impossible for her to have it reconnected. Now Raynaldo had provided this added symbol of her new status in Hollywood. Hollywood!

She touched the telephone, a pale lavender color she had chosen. She always thrilled to its ringing, although lately she had begun to fear it might bring unwelcome news about Juan or Gloria. About what! Well, if it rang now it would be only one of her employers wanting her to change her usual day of work for them. They always assumed she had nothing else to do except work for them. One woman had even asked her to work on Sundays as her "regular day." Amalia had informed her frostily that that was "God's sacred day" and that it was a sin even to *ask* anyone to work then, although — God knew this — she didn't, couldn't always go to Mass; but, if not, she made sure to say a few extra prayers — and, of course, she *did* work on some Sundays, when she had to — that once to provide Manny with money when he was in jail; and yet — she paused on this wondrous memory — he hadn't taken it, had signaled from behind the glassy partition that separated them that he wanted *her* to use it.

She heard Juan's voice, Gloria's laughter. Since Manny's death, that was the only time they laughed, that way, when they were together.

Would they be glad Raynaldo had not come back last night, after their quarrel at El Bar & Grill? Would they hope he had left permanently? What a thought! Amalia chastised herself. Whatever the source of conflict — if there was any — it was temporary. There was no reason why they would not love Raynaldo like a father. She would tell them that he was on one of those jobs that kept him away overnight when freight was heavy.

She stood at the bathroom door, and she looked into the living room that turned nightly into a bedroom. Their backs to her, her children sat in their "beds." They hadn't dressed yet, Juan in his shorts, so white against his brown skin, Gloria in one of those slips she only slept in — God knew there couldn't be anything under the tight skirts she wore. *When did they change toward me? Why? What do they have against me?*

Those questions recurred, unwanted, more and more now. Had the change begun after Manny's death? No — they had been loving in that punishing time. Had they begun to change before that? — that time when Manny came home on drugs or drunk or God knows what and she heard him talking to them? What had he told them? There was nothing to tell. Of course there was that terrible time — just after Manny's murder — when she had forbidden them to call her " 'Amita" because that belonged only to her first son and the wound of his death was too fresh. But surely they understood that. And hadn't she hugged them right away, demanding they *must* call her " 'Amita"?

Were her son and daughter aware of her as she stood watching them now? Hadn't they heard her in the bathroom? The new sadness she had detected earlier tugged at her.

It wasn't a new sadness, she knew, it was an extension of the sadness she had known from long before that forlorn day when she had stood in front of the Los Angeles Greyhound bus station and wondered how to get to Torrance, that desolate day when the heated winds were thrusting in from the desert.

Only later would she learn that those winds, which follow a tense, hot quietude, have the name of a saint, "Santa Ana winds" — "Sant' Anas." It would delight her to discover how many streets, plazas, nearby cities are named after saints — Nuestra Señora del Pueblo, San Vicente, Santa Monica, San Diego, San Juan Capistrano. She would come to love the city of angels and flowers and saints' names. But she would also come to fear the ominous winds and the scorched odor that permeated the city during the season of fires, the floods she heard about that swept distant cliffs into the ocean — and she would come to hate and fear the prospect of earthquakes — and the presence of gangs. But all that came later.

When she finally managed, the day of her arrival in California, to reach Torrance, she was sweating and weary to the point of tears. She had reached her destination after transferring from bus to bus. She arrived when the sun was setting on the flat city of small houses and plastic apartment buildings; the city where she was sure she would find Gabriel, a city she came to hate.

She rented a room from a Mexican woman — there was a scattering of Mexicans in Torrance, she quickly learned. In the room, after she had located on its only table her statue of the Holy Mother and its plastic flowers, she sat staring blankly at blemished walls. Manny joined her pensiveness, holding her hand. Juan slept. How long would the money she had saved, for this, last her?

First, they had to eat. She left her two children with the woman she had rented the room from, and she went to the giant supermarket she was given directions to.

"Aren't you that movie star?" a hefty, reddish-faced woman with pants that squeezed her flesh into lumps asked Amalia as she was checking out with milk and a package of cinnamon rolls.

"Which one?" Amalia thought the woman might say Maria, la Maria, Maria Felix.

The woman frowned. "You have an accent and you're too dark. No, you can't be Ava Gardner."

At the news rack, Amalia searched for a picture of Ava Gardner.

She found one. The American movie star looked like Maria Felix!

The next day, with Manny and Juan, she took a bus to the only "airplane factory" near Torrance. She was there early when hundreds of workers went in with lunch pails. Again with her children, she returned when the workers were leaving in the afternoon. She did not see Gabriel.

Her money had run out. She found a job doing housework. For almost half of what she earned, she left Manny and Juan with a Mexican woman who lived in the same building and who had three children and bristly bleached hair.

The American woman Amalia worked for asked her why she did housework. "You could work in a cafeteria or even in a hospital tending to, you know, things."

But she didn't tell me I could be a secretary like her, Amalia thought. Once again, she simply accepted doing housework, a line that intersected the course of her life. Too, she liked being in pretty apartments in California, and she was paid in cash, without deductions, and that was essential to her day-to-day survival.

The woman let her go after one week: "Amalia, I really can't afford—" she began. "My husband likes women like you," she blurted.

"What kind?" Amalia tried to keep anger out of her voice so the woman would get her another job.

"Oh, you know," the woman stumbled, "Spanish, and—" She waved her hands, outlining ample breasts. "But, look, I have a dress for you, I've outgrown it." She tried to laugh.

"I'm Mexican-American, not Spanish," Amalia told her, "and I don't care if your husband likes women like me, I don't like men like him, and I don't like your dress, it would look like a sack on me."

By herself she returned to the airplane factory. This time she stayed through two shifts of workers. She did not see Gabriel.

A distant relative she contacted told her she should leave Torrance and move to East Los Angeles. "What are you doing out there with the rednecks?"

Amalia, Manny, and Juan left Torrance. Her distant relative located a place for her, a pinkish bungalow in a small court. It was old, not exactly well kept. She tried to make it pretty with her blessed statue, religious pictures cut out from old calendars, and paper flowers. She sewed a bright cover for the gutted sofa Manny and Juan slept on.

In East Los Angeles, populated almost entirely by Mexicans, Gabriel found *her*. He told her how much he had missed her and that he couldn't get his baby out of his mind. Amalia showed Juan to him; he had now begun to walk.

"Jesus Christ!" Gabriel said. He would back away from the boy, and then return to study the little creature he had produced. "I want to move back in with you," he told Amalia the same day.

He was kinder to her than ever, kissed her after sex, bought her a dress. He tried to play with Manny, throwing a ball at him a couple of times. But Manny would just let it drop. Then Gabriel would stare at Juan and say, "Jesus Christ!"

After he had stayed out all night a second time, Amalia accused him of returning to his "old ways." Gabriel slapped her. She fell to the floor, hunched quietly. He pulled her up. Manny rushed at him, battering him with his fists.

Gabriel left her again, and Amalia became a *divorciada* a second time. Since God understood her first divorce, thanks to Father Ysidro, He would understand this one, Amalia never doubted.

Times she did not work — she continued to do housework by the day — Amalia explored the blocks of this new city. Even with her two children at her side, she elicited admiring looks from men, and what was wrong with that? She liked East Los Angeles. There were flowers and vines everywhere, all shapes, all colors, and they decorated even the poorest neighborhoods. In wreckage yards — which were everywhere, too — enormous yellow sunflowers with brown velvety centers peered at twisted chrome veins on mangled metal bodies. Along every street were rows and rows of palm trees.

And near her house was the chapel of Nuestra Señora de la Soledad, Our Lady of Solitude. Atop the yellowish church, Our Lady welcomed Amalia. Inside, within a large silvery shell enclosed in a gleam of blue, a statue of Our Lady of Guadalupe stood on a gathering of red roses. Before her, a statue of the peasant Juan Diego knelt, gazing in awe at her divine radiance. Amalia would always spend a few minutes there, especially when there was no one else nearby. That way, she felt even closer to the Holy Mother.

Every Saturday night on Whittier Boulevard the young men of East Los Angeles would display their "customized" cars, growling machines worked on constantly, often prized '50s "Cheveez"; cars silver-sprinkled red, green, blue; purple birds or fiery flames painted on the sides and hoods. Flaunting their budding sexuality, girls rooted for the best cars, the best-looking drivers, the members of their favorite *gangas,* or the lowest "low-riders," cars that almost touched the street and bounced up and down, to applause.

Amalia liked watching the "parades" — although seeing the exuberant girls there reminded her that she had had no real girlhood. And Manny delighted in the display of cars, especially the antics of the drivers. He seemed to come to life then, out of an entrenching sadness that haunted Amalia, that she saw in his hurt eyes.

One night, police helicopters hovered over the unofficial parade. Suddenly light poured down in a white pit. Squad cars rushed to block the side exits off the boulevard. Police motorcycles tangled in and out of lanes. Young Mexican men rushed out of cars. Some were pushed to the ground. There were screams. The police pulled out their guns. Amalia ran home with Manny. "*No es nada,*" said a woman who lived nearby. "Just the usual harassment."

Increasingly, Amalia noticed sun-glassed Anglo police prowling the area like leisurely invaders in their black cars. She saw young Mexican men — boys — sprawled against walls while cops frisked them. She saw those same young men, young men like them, in bunches — *klikas* that form the gangs — roaming the streets or idling; and she felt afraid of the police and the gangs.

Sometimes Amalia would take some extra time to walk to a more distant bus stop so that she might pass the small plaza off Boyle Avenue on her way to work. At that corner, near a doughnut shop, there would already be a cluster of *mariachis,* from whom, throughout the day but especially toward evening, those wanting to hire a band for birthdays or weddings, or to play at a dance or a bar, would make their choices while sitting in their cars. The *charros* for hire stood already dressed in their *trajes,* tailored pants and jackets, black or blue, lined with silver. Guitars, trumpets, accordions, violins at their sides, they sometimes practiced their music right there on the street, songs of love and lament.

Amalia would walk past, a bright flower in her hair, and with a slight toss of her hips she would encourage approving remarks and — her real goal — also a few strains from a guitar, perhaps something from a Pedro Infante song from way back, her mother's sweet time of two-day weddings.

◆ 44 ◆

She especially liked the murals scattered about the area — imagine! — paintings as colorful as those on calendars, sprawled on whole walls. One of the prettiest was of a bride, in white swirling veils, accompanied by her new groom. Colored confetti rained on them and on the lovely bridesmaids and handsome escorts, all joyous.

In a spottily green park, where young Mexican men bunched together, idling, smoking — Manny stared at them and Amalia coaxed him away — there was a wall painting that fascinated and puzzled her, and she went there often to look at it: A muscular Aztec prince, amber-gold-faced, in lordly feathers, stood with others as proud as he. They gazed toward the distance. Behind them on a hill pale armed men mounted on horses watched them. At the opposite end of the painting brown-faced, muslin-clothed men stared into a bright horizon. They were the ones whom the Aztecs were facing distantly.

Today, standing before it with Manny while Juan played nearby on the patchy grass, Amalia must have shown her bewilderment, because an old Mexican man who had been sitting nearby on a bench came up to her and explained: "The *conquistadores* are about to subdue the Indians with weapons, as they did, but over there" — he pointed to the band of muslin-clad men — "are the *revolucionarios,* who will triumph and bring about *Aztlán,* our promised land of justice."

Amalia thanked him for his explanation. She continued to study the mural. There were no women. Where were they? Had *they* survived?

"— saw it, a glimpse of it. No, we *demanded* it."

Amalia hadn't been aware the old man had remained standing nearby until she heard his emphatic words. "What?"

"A short time ago when we demanded justice." He frowned. "It seems so much longer. But it was right here, in East Los Angeles, when they tried to kill us on the streets."

"Who?" Amalia was not sure she wanted to hear.

"The police," the old man said, "when we protested in the streets, thousands of us, because so many of our boys were being killed in that terrible Vietnam. Why, my own grandson died there." He made a sign of the cross in memory.

Amalia made one with him, and she coaxed Manny to cross himself, too.

The old man shook his head. "Our sons were fighting for the

country, and yet we were being treated—" he paused, choosing careful words "— without *dignity,*" he finished. "We marched in the streets," he said proudly, "and we shouted, '*No más!*' No more abuse. *No more!* . . . Then a thousand policemen gassed us, beat us with their clubs. Yes, men, women, children. One man was killed."

Amalia remembered something like that. When she was still in El Paso? When she was in Torrance? She wasn't sure, because for her that had been only the time of Gabriel.

"We rioted," the man said. "*I* threw something, a rock, I can't even remember what, I just wanted them to know that *I* was there, too. 'No more!'" he echoed his words from that time. Then he looked about him. His voice was quiet. "But nothing's changed," he said to Amalia.

Amalia needed to move away from this man's troubled memories. So she said, "*Buenos días,*" with extra courtesy, and walked away. Until she had almost reached her house, she wasn't aware that in her mind she had kept repeating the man's words, "*No más*— no more," without knowing why.

When Gloria was born, the daughter of Gabriel, it was difficult at first for Amalia to think of her and Juan as children of the same father, because she thought of Gabriel now as two men, the one she had married and who had left her, and the one who had found her only to make her pregnant again.

In her house Amalia would sometimes stand apart and watch her children. Imagine! They were hers and they loved her, perhaps as much as she loved them. She was proud of this: Her children had enough to eat, and she sewed and altered their clothes because she did not want anyone ridiculing them for being poor. She made ruffled dresses — out of her own — for Gloria, so that she looked like a flower.

Juan was always laughing now, like Gabriel when she had first met him. At times completely silent, Manny would watch over his brother and sister protectively, clearing away any possible hazard in the house. For a time Juan had terrible stomachaches, and Amalia soothed them by putting warm towels on him, the way Teresa had said would help. There was no heating in her unit; and so on cold California nights Amalia would leave the gas burners on. If the gas was turned off because of late payment, she would bring Juan and Gloria into her bed with her — Manny was growing up.

She met a new "boyfriend." He looked like a Mexican gypsy. He even wore a red-print handkerchief like a bandanna around his forehead when he worked without a shirt in the car-garage he owned. His name was Emilio; was there a saint by that name? she had wondered, and thought there was. His garage was only blocks away from where she lived, and she was with him only in the room he occupied behind it, and only when her children — he knew about them, had seen her with them — were being cared for by one of the older girls in the court who kept them when she was at work.

He gave her a present, a pair of gleamy green earrings, loops within loops, which, delighted, she put on immediately. He told her he loved her and wanted to move in with her — a man shouldn't be without a beautiful woman.

She considered it. Every day now there was another bill to pay, left unpaid — and nobody who wasn't blind could say he wasn't handsome, and hadn't he given her this beautiful present? What would she tell the children when he moved in? She deliberated claiming he was Gloria and Juan's real father, but then she would have to explain Gabriel. Did Juan remember him? Not that well, and Gloria had never seen him. Manny, of course, would. She could see his enormous eyes on her, asking — what? She might tell them that she and Emilio had run off and married. Well, she would think of something.

She invited him to visit.

"Bastard!" he shouted at Manny for spilling coffee on him.

"Bastard!" Manny mimicked. Juan giggled. Gloria began to cry.

Amalia continued to see the Mexican gypsy, but only at his place. He still wanted to move in, assuring her that everything would be all right and that he had a way with children. He had just been edgy that day — and, he whispered to her, he was thinking it might be time for him to join with a good woman "permanently." Well, she might reconsider, she told him. Would he marry her, be a father to her children? Yes.

At home, Manny's eyes followed her as she moved from one room to another.

The affair with Emilio ended when he told her that his wife — "I didn't tell you I was only separated?" he answered her look of surprise — was coming back to live with him.

A woman in the court of bungalows told Amalia she might make more money working at one of the "clothes factories" in downtown Los Angeles — "sewing sweatshops," a reporter doing a television story on conditions in the city's garment district called them right after Amalia had started working there. That humiliated her, but she eventually decided that was an accurate description.

On the top floor of an old six-story building — just blocks away from glassy new ones — electric fans churned only hot air while dozens of Mexican women sewed steadily in crowded rows of buzzing machines. Under long tubes of icy fluorescent lights, even garments that would eventually boast famous labels appeared grayish on metallic racks here. By the end of the day steam from pressing irons was heavy with the odor of sweat. One woman brought her two-year-old child with her, keeping him secretly by her machine.

Still, Amalia told herself, this might be a move up from housework; she might become a "supervisor," the owner, Mr. Lewis, told her when he hired her eagerly. "*If,*" he said to her, "you play your cards right." He was a short, thin, craggy-faced old man with a full head of still-dark hair. He constantly pushed up the right sleeve of his shirt to expose a wiry biceps. That prospect — of "moving up" — made the job bearable for Amalia, that and her friendship with Rosario, a small but powerful older woman who, Amalia knew immediately, was the intelligent one of the bunch.

The other women — when the owner was not there overseeing them — would gossip over the sound of the pick-picking of their machines and especially during their lunch break. Most often they would discuss the serials they watched on Mexican television. Some of the women lamented that they could not watch the daytime American soap operas. "Good," Rosario said, and so Amalia kept to herself that she enjoyed following the stories the women discussed, about errant women and faithful husbands, errant husbands and faithful wives, and, always, loyal mothers who believed in God and the Virgin Mother.

Amalia was often teased by the other women because she wore pretty dresses scooped to display her breasts. "La Elizabeth Taylor," one called her, and another said, "You look like you want to be discovered for the Night of Stars," referring to a Mexican variety program they all seemed to watch on Sundays. It did not help that Mr. Lewis, the owner, who was usually drunk by late afternoon, sought Amalia out, peering into her blouse.

"Play your cards right," one of the women said to Amalia, apparently echoing Lewis's familiar words, "and he might marry you — he's a widower, and horny." The other women added their mock encouragement. But she would *never* marry for money, Amalia thought, God would never forgive that.

"It's about time for a raid from '*la migra*,'" Rosario warned Amalia. *La migra* was the Immigration and Naturalization Service; a "*migra*" one of its agents. Sporadic raids occurred when several *migras* would appear suddenly and one would bark, "Workplace survey!" The stern men would then interrogate the workers about their "papers." Amalia assured Rosario that she always carried her birth certificate — "from Texas" — with her.

Still, she felt horrified when two men did appear one early afternoon. "*Cálmate*," Rosario soothed Amalia, "those are just building inspectors. Watch what happens."

The two men wandered about the premises. Red-faced with anger, Lewis followed them.

"Bolts of flammable cloth blocking exit corridors," one of the inspectors, displaying hairy arms under short sleeves, dictated to the other, fat, wheezing, who scribbled on a long yellow pad. "Electrical cords wrapped around water pipes," the hairy man continued his list of observations. "Security gates locked, unopenable, blocking fire escapes and stairs." Then the three — the two inspectors darkly serious, Lewis speaking hurriedly — disappeared into Mr. Lewis's office. The frowns on the faces of the two inspectors were gone and Lewis was smiling when they emerged.

"In a fire we would all burn," Rosario said dourly.

Amalia convinced herself that the older woman was just exaggerating, because everything remained the same at the sweatshop — Amalia now called it that herself.

At lunch, one of the women, Milagros — Amalia marveled that so ordinary a woman could be named Miracles — had launched into a spirited recounting of her favorite television serial, "Lágrimas de Honor": "Aurelio has just discovered that his rich wife — her name is Blanca or Concha — one is his mistress, the other is the wife —"

Blanca is the wife, Amalia said to herself. Because "Blanca" means "white" — pure.

"Well, the wife — yes, her name is Blanca — has just confronted Concha, his mistress," Milagros was going on. "Blanca told Concha she knows she's having an affair with Aurelio, although it's clearly not Aurelio's fault, he's a good man seduced. Yes, says the brazen Concha, and right under your nose. You mean while I was pregnant with my little Anuncio? Blanca demands, although she's so over-whelmed by the terrible affront that she has to sit down with her rosary in order to keep from fainting. Precisely, that vile Concha says."

"She's an evil woman, that Concha," another woman offered.

Amalia noticed that Rosario was eating her sandwich with her head lowered.

"She's evil all right," Milagros said. "Last week we learned that once — in a hospital officiated over by holy nuns — she had pre-tended to be a nurse, to that sweet old man who had made his peace with God and was ready to die; she was there in order to get his enormous wealth, which he was leaving to his son and to the Church."

"Why else would a woman like her be in a convent?" a woman assumed.

"Don't ask me how she got away with the impersonation," Mila-gros resumed, "because one look at her, with her lacquered nails and that bleached hair and you'd know she's not an angel of mercy. Of course it's all inevitable when you consider that her mother had once been involved in a ring of fake jewelry, including holy trea-sures, and that her father — But before all that, Blanca could not give her full attention to Aurelio, during that crucial time when he was involved with those trouble-making godless unionists —"

Amalia saw Rosario's head jerk up.

"— and Concha knew that. Blanca had fallen into a deep de-pression because, despite her devout prayers, the birth of her child —"

Rosario set her sandwich aside as if, Amalia thought, something, not the food, had disgusted her profoundly. The older woman made her way toward Milagros and asked her quietly, "What is godless about unionists?"

"What?" Milagros had already forgotten what she had said earlier.

"What is godless about unionists!" Rosario raised her voice, and some of the women looked at her, puzzled.

Amalia began to suspect that Rosario, who was so smart, stayed here in order to question the women this way. Now she hoped fervently that no one would come up with a good reason why God did not like unionists.

"I'll tell you what's godless about unions, Rosario," the woman who brought her child to work was volunteering. "That if you join one you'll get fired."

"Or threatened with *la migra*," another woman added.

There was approving laughter, and then they all returned to the buzz of their sewing machines.

Well, Amalia thought in relief, they certainly hadn't convinced *her* that God wasn't on Rosario's side, whatever that was.

That same day, they discovered Mr. Lewis was not a widower. His blonde wife — years younger than he was — came to pick him up. She was a pretty woman, Amalia knew; why deny it? — and she might have looked even prettier if she had known how to do herself up better. She wore plain clothes, expensive, though. She had a pampered complexion — that was obvious — but you hardly even *saw* the makeup she wore. Her breasts were a good size — you could tell despite the loose-fitting blouse, Amalia allowed — but her own were fuller, and —

"What a pretty dress," Mr. Lewis's wife came over to her and said.

Amalia thought: What a stupid woman, doesn't she know I'm sewing a shirt now?

"Did you make it yourself?"

Then Amalia realized the woman was asking about *her* dress, a low-cut one, yellow with large purplish dots, a favorite that never failed to arouse enthusiastic whistles from the men working in the garment district. *Made it herself!* Amalia felt her face hot with humiliation. "No, I *bought* it," she managed to say. She was about to add, "And it was expensive" — but she knew this blonde woman's clothes had cost at least a dozen times what she had paid.

"I'm sorry," the woman seemed honestly flustered.

That annoyed Amalia even more. She could understand a remark of envy, but this woman seemed to have meant her comment genuinely. Seemed to! Amalia brushed away any good intention. She's jealous of my breasts, she resolved it, and added: What would she think if she knew her husband is always hovering around me? Then confusion, anger, and hurt mixed.

Rosario placed a reassuring hand on hers. "She meant it looked much too fine to have been bought, *corazón.*" She called Amalia that, "heart."

Amalia said softly, "Thank you."

Increasingly, Amalia listened to Rosario because she was always eager to figure things out, and the world was baffling. Even so, it seemed to her that Rosario brought up only problems, always about injustice, and Amalia wondered about the solutions.

As Manny grew — he was ten, Amalia marveled — he became moodier, but, also, more wonderful to her. He brought her a small present, a shiny pin, which he attached to her chest. Oh, where had he got it? Amalia did not want to ask him. He was in school but never seemed to carry any books — and he never spoke about anything that occurred there.

Amalia returned home to the odor of glue. Manny seemed dizzy, almost falling. That sent Juan, five years old, into convulsions of laughter. Amalia told herself she was smelling paint, someone in the unit had finally decided to paint some walls — and Manny was just clowning for Juan.

Soon after, she came to find Juan and Gloria each with a pint of expensive ice cream. Their faces were smeared from their efforts to gobble it all. "I bought it for them," Manny told her.

"Why don't you carry any books to school?" She decided on a less disturbing question.

"I do, but I hide them," he told her. "Because if they see you with books, they'll jump you."

They . . . ? Gang members. No, they couldn't exist in grammar school. Amalia did not ask Manny any more questions.

"Workplace survey!" Two burly immigration inspectors appeared one early morning in the sewing factory. The large room was suddenly charged with quiet tension. The two *migras* scanned the rows of women, who looked down intently at their machines. Then the two men walked slowly along the narrow aisles, stopping abruptly to demand to see the papers of one or another of the women; backtracking suddenly to question someone who had sighed too quickly in relief at having been bypassed. A few of the women were now lining up quietly, knowing they would be taken to Customs.

"Your papers."

Amalia was indignant. Did she look like an illegal? Didn't this man see that her dress was pretty, fresh, that she wore sophisticated makeup? She answered in her best English that she was an American citizen, born in El Paso, in Texas.

Still, he demanded her papers.

Humiliation deepened. Amalia fished into her purse, showing it off, a *modern* purse.

Before she could find anything to show him as proof, the man walked away, winking at his partner.

"*El cabrón* had his eyes on you from the moment he walked in. I saw him. He just wanted to try to look down your dress," Rosario assured her.

That was it! But Amalia was disturbed that she had felt humiliated, in a way she didn't want to feel, at being mistaken for an illegal.

There was an uglier incident.

Jorge, a slight sixty-year-old man who gathered the clothes from the women, had been stopped by one of the inspectors. "These papers are forged."

"They are not." Jorge stared evenly at the man.

"Come with us." The man reached for Jorge.

"I will not. Check those papers again."

The man grabbed at Jorge. The women gasped.

Rosario stood up.

Jorge resisted. The two men wrenched him down. "Kneel, motherfucker!"

"I'll kneel to God, not to *cabrones*," Jorge said.

Another inspector hit Jorge at the knees, to force him down. The first one pushed on his shoulders until Jorge was crouched before them.

Rosario ran to Lewis's small office. He was hard of hearing, and so she yelled loudly, "There's trouble, Lewis!"

Amalia wished *she* had done that, but she had felt so trapped by fear she could not even stand up.

Lewis came out. "Hello, boys. Some trouble here? Jorge's a little too defiant for his own good — I know that — but his papers are in order."

The men released Jorge. He stood up. "*Cabrones.*"

"Now, now, Jorge," Lewis soothed. "These men are just doing their job, and they do it damn well, too. Why, look at how often some of these women fool *me* into thinking they're legal. Wouldn't hire them otherwise."

Rosario stared coldly at Lewis until he looked back at her, and quickly away.

The men left, wishing Lewis a nice day.

Rosario went to Jorge, talking to him, holding his hand.

At lunch, the women were chattering about their television serials. "Well, Blanca couldn't believe the rumors the servants were circulating, she's such a holy woman . . ."

Amalia noticed Rosario staring hard at them, and so she made it clear she was not listening to the babble; she sat closer to Rosario.

Milagros continued, "But Aurelio took her to the church, and there in full view of the Holy Virgin he confessed to her that once he had—"

Suddenly trembling, Rosario shouted at them: "*Estúpidas!* Don't you care about what happened to Jorge just now? Don't you care about the women who work next to you?—arrested and sent back without even their wages! For God's sake, don't you see your own sons shoved around by cops only because they're Mexicans? Don't you wonder why they join the terrible *gangas,* and take *drogas?*" She inhaled and then said with added disgust: "And then they turn into killers of their own people!" Her brown face darkened. "Haven't you seen the women line up to visit their sons and husbands in jail?" She shook her head, over and over. "Why so many of *us?* People desperate—" she began to stammer. "Don't you care? Don't you *see?*" Her words choked, stopped.

For long minutes, all the women were quiet. Then Milagros addressed Rosario. "What are you babbling about, *mujer?* Do *you* know?"—and they all laughed, and Milagros continued her account of the tribulations of Blanca and Aurelio, who "finally did what they had to do, turned to a priest for God's counsel."

That was the first time Amalia had seen her friend perspire. She put her arm about Rosario, to still her trembling. "Today near the border *la migra* shot and killed a fourteen-year-old boy they said threw a rock at them," the older woman said softly, "and when the people gathered to protest with the boy's parents, the *desgraciados* turned up their loudspeakers to laugh and insult them."

Amalia avoided passing Emilio's garage. She did not want to risk seeing his wife. She resolved that if the opportunity presented itself again—and who was to say it wouldn't?—she would be much more careful in choosing a boyfriend.

Rosario came to work laughing furiously. She had read an account in an American newspaper that claimed that maids were in such demand in Beverly Hills that they were being courted with huge salaries and presents. "'Cars, jewels,'" she translated from the article. "'Even so, there aren't enough maids to go around,'" she finished reading. "*Desgraciado!*" she addressed the writer of the article. "Then why are so many poor women looking for work every day, and working for less than a dollar an hour?"

Milagros said, "Well, I think we should all take a bus right out there now and get one of those jobs so *we* can get presents and be rich."

The women burst into laughter with her.

"I'd ask for a dishwasher, but I don't have any dishes," a woman said.

"I'll demand a refrigerator, maybe one that works," said another.

"You have to have food to put in it, *mujer*," another reminded.

"A green card so I could become legal — and a color television," another called out.

"A good husband," Amalia joined the laughter.

Even Rosario was laughing with them now.

The laughter stopped abruptly.

The rest of the day there was a rare silence among the women. It would be broken occasionally by one or another of them announcing without laughter what she would ask for.

In the next days Amalia would have left the sewing factory, except that Mr. Lewis took her aside and told her he was going to give her a raise because she was such a good worker, might become a supervisor — "if you play your cards right."

"And Rosario?" Amalia knew that Rosario worked harder than any of the others, as if to stop herself from thinking.

"Who? Oh, her. Why, yes. Damn good worker, that Rosie, *damn good.*"

Amalia did leave soon after when Lewis offered her a "much larger raise" if she'd work "overtime" that night. He emphasized his meaning by brushing her arm.

"I am not a *puta.*" Although she was infuriated, Amalia only managed those words because now he was holding her hand tightly and she felt the beginning of the numbing fear she dreaded. But a few women were still gathering their belongings before leaving for the day, and Lewis walked back into his office.

Amalia returned to doing housework by the day, welcoming the certain freedom it gave her at the same wages. She made sure to make Sundays special for her children, if only by taking them for a walk. She was proud that that never embarrassed Manny, growing so fast. She did not mind if on those outings she encountered an attractive man to flirt with. She avoided a mural that had startled her recently: A tall, plumed Aztec held a bleeding, dying city boy in his arms. Amalia had clutched Manny's hand.

The people she did housework for had very little reality for Amalia, only outlines; a newly divorced woman, a single man, a married couple with children in school. She was no longer surprised at how often the women gave her dresses they had no more use for — and that she wouldn't be found dead in, thank you; nor at how often some berated her with their problems — as if she didn't have any, none. With some of her employers, she pretended to know only enough English to get by, and so to limit any conversation with them, conversation which was always about them. Their pretty houses were much more real to her than they were. Eventually — she was a good worker, recommended to others — she retained only jobs where the inhabitants would be home briefly, if at all, while she was there.

She learned not to work after certain hours in exclusive areas. From others on the buses she rode, she had heard that Mexicans and black people were routinely stopped and questioned by Beverly Hills police. When that happened to her — a fat motorcycle cop asked her what she was doing as she stood admiring a garden — it humiliated her deeply; he kept referring to her as a "pretty *muchacha*" — a girl! From then on, she always carried another blouse, sweater, or coat folded neatly to wear fresh as she traveled to the bus on her way home. As soon as she was on the bus, she would remove the sweater or coat and flounce up a ruffle on her blouse.

To keep afloat — and as the children grew it became more difficult — she occasionally took in piecework to do at home. Her children would help. Gloria would adjust the expensive labels, Juan would glue them on the garments, and Amalia would sew them. When Manny was home, he would fold the items with exact care, sometimes making them all laugh by creating a grotesque face out of one of the garments.

At every available opportunity, Amalia would go back to the "sewing sweatshop" to visit Rosario.

"I'm sad, Amalia," Rosario told her as they sat during a break in the hallway of the factory. "Very, very sad."

"I know," Amalia said.

"Those women —"

Amalia thought she understood. "But what can they do?" She was careful not to say "we."

"Nothing," Rosario said. "That's what makes me so sad."

Manny had started running around with three older boys. He was fifteen, they were seventeen. He would still sit looking intently at Amalia, as if something puzzled him. He adored his half brother and sister. He startled Amalia one afternoon. He walked in with long, deliberate strides, an exaggerated gait. He hunched his shoulders.

Juan laughed, delighted.

"*Soy muy chingón!*" Manny boasted. "Real tough," he interpreted the language of street gangs. "Every *vato* looks up to *me!*"

Sad, angry, bewildered, Amalia could only stare at him.

He was growing lean and sinewy, though not tall. His hair was black and wavy; he had liquidy brown eyes. To Amalia he looked even more like an angel. When he kissed her now, it was always with the promise to buy her extravagant presents, do wonders for her. Amalia was sure her love would keep him out of trouble.

She discovered — from the sister of one of the older boys who visited a girl in the courts — that her son was one of the toughest *vatos* in "East Ellay" — a "*vato loco*," a gang member of extreme daring. He boasted that his father was in prison. In an initiation for membership in the *ganga*, he had not only lasted the required thirty seconds of pummeling by those who were already members — to test his courage — but he had demanded they extend the count thirty more seconds, then thirty more — until he was aiming his fists at nothing because the other boys were only circling about him now and staring.

Her son! Her Manny! No. He would have had to become someone else. Amalia said to the girl who had reported all that with admiration: "How can you know so much? You just carry rumors, that's all."

"*M'ijo,* what —?" she started to question Manny that day.

"I want you to be proud of me, 'Amita," he interrupted her. "If I'm the toughest, I'll be able to protect you against *everyone.*

Nobody will ever hit you or yell at you again." He pressed his head against her chest.

She clasped him, and she hated Salvador and loved her son, and hated . . . and loved . . .

He came home drunk and Amalia refused to talk to him for two days.

At the sewing factory, Milagros surprised them all one day when Amalia had gone to see Rosario. After a recitation of what was occurring in the tumultuous lives of the characters in her serials, Milagros announced bluntly — she looked down and her voice grew tense — "My son is in a gang, he's doing bad things, a man from the county says I should have him committed to the court, to a detention home as an incorrigible. He's doing terrible things!"

"Do whatever you have to do before he's killed or kills someone," Rosario urged her.

Bruised from a terrible beating by her husband, Teresa arrived from El Paso unannounced and with her grieving statue: "I'm staying with you a few days," she said. Amalia bought a cot for her, and the old woman slept in the bedroom with her, wheezing in a way Amalia did not remember.

Juan was ten, Gloria almost eight — both happy children, Amalia was certain. They went to school; and so she did not have to worry about leaving them with Teresa, whom they all merely looked at and avoided. God knows, the old woman was capable of filling them with all her recriminations against her own daughter.

When Manny came home drunk again, Amalia told him she was going to court to have him declared an incorrigible unless he changed his ways. She did not look at him, and he did not answer.

"What do you intend to do to your own son?" Teresa demanded in the morning.

"I only wanted to warn him."

"Threatening your own flesh with incarceration. God help us when a mother turns against the flesh of her womb."

Amalia knew she would never be able to turn her son in for incarceration. But there was no way to thwart Teresa's judgments.

Only a few days later, a neighbor called out excitedly to Amalia, "Your son's going to be on television! They announced it on the news, my son says it's about Manny!"

Amalia watched the newsclip while Teresa stood rigidly behind her. With the child's face he never lost, Manny leaned against a car on Whittier Boulevard, his arms crossed before him. Two other boys stood uncertainly with him. About them, traffic had halted. Policemen rushed toward the three.

Juan and Gloria peered excitedly at their brother on television, encouraging him not to move.

Amalia stayed up to watch the newsclip of her son again. She was fascinated, terrified to see this defiant little stranger. Where was he now? The two other boys with him had been arrested, but he had avoided the police, the announcer said.

Manny managed to run home, sweating so much he had taken off his shirt, so that Amalia saw, in shock, that he was no longer a boy, was a young man.

"'Amá!'"

"*M'ijo!*"

Amalia screamed at the cops who came with guns to the door, "Leave him alone, he's scared, he's a child, can't you see?"

Manny was sent to juvenile home for hot-wiring a car, driving it with the two other boys into the midst of the busy street to display it to the gangs that paraded there. He had remained, challenging anyone to make him move.

Dressed now only in black, Teresa stared accusingly at Amalia.

"I did not turn him in," Amalia said to the somber presence.

Clutching her black-beaded rosary, Teresa answered only by praying aloud: "... blessed is the fruit of your womb ..." She stopped and said to Amalia: "You killed your own firstborn child before he had a life."

From the rape you knew happened! Amalia wanted to shout but couldn't form the words.

Then Teresa returned to El Paso — "to my husband, who needs me."

"God will remember," she said to Amalia and Juan and Gloria, "that I never divorced my husband."

Strange, to receive a letter from her son, Amalia thought the first time Manny wrote her from the juvenile home. It was a letter full of expressions of regret for causing her pain, and even more expressions of his love for his "'amita." What a beautiful letter — and what beautiful handwriting! Of course she was not surprised by how smart her Manny was because he was her son.

And Salvador's. She remembered that more and more now.

Emilio reentered Amalia's life. The "Mexican gypsy" — he still wore a bandanna handkerchief about his forehead although he was not at his garage — waited for her at the bus stop when she returned from work. His wife was gone — and what a mistake that had always been, but he had learned from his experience. "I've missed you very much, Amalia. I'll be good to you," he promised. "I'm sorry I was so stupid. I'll prove to you I love you." He sighed.

Why did she think of Gabriel? Because Emilio was returning to her the way her second husband had? Or because he had sighed, that way, that long? Like Gabriel. Yes. She remembered that, how often Gabriel had sighed. And Salvador . . . Yes. No, never! But her father . . . ? She pushed away those odd thoughts. "Emilio," she said aloud because she wanted to confirm something — and did. Hearing the name this time, she was sure there *was* a saint with that name. That helped her decide — that, and the sad way he was looking at her — that she could believe him, and she did, at a time, remember, when she was lonely, missed her son constantly, more each day, week, month.

She was with Emilio, the first times, only in his room. He held her with more tenderness than she remembered. He wanted to move in with her, as they had first planned, and, God knows, it would help during a most difficult time of making ends meet.

He came over, on a very cold California morning when he knew her children were in school and she was staying home to do some piecework she was behind on. To warm the house, she had left the stove burners on in the kitchen.

He kissed her, so gently.

She was in the bedroom — afterward — dozing, with his head on her breasts, when she heard the front door open. In her slip, she rushed out of the room.

She faced Manny.

"'Amá . . ."

"M'ijo!" Quickly, she shut the bedroom door. She wanted to rush to her son, hug him, kiss him, tell him how much she'd missed him. But he looked . . . different. . . . Had he run away?

"No," he told her, "I got out early because I was good." He spoke very, very softly, slowly. He opened his eyes, wide, as if he were trapped in a dream he was trying to wake from.

"You're on drugs." She knew it from hated memories of Salvador. "You just came out and already you're on drugs." She moved into the kitchen, away from the shut bedroom, into a warmth she needed desperately now.

He followed her. "No, 'Amá." He tried to open his sad eyes wider, to show he was alert. "See?" He held out his hand as proof.

She backed away. "What's that on your hand?"

"A tattoo, a burning cross," he said.

She felt terrified and angry. She was aware of how sheer her slip was. She felt her nipples pressing against it. She saw her son's hand held out toward her. Furious, she grabbed it, the hand with Salvador's tattoo, the tattoo she had come to despise almost as much as she had despised him. Manny wrenched away, against the lit stove. She still clasped his hand when he tried to yank it away.

He screamed.

Then she smelled singed flesh and saw her son's hand over the flames of the burner. She pulled him back and began to sob.

"'Amá, 'Amita, don't cry, it was my fault, please don't cry. When you cry —"

She licked the burn, to soothe it. She held it to her breasts, the way she had when she was nursing him and he fell asleep. His head burrowed there now. Then he looked up, toward the kitchen door.

Emilio stood there naked.

Manny's dreamy eyes searched Amalia's.

Emilio leaned against the door, his arms outstretched, hands propped on the frame, three heavy, dark patches of hair on his body. That's how Amalia saw him — shocked — through Manny's eyes. "I was with him only because I wanted to have a father for you when you came out!" she cried out to Manny.

She was still nursing her son's hand when — minutes later — she heard the front door close and knew that Emilio was gone.

After that, Manny became an intimate stranger to her. He would watch her even more closely, at times he didn't even seem to hear her talk to him, just watched her. She did not want to think about the fact that Manny had never seen Salvador's tattoo — Teresa would have told him only that his father was in prison; Amalia did not want to think of that tattoo as an inheritance. She avoided looking at the whitish scar the burn had left.

She began to notice her other children more and more. Why,

Juan was such a happy boy, laughed a lot, so different from Manny. Well, they didn't have the same father, after all, and Gabriel had laughed a lot, like that; so what her two sons had in common would come from her. But she wasn't sure what that was. She knew only that when she tried, she had a difficult time remembering when Manny had laughed like Juan, actually laughed, laughed happily. Of course, he *had,* she knew that, he must have, every child laughs and is happy. It was just that she couldn't remember a specific time. That was only because he gave the impression always of being . . . so pensive, even as a little child. What was he always thinking about?

She began to notice Gloria was prettier than a girl her age should be. Well, there was no question about where *she* got her looks, was there? . . . When Amalia was delighting most in Gloria and Juan that way, into her mind would flow a memory of Manny — perhaps, often, in the angel's costume she had sewed for him for the Posadas; when he covered her chest after the Immigration check into California; when he retrieved the flower she had thrown on the floor when Gabriel was leaving her . . . And then, all the joy she might have been feeling for her two younger children would vanish, and there would be only a sadness that ached emptily.

When, on her way to work, she saw Emilio with another woman — and nobody could say he didn't like women with impressive breasts! — she did not care, did not care at all.

With increased credentials for toughness now that he had been incarcerated, Manny became the leader of one of the toughest gangs in East Los Angeles — that's what the girl who reported to the women in the court about the activities of *gangas* said. When Amalia confronted him, he promised — "with all my heart, 'Amita" — to be "good."

He was in trouble again — stealing; back in detention.

When he returned this time, he got a series of menial jobs after school — which he attended only off and on; he worked stacking boxes in a store, worked in a car-repair shop. He would give Amalia whatever he earned, but he didn't keep a job long and his wages were not nearly enough to help her support a full family. Amalia knew she would have to do something very soon.

She met Raynaldo at La Casa Bonita, a combination bar and restaurant, perfectly respectable; in the tradition of Mexican restaurants, it had a "family entrance" into a section apart from the bar. She had started stopping there on Fridays for a beer, sometimes two, to relax her after work. On Saturday nights she might return, have another beer, two, never more, and none, ever, on weeknights — except one now and then with dinner on special occasions.

She had seen Raynaldo there before, noticed him looking at her, but she was not interested in him. He was not the handsome man she was attracted to. He was perhaps ten years older than she. He wasn't fat, no, but he was a large man, certainly sturdy. He did have a full head of wavy hair, which was graying.

One night he spoke to her, and she allowed the conversation, and then again on another night, and then she met him there one Saturday for a good dinner. He appreciated her, called her "beautiful," was kind, made apt jokes that everyone in the restaurant laughed at. So Amalia allowed the courtship, something different.

She visited his rented room, uncommonly neat for that of a man, especially a single man. He kissed her, just that.

It was only after several "dates" — he called them that — that he asked her if he could make love to her. They went to his room, and she let him. Oh, she didn't enjoy it, what was there to enjoy? He was urgent, clumsy. Afterward, he held her closely to him as if he were protecting her with his whole body. The next time she saw him, he readily admitted — but with embarrassment, which touched her — that he was married but permanently separated from a woman in Denver. A divorce, which both wanted, was pending. When that was final, soon, he wanted to marry "a good woman." "And if she's beautiful," he told her with a smile, "so much the better."

Sometimes, in his awkward urgency, he would hurt her during his lovemaking, but never deliberately — as she had always suspected the others had, at least at times. When she winced at his pawing and pressing, he would apologize quickly. And he never stopped holding her protectively, afterward.

Amalia decided: He would be a good father to her children; he loved her; and he was a kind, generous man with a steady job.

She arranged to introduce him to her family at dinner. She made fat *chiles rellenos,* which she knew he loved, and a rice casserole with pieces of chicken; puffy *sopapillas* sprinkled with cinnamon

and sugar for dessert; an extravagant meal that he kept compli-
menting enthusiastically at almost every bite.

Manny did not look at him. During dinner he had entertained his
brother and sister by making funny faces at them. Then, silent, he
kept his eyes fixed on the table, and Juan and Gloria followed his
lead, giggling.

When Amalia saw Raynaldo studying her family, she was proud.
Two good-looking sons and a pretty daughter, and — the Holy
Mother would not deny her this small vanity — she herself did not
look unattractive in a creamy dress that hugged the ovals of her
breasts.

Raynaldo cleared his throat. Amalia had rehearsed with him the
words he was to speak. He said to the children: "I want to be a father
to you."

Manny smiled and Amalia felt relieved. He said: "No, you just
want to fuck her, you want to fuck our mother."

Juan laughed, Gloria looked puzzled.

"*M'ijo* . . ." Amalia heard the pleading in her voice.

Manny pushed his plate off the table, and it shattered.

That night he did not come home, nor the next night. Amalia was
despondent, asking everyone in the neighborhood if they knew
where he was. He returned, early one morning, when she was in
the kitchen, unable to sleep.

"Where have you been?" Her love rushed to her son, but her
voice was cold — from worry that was now anger.

He sat down with her at the table. "'Amá," he said, "when I was
gone, I slept in an alley, near a trash bin so no one could find me.
A baby woke me up with his crying. Someone had abandoned him
in the garbage."

Amalia clenched her hands, warming them. "You're lying. That's
an ugly story. What mother would ever abandon her child to the
garbage?"

"It's true," he insisted, in a soft, almost whispering voice. "There
was a baby in the garbage, abandoned, crying."

"You're lying."

"And when I was away," his voice was lifeless now, "I fucked a
girl, 'Amá, in an abandoned house."

"Manny!" She would have been angrier with him for using that
word except that he was speaking even more softly.

"I'm not lying, 'Amá. I met her in one of those places where girls and guys go with hair dyed different colors. And, 'Amá, her breasts were real small." He held out one hand, vaguely.

The hand with the white scar. Amalia stood up angrily. "You're on drugs. If you're ever like this again, I don't want to see you!"

His eyes closed. He fell asleep on the table.

When Amalia came home from work, she found him sitting on the floor with Juan and Gloria. Gloria was inspecting the burn on his hand, as if trying to smooth it with her fingers. Amalia paused, tensely, watching them. Juan was the first to become aware of her. He looked up at her. Angry? Puzzled? Then Gloria left the room and Juan followed her.

"What did you tell them, Manny?"

He shook his head.

The next day — and for days following — Manny was changed, her Manny again, the son she had raised. "I'm going to be good now, 'Amita, I promise." He was even friendly to Raynaldo when he returned for more visits.

Amalia rushed in breathless with excitement on a Saturday afternoon. Manny was sitting on the floor teaching Gloria and Juan a card game.

"Raynaldo and I went to the courthouse and got married!" she announced to her children.

She was relieved that Manny said nothing and that Juan and Gloria seemed to accept it as if it had little to do with them.

It was a lie. She and Raynaldo had not been married, but claiming that would allow Raynaldo to move in that night. She had considered, but rejected, saying they had been married in church — she would adjust that later. She *had* coaxed Raynaldo to bring over a cake to celebrate that evening.

She avoided the children until then. Manny went out, but that was no different from other times.

Raynaldo came over with a colorful cake decorated in red, blue, green, yellow. He also brought a bottle of sparkling wine! Manny returned, and Amalia hugged him in gratitude.

They all gathered about the cake. Amalia almost convinced herself that what she had told her children was true — and it would be, as soon as Raynaldo's divorce was final.

She marveled at how happy Juan and Gloria looked, devouring

the cake. They were happy because now they had a father at last, Amalia knew. Tensely, she passed a slice of the cake to Manny. He took it.

Perhaps the inevitable course of her life might contain some peace, Amalia thought when Manny ate the cake and looked up at her smiling and she saw again the purified part of Salvador.

4

◆   ◆

*I*N HER STUCCO UNIT in Hollywood, Amalia remembered
Manny's smiling face when they had celebrated her "marriage" to
Raynaldo. Who would have thought that only a short time after that
day, she would sit in a courtroom and hear that very same boy —
her beloved son — called a murderer!

Now, the hot stillness of this day that had begun with the impression of a silver cross in the sky — *no more about that!* — persisted.
Still early morning, and the day was growing hotter. Would there
be one of those dreaded Sant' Anas today?

Amalia had remained for more seconds quietly watching Gloria
on her pullout bed and in her slip, and Juan in his shorts and on
his cot — sitting there without any embarrassment, still talking in
the living room that turned into their bedroom. Had they lowered
their voices when they detected her presence? Why didn't they run
to her, hug her, wish her a good morning, as they once had?

"Gloria! Juan!" She called out to them because she felt suddenly
angry, suddenly alone.

Her two children turned quickly to face her.

Oh, how beautiful they are, Amalia thought, as she did often.
Strange that so many people do not realize how beautiful Mexicans
are. They just don't see us, Amalia knew. Look at Juan — every sinew
on his body showed, that's how lean and strong he was, and not
quite eighteen. He combed his black hair back, only a strand over
his yellowish eyes now, eyes surprising with his brown complexion.
He was not tall, no, but he wasn't short, and he was so ... mature,
masculine. And why shouldn't she think that of him? He *was* her
son.... But the tinge of shame had come from the memory of
Angel, last night, and that extra beer.... She turned hurriedly to
bask in her daughter's fresh prettiness. Without makeup, Gloria's

face was flushed with its own coloring. She had hazel eyes, and her skin was as smooth as tan silk. She would inherit her mother's breasts, Amalia knew proudly. She already had a way of tossing her head to display her dark hair, the way she, Amalia, did when she was being . . . well . . . a *woman*. But Gloria was a girl, only fifteen.

"Hi, Mom," Gloria said easily.

Mom! Amalia hated that word. It made her feel fat and vulgar and ugly, like some of the women she worked for. Why couldn't Gloria call her "'Amá," the way Juan now often did? Sometimes he even called her "'Amita" — and when he did, she would quickly evoke her dead son, as if to assure *him* that the cherished designation still belonged to him.

"'Amá —" Juan said the word cautiously now, as if to please both her and Gloria.

Why did he feel he had to borrow his sister's new defiance? *About what?* When they began to dress, Amalia moved into the kitchen — more aging furniture, more barred windows. A picture of the Blessed Mother remained shiny because it was periodically replaced, most often from religious calendars. Here, too, were the graying paper and cloth flowers with which she had gradually tried to overwhelm the house.

It had seemed prettier when she first moved in, when Raynaldo made it possible to leave East Los Angeles. Yes, and everything had seemed so right that night they had celebrated her "marriage" to him.

That night, after the cake celebration, and for a time after, she muffled the sounds of Raynaldo's lovemaking by hanging blankets on the door of the bedroom — that's how sensitive she was to her children — so they would accept him as the father she knew he wanted to be.

And for a time they did accept him as that — Gloria and Juan did. It had been difficult to tell with Manny because soon after he was in trouble again.

Juvenile home, county detention camp, youth authority, detention center, youth training school. . . . Amalia could not keep the names straight. Manny was in and out of them. She was no longer sure which one it was, even when she rode by bus to visit him. He was there for fighting, then for stealing. Even the exact charges, Amalia could not remember.

More and more she prayed, not for anything, exactly, but just to express her faith. She went to confession and confessed the usual things, anger, impatience. And, more and more, she prayed to the Holy Mother, feeling that God had created the Blessed Lady — in part only, of course — to "soften" His most mysterious and difficult ways.

Manny was "away" again — that's how she referred to his absences. To lift her spirits, Raynaldo had begun taking her on Sunday drives in his old but pampered Ford, which he took regularly to be washed and sprayed with hot wax.

"What a beautiful neighborhood!" Amalia said as the shined car drove into Hancock Park. Unlike those in Beverly Hills, the marvelous houses here were not hidden behind walls and tall trees. There was one proud old mansion after another for anyone to admire.

"I know you like rich houses," Raynaldo explained his choice.

Trees arched their branches over the wide streets, creating a green, leafy tunnel. It seemed that only houses and those trees claimed the area — no one was out.

"That one!" Amalia said aloud, pointing to the most beautiful house. She had been playing a game with herself, that she could choose any house she wanted. She had chosen one with marbled steps that swept toward two stories, colored panes of glass —

A gunshot!

Raynaldo dodged, Amalia crouched.

"I've had a blowout," Raynaldo lamented.

The loose rattling of the ripped tire confirmed that. He drove to the curb of one of the great houses. He and Amalia got out. No one stirred to acknowledge their sudden crisis except a black maid, who peered out.

It was then that Amalia realized the origin of her earlier game. Once Manny had consoled her, after returning from a detention home: "'Amá, I promise you I'm going to be good, I'm going to be rich, and then I'll buy you the most beautiful house in the world. All you have to say is, 'That one!' and I'll buy it for you."

On another Sunday, Amalia saw something that disturbed her for days. They had driven to the Griffith Park Observatory, where she had thrilled to the make-believe sky. Now Raynaldo said he wanted to take her to a place one of the men he worked with had told him about, in West Los Angeles, a dance-bar where they played the romantic ballads she loved. He finally found the place, only to discover that it had been converted into a brawly cowboy club. Women with giant blonde hairdos and western shirts stared at Amalia in her velvet dress. She stared back at them.

Raynaldo drove home on Santa Monica Boulevard. It was night. Along shabby blocks, Amalia saw young men in their late teens, some perhaps younger, others in their early twenties, difficult to tell. They stood idly, alone or in small groups. Many were shirtless. They kept eyeing cars that drove by slowly and stopped on side streets. She saw one shirtless young man walk up to a car, talk briefly before the open window, then get in. The car drove away.

"They're boys looking for men who pay them," Raynaldo said knowledgeably.

Prostitutes — those boys? Amalia was confused and angered. She had never understood how one man could desire another. A man's thing belonged between a woman's legs. That's why God had made them the way He had. It baffled her even more that those boys had not looked like *maricones,* the effeminate men anyone could tell were —

A screech! Brakes! Shouts!

A carload of burly young men with clubs and bottles jumped out of a car and attacked a cluster of idling younger men. Just as suddenly as they had appeared, the attackers fled, laughing, leaving two boys bleeding on the sidewalk.

"*Qué horror!*" Amalia screamed.

Now, often, she talked about moving away from East Los Angeles. She saw more and more of the gangs, more of their graffiti everywhere. She paused once before one wall across which was scrawled in red, bleeding paint:

AZTLÁN ES UNA FÁBULA.

Aztlán? A fable? Where had she heard that name? Oh, an old man before a mural had told her — She could not remember, but the scrawled words continued to haunt her.

She learned increasingly about gang fights, violence, raids on the homes of rival members. Manny would be out soon. She knew how difficult it was to leave a gang, an even more brutal initiation than the pummeling required to join.

"I'll find a house somewhere else, *preciosa,*" Raynaldo promised.

He had just been given a raise. Now his job required him to work overnight at times, unpacking goods for a chain of groceries in and outside the city. Amalia would have grown suspicious about that with any other man, but she trusted him, believed him immediately when he informed her that his divorce was taking longer because some complications with his wife had occurred, not serious. Amalia was surprised at how much she missed his burly arms about her the mornings he was gone.

Except for the fact that Manny was still "away," things were much better than before. She could afford meat now and then, to make her special *picadillo,* and decent cheese for her favorite *entomatadas,* and chicken, which Gloria and Juan loved fried.

On her way from school with another girl, Gloria was walking past a small triangular park bordered by bushes with giant white blossoms when a car sped by and a gun fired out of its window at a teenage boy. He thrust himself on the ground, and the bullet grazed away from the pavement where the two girls had flung themselves. A gang shooting. . . . For days, Gloria refused to go to school. When Juan volunteered to escort her, she insisted they walk several blocks out of the way to avoid the deadly park. Soon after, a boy was stabbed in a school corridor. A gang ambush.

Sometimes distant, like echoes or omens, now there were more gunshots heard in the neighborhood. *"Las gangas,"* older people said, and soon began to add: *"La jura,"* because as police cars increased, so did the sound of bullets. In other cramped neighborhoods, too, in communities with beautiful names — Pomona, Florence, Echo Park — violence swept in, intended victims and bystanders felled by gang bullets, cop bullets. There was talk of barricading certain areas "to contain the violence, seal off drug zones."

Like living in jail, Amalia thought. And soon Manny would return to this.

She came home from work to hear an old man who lived nearby bragging to a cluster of boys, children, that in his day *"las gangas"* had real *"huevos"* — balls, real courage. *"We* used to *face* the other *vatos,* bring them down with *chingazos."* His wrinkled face brightened at the memory of the blows he had inflicted. "Sure we had to use weapons sometimes, I ain't saying we didn't, but only now and then and always one-on-one. Nowadays the *vatos* drive by in their cars, shoot, run away, get their courage from *drogas,* not *huevos.* That's not the real man's way. If you got class, you don't shoot no babies, no women, you don't run away." His voice gained authority. "And we *dressed, manos*—pegged pants, classy hats, pocket chains." He shook his palm, low, from the wrist, a wordless gang expression of grandness. "*Everyone* knew who we were."

Amalia rejected the memory of Salvador—he had said something like that.

"When we were real *chingones,* the toughest, that's when we *made* the *gringo* cops recognize us." The old man studied the boys listening intently. "That's one thing ain't changed, the only time they see us."

"And when they put you in jail," Amalia said angrily.

The old *veterano* was quiet for moments, his head bowed. Then his memory of grandeur resurged: "We even took on the U.S. Navy once, *manos*—you know that?" he asked the rapt boys. "Ever hear about the zoot-suit riots?"

The boys nodded. One said his grandfather had been in them.

"That was *us.*" In a long, slow arc, the old man's palm swept down, even lower now, the gang gesture of greatest pride. "And then some of us even joined the navy later, *manos!*" He laughed. Then he frowned. "But we *belonged!*" he said emphatically.

That night Amalia said to Raynaldo, "If we could only move away from it all."

"We will," he assured her, and held her hand.

A letter came:

Amalia—

Your father is dead—I am coming to live with you—there is nowhere else.

Your Mother.

Teresa arrived from El Paso with her Dolorosa. She cleared a table at the entrance on which Amalia had placed "fresh" cloth flowers to thwart what she had suspected would happen, and did: Teresa set her mournful statue there, to command the house. She handed the flowers back to Amalia.

Amalia repeated the story about her and Raynaldo getting married at the courthouse. She went on to embellish that they had even gone to a Catholic church, on their own, to exchange "sacred vows under God's watch."

Teresa said, "God doesn't believe lies, and neither do I."

"Our mother's not lying," Juan said firmly.

"She's telling you the truth," Gloria said.

That evening the old woman seemed quickly to "accept" Raynaldo. Out of convenience, Amalia thought, and crossed herself in case there was something sinful in thinking that.

Often startling them awake with her hacking, Teresa slept on what had been Manny's cot, in the room with Juan and Gloria.

Raynaldo found another house for them. In Hollywood! He took Amalia to see it.

It was a bungalow in another of the ubiquitous clutches of stucco courts that proliferate throughout Los Angeles. It was near Western Avenue and Fountain — and it was pretty, Amalia tried to convince herself. If not, it was certainly better than the unit in East Los Angeles, and far better than any place she had ever lived in. She was excited to learn from the only Anglo who still lived there, with his wife — but not for long, they both looked to be at least eighty to Amalia — that the court had once been inhabited by "movie people."

"Movie stars?" Amalia was hopeful. Ava Gardner . . .

"No — grips and extras," the old man said.

Amalia didn't understand what they were, but, she reminded herself, as she would often, it *was* in Hollywood. It was also close to the tangle of freeways, but: "You can imagine the sound of the traffic is the sound of the ocean — someone told me that," Raynaldo advised her. That would be difficult, since she had never been to the ocean. Her enthusiasm dampened when she saw that other houses in the neighborhood were beginning to decline, windows left broken, patched. But each unit in the court did have a small "garden" — only about two feet by four — and there was a rose bush toward the back. The unit was flanked by stubby palm trees. From one of its windows you could see — in the distant hills — the giant HOLLYWOOD sign. This disturbed her: A few blocks away, on Sunset Boulevard, along a strip of fast-food stands and seedy motels, exaggeratedly painted women paraded the streets. Still, there was this: She saw no sign whatever of gangs in the neighborhood.

They moved there.

Juan and Gloria kept joking about being "movie stars" now that they lived in Hollywood.

Raynaldo turned a small porch into a bedroom for Teresa. Amalia placed her mother's statue on a table there — "a *special* table, just for her," she told the old woman; but Teresa insisted she wanted to share La Dolorosa with everyone. She located the somber black presence again in the living room.

Amalia marveled at her mother. Despite her now constant wheezing, she still had so much energy. Perhaps too much. Soon after they had moved into the new neighborhood, she set out to investigate her surroundings. She came back indignant. "Who would have thought I would come to live so near Filipinos and Protestants." She had discovered that several blocks away from this area that was populated mainly by Mexicans, there were pockets of other groups — Armenians, Asians, a smattering of black people. To Teresa they were all "Filipinos" because there had been some in the tenement where she had lived and they had been Protestants. "I saw stores with names written in God knows what language. Certainly not Spanish. And all those Protestant churches — one with a star instead of a crucifix." She made an eternal sign of the cross, punctuating each movement with a stern look at Amalia.

Teresa's hacking often wakened Amalia, especially on nights when Raynaldo was away.

Still, in this new neighborhood, Juan and Gloria were going to the good school nearby — even some Anglos went there, and there was no sign of gangs, no territorial graffiti. When Manny returned, he would be away from the dangerous former neighborhood.

It was around that time that earthquakes invaded Amalia's fears. That was when she saw the wall split apart before her eyes. She thought the world had exploded. It had not, and what had occurred was called a "moderate earthquake." That annoyed her — it had not seemed "moderate" to her.

Soon after, she went to visit Rosario at the sewing factory. Rosario now ate her lunch late — "to avoid listening to Milagros's accounts of her serials," she told Amalia. They were sitting on the stairs in the hallway of the building and eating Amalia's homemade *chiles rellenos* when Milagros ran past them and into the sweatshop, blaring the news that the Mexican tabloid — in her hands — was predicting that the Big Earthquake would occur at exactly 1:34 that afternoon. It was the same earthquake that a famous astrologer had centuries ago foreseen for this very date — and a "seer" down the block had further confirmed it in the newspaper.

The Mexican women — and the Nicaraguan, Guatemalan, and Salvadoran women who now worked there — all hastily gathered their belongings, because it was 1:29, five minutes before the earth would tremble disastrously.

"Bunch of *supersticiosas* — still believing in witches," Rosario chastised them. "No one can predict when the Big One will occur."

"I'm not waiting to find out if it's today," said one of the women.

"Not me either," said another. Soon they had all fled the sweaty factory. Rosario kept eating her *rellenos*. Amalia was torn with conflict. She wanted to believe Rosario — who was, after all, the intelligent one — and to stay with her to show she was not a *supersticiosa*. On the other hand —

"Are you *sure* it's not going to happen?" She asked the older woman.

"No one can tell." Rosario kept eating.

Amalia longed to stay. But at 1:32 she ran out into the street.

The news had spread. Women from the sewing factories in the garment district, Anglo secretaries from glassy office buildings, businessmen in suits, skid-row bums from Main Street — all gathered outside, looking up as if the earthquake would descend from the sky. Several tried to laugh. Amalia looked for Rosario. Nowhere.

Now it was 1:33.

Then it was 1:34.

Amalia closed her eyes and braced her feet.

It was 1:35.

Buildings — new chromy ones — were impassive in the hot day.

"Well it *is* earthquake weather," said an Anglo businessman, laughing.

"Hot and still," confirmed a secretary.

Then it was 1:40.

Someone said, "What the hell," and went back to work. Some still checked their watches. Then everyone laughed and they went back into their buildings.

Amalia whispered to Rosario, where she had remained eating on the steps: "I didn't believe it."

Rosario didn't even look at the women coming back, did not gloat.

"There won't ever be a Big One, will there, Rosario?" Amalia asked hopefully. But when she saw the older woman about to answer after peering at her for pensive seconds, Amalia excused herself to go talk to Milagros, who greeted her with her usual "Here's la Liz Taylor!"

At least, Amalia consoled herself about having rushed out with the other women, *she* had not been like so many of the new aliens who for days refused to return to their apartments and slept in parks. She felt even better on learning that many very rich people had fled the city in airplanes during that time.

"What worries you so terribly, Rosario?" Amalia asked her friend on another occasion, when the tiny woman was sitting on the familiar steps of the old building.

At first Rosario only shook her head, as if thrusting away the possibility of any answer. Then she touched Amalia. "*Mira, corazón* —" She spoke slowly, softly, as if to contain words that might otherwise explode out of her: "Every day hundreds — a thousand now — are arrested crossing the border — *every day!* — risking danger because they're hungry, fleeing poverty, risking *la migra* hunting them down like animals, with horses, helicopters, brutal ambushes to keep the desperate people away — *and from what?* From jobs no one else would take!" Her voice had risen with anger: "Thieves rob them of their savings, women are raped, people murdered." She breathed deeply, continued slowly as if to make sure Amalia understood her full despair. "And if they make it across? More horrors." She shook her head in disgust. "Two men escaped a ranch in Somis — yes, escaped, *corazón* — through barbed wire. Beaten, their heads shaved, worked sixteen hours a day for fifty dollars a week, charged five dollars for a gallon of milk. Amalia, *corazón* —" Her voice almost broke. "Families end up separated in detention camps. Jorge told me of a man who sold his home to pay a *coyote* more than a thousand dollars to smuggle him and his wife across, and the *coyote* left them — his own people! — left them abandoned in a hovel in the desert, without food, water. His wife got her period —" Her voice was harsh with rage: "And those who reach the cities? Slums! The streets! Terrorized by *gangas* and violence and the *migra* always tracking them down. Illegals? Huh! How can a human being not be legal?" Her voice softened, a whisper: "*Corazón,* a human being has the right to eat, to have a home, work —"

"And to worship God and the Holy Mother," Amalia added, assuring Rosario that she understood, and cared.

Rosario smiled. "Yes, that. But many times the Church—" She pulled back. "*Corazón,* at this very moment, Jorge's family—" She stopped abruptly. She said quietly: "For all the destitute people, it's like living with a loaded gun held to your head."

A loaded gun held to your head!

Just the words terrified Amalia. A loaded gun held to your head!

When Rosario returned to work and Amalia remained at the steps for a few moments, she was astonished to see — again — how tiny and frail her friend was.

Well, Amalia thought later, despite all the miseries, there was always faith in God's ways, although Rosario had certainly made them seem even more mysterious, hadn't she? Amalia had often wondered — but had never wanted to ask — whether Rosario had strayed away from the Holy Church. No, she assured herself, because her name meant "rosary" and what was more Catholic than that? Whatever! God, if only through the Miraculous Mother, would be sure to extend His compassion to someone like Rosario. Of that Amalia was sure.

There was a time with Rosario that Amalia cherished especially. She often evoked it because she understood part of it and wanted to understand all of it. Rosario had said to her: "You're a very smart woman, Amalia, perhaps smarter than you know — but what good does it do you, *corazón?*" Amalia was flattered, then immediately puzzled. "What should I do, Rosario?" she asked. "Think," Rosario had said. "Just think."

Things were changing for the worse in the garment district of downtown Los Angeles. Thousands of new aliens were seeking work, any work. Men, women, boys, girls from countries south of Mexico, with no papers, worked up to sixty-four hours weekly for $50, and they did not complain because if the sweatshops closed they would have no income at all. More and more women brought their children to work with them, tucking the smallest on rolls of material stacked against walls.

Rosario informed the women at Lewis's shop about all this, her voice furious with new indignation. Once — and Amalia increasingly adjusted her housework hours so she could see Rosario, and, too, listen to Milagros's accounts of the romantic travails in her serials — a middle-aged Anglo woman and a young Mexican man from a group called La Familia del Pueblo — The Village Family — rushed in passing out pamphlets that spelled out in Spanish the rights of garment workers. Many of the women threw the pamphlets away nervously. Rosario picked them up and placed them assertively next to their machines.

"You got no business here," Lewis was shouting at the invaders.

"Just information." The Anglo woman faced him. She had bright red hair and deep-set, pained eyes.

"I run a fair shop."

"Then there's nothing to fear, sir," the Mexican man said.

So handsome, with gleaming white teeth, Amalia noticed. Of course he would be a devout Catholic.

"No need for those pamphlets in a *fair* shop," Lewis emphasized to the women when the invaders had left.

"*Fairer,*" Rosario admitted, and mumbled: "Imagine what it's like in the others."

"The others" were unlicensed shops burgeoning in declining buildings nearby. Most often, Koreans, who spoke neither English nor Spanish, were identified as the owners, but no one was sure — the Koreans claimed they were only "managers" for invisible small contractors; and the landlords of the aged buildings and the manufacturers whose labels would be attached to the garments produced in the sweatshops claimed ignorance about the contractors.

"Those Oriental owners don't know our fair American ways," Lewis declared, separating himself from the unlicensed sweatshops that did not even bother to post a company name over their workrooms. "That's why there're so many damn inspectors now." He avoided Rosario's cold stare. "And who the hell can compete with those new shops?" he complained in a sullen mumble.

Soon after, women on the buses were warning about a *migra* agent terrorizing the garment district, demanding to see the work papers of lone women, "arresting" them, handcuffing them — and raping them and abandoning them miles from the city. That even made the television news — at least three women were known to have been attacked.

So Amalia decided to stay away for a time.

Then Manny returned, a man now. Amalia welcomed him with love and sadness.

He seemed to get along with Raynaldo, quietly — and even Teresa appeared to be growing fond of him. Once she called him "*m'ijo*" — and Amalia resented it. He did not complain about Teresa's coughing, though he slept on the floor near her cot.

One night he gave Amalia money, several bills. "I don't want you to be poor," he told her. She longed to believe what he told her — that he had gotten a job. And he *was* gone all day. And *not,* Amalia assured herself without daring to ask, because he was going back to his old neighborhood.

Another night, when Raynaldo was gone, Manny sat on the floor laughing and playing cards with Gloria and Juan. He kept explaining the rules of the game to them, patiently; but — Amalia saw this and marveled at how wonderful it was to have all her children with her serenely — he was making sure that Gloria would win, and then Juan, and —

Two policemen burst into the house with guns drawn.

Manny stood up with his hands raised. "'Amá —" That's all he said, a whisper.

Amalia rushed over to hold him. "*M'ijo!*"

A cop pushed her away roughly.

Manny strained toward her. A cop threw him to the floor, hand-cuffing him.

In a corner, Amalia held Gloria and Juan.

Amalia sat in a courtroom in the Hall of Justice in downtown Los Angeles and heard her son charged with attempted murder. In that courtroom she came to despise — and she went alone, did not *want* anyone with her — she learned — for certain, finally — that her son — who listened fascinated as if people there were talking about someone he did not know — dominated one of the toughest gangs in the city, along with Indio, his age. Both were *vatos locos,* the most reckless. Sometimes he and Indio led others in what seemed to Amalia to be no more than childish pranks — couldn't they see that? — raiding an orange grove and feasting on fruit; other times they led them into pointless danger, riding a "borrowed car" to the police station, and, horn made to stick, leaving it there as the *klika* scattered in every direction. On *roca* or *polvo* — crack or angel dust — Manny became fearless, one terrified boy testified.

In that courtroom, Amalia discovered a whole other life that belonged to her son: After a series of *pleitos* with a rival gang — skirmishes that augur a major confrontation — and only minutes after the name of Manny's gang, scrawled on a wall, was spattered with paint — a car sped by Indio's house, a shack surrounded by sunflowers — where Manny, Indio, and another boy drank beer, smoked. "*From Chuco and his boys!*" Those shouted words were followed by three shots. Indio was dead. Manny went, alone, to confront the invaders on their own turf. Backed by his own home boys, the young man named "Chuco" — because a distant relative had been a famous *"pachuco"* — met him. At the sight of the slight young man standing before them unarmed, they heckled, laughed, taunted.

Manny said to Chuco: *"Estás escamado, ése. Te rajas . . .* Even with all your home boys, you're scared shitless, man. I'm facing you like you couldn't face Indio, and I don't even have a gun. *No tienes huevos."*

"I don't have no balls, huh, *ése?"* Chuco brought out a knife. Lazily he cleaned his nails with it. He said very slowly: *"Tu madre está chingada."*

"I'm a son of a what?"

"You heard me."

It was then that Manny went out of control. He knocked the knife from Chuco's hand, grabbed it, wrested him to the dirt, and held the knife over his throat.

"Say that again, *cabrón,* and I'll kill you."

When they saw the knife touching Chuco's throat, the others didn't move.

Chuco tried to twist away on the ground. The knife tore across his chest in an eruption of blood.

"And all the time he was crying," the frightened boy who had told that account of the fight said about Manny.

My son was defending me! That was Amalia's first thought as she sat in that punishing courtroom and heard of the incidents that had led her and her son here. It had happened because Chuco made that ugly insult to a mother. Amalia could not repress a moment of pride out of the pain, pride in her son's love for her. But quickly that triumph was drowned in the reality of what was occurring in this gray room. It had been an accident. She was sure of that as she stared at her son sitting nearby, looking even younger, a boy, a child. Who could possibly think *he* had attempted murder? . . . And if the boy died it would be murder.

When that day's eternal session was over, Amalia saw her son handcuffed and taken back to jail. *He was defending me!* This time the pride she was able to extract from that thought was pulled away even more quickly by an overpowering sense of helplessness and sadness, and an anger which spread out to everything.

She stood alone in the corridor outside the courtroom where her son's life was being reduced to one violent act. It was as if nothing but that existed, not the many times of sweetness that had occurred between her and her son, nothing but the knifing of a stranger nicknamed Chuco, who had killed another stranger named Indio. Amalia was thinking that when a woman in a black-dyed dress held her hand tightly and said passionately:

"Your son was right to go after that savage, that Chuco, who murdered my son."

Amalia faced Indio's mother. In that moment, another woman Amalia had seen in the courtroom — a thin, dark Mexican woman with eyes full of loss — looked at them and called out:

"*Las gangas, las gangas malditas.*"

Amalia recognized her as Chuco's mother.

The three women nodded, yes, the cursed gangs were to blame. Now Chuco's mother stood with them, the three women bound by mutual grief. They held one another's hands. Then the moment passed. They looked away from each other and separated.

Amalia needed to talk to Rosario. Who else would know what to do, what to feel?

"She's gone," said Milagros, at the sewing factory.

"Gone? Where?" Amalia believed the absence immediately.

"Who knows? You hear so many stories," a woman nearby said.

"I told you what happened," another woman asserted. "Jorge's disappeared, too. He paid a *coyote* a thousand dollars to bring his daughter and her husband across the border and the *coyote* abandoned them, and Jorge killed the *coyote,* and Rosario took them all in and *la migra* caught her —"

"No," a Guatemalan woman said, "Jorge killed one of the men of *la migra,* the one who found his daughter and her son in the desert and —"

"Whatever," the Guatemalan woman said. "They caught Rosario."

"Caught her —?" Amalia was grasping it all instantly, wishing she could disbelieve it, but she remembered that Rosario had told her something like that one day, about a man and woman abandoned in a hovel in the desert by a *coyote,* and something about Jorge —

"She's probably in jail," a Salvadoran woman said, "just like in my country."

"No, she ran away before they could arrest her," another woman offered.

"All I know is that I miss her," Milagros said.

Amalia walked silently away from them.

Milagros followed her to the hall. "Amalia, come and see me, please. To talk."

Then she knew more about Rosario! Amalia promised and took the address Milagros had scribbled on a piece of paper.

The public attorney appointed to represent Manny told her to get there "an hour early" when she went to visit her son in the Hall of Justice. She arrived even earlier on a sweaty afternoon to find that people were already lined up for a whole block to visit their own inmates. Almost all were women, many with children, several pregnant. Some sat on the sidewalk, on newspapers. Older children attempted to play in the street. Most of those here were Mexicans and black people. Very few were Anglos — only here did Amalia remember them looking out of place.

Along the jagged line, vendors hawked cold drinks, hot dogs, syrupy popcorn.

A slender woman stood hesitantly near her. Amalia saw a look she had come to recognize in the courtrooms on the faces of mothers whose sons were in trouble. "Your son —?"

The woman nodded. "*M'ijo, sí.*"

There was something more in her anxiety, something added, Amalia detected. The woman seemed to want to pull away from her at the same time that she lingered. When they had reached the end of the line, the woman said hurriedly, "I hope everything will turn out right for your . . . son?"

"*M'ijo,*" Amalia confirmed.

The woman rushed away.

Only then did Amalia notice that there was another line on the opposite side of the entrance to the Hall of Justice. A younger, pregnant woman in a bright dress noticed Amalia's confusion. "That other line is for the visitors of the *maricones.*"

Amalia did not know what to think. She didn't like homosexuals any more than the next person — sometimes they disgusted her; but why should their families — their mothers, that woman she had just talked to? — be separated as if they shared contamination? "Of course, God *does* forbid that sternly," she addressed her own confusion. She remembered the doubled pain on the face of the woman who had fled from her, who was here to see *her* son. "But that woman —"

"I wouldn't feel that sorry for her," the pregnant woman said. "She's a *divorciada.*"

A divorced woman! But God understood *that,* Amalia knew. She had clarified it with Father Ysidro. Now she avoided even glancing at the separated line. She also avoided the pregnant woman, distancing herself by letting two women get ahead of her in the line.

"I've been here for two hours," a black woman said to no one. Her sweat was drenching the child she cradled in her arms. "Hate that building." She did not even look at the looming Hall of Justice. "Can't even buy a cold drink." Her perspiration dripped onto the child's face, eyes, and he began to cry.

"I don't even know why my husband is here, and he doesn't either. We can't understand what they're saying," a Mexican woman complained to everyone.

"Well, I know why *mine* is here — because he tried to kill me," another joined in.

"Then why are *you* here, *mujer*?"

"Who else has he got, woman?"

"My son did not —" an older black woman asserted with indignation.

"— drugs —" . . . "— resisting arrest —" . . . "What will we do now?" . . . "— *las gangas* —" . . . "— *drogas* —" . . . "— no job —" . . . "What will we do now?" . . . "— the police said he —" . . . "I don't know why, *mujer!*" . . . "— the gangs —" . . . "drunk but he —" . . . "What will we do now?"

As their time in line stretched, the women looked drabber, poorer, more desperate, and their words became one terrible lament punctuated by the crying of children as Amalia waited to see her son.

The line began to move now. At the entrance to the Hall of Justice, two guards checked purses, cleared the visitors. A square-faced woman in uniform — *could* she be Mexican and work here? Amalia wondered — barked in English and Spanish that they were to surrender "any weapons, knives, guns, drugs" they were carrying. Amalia closed her eyes as if that would allow her to endure. She felt as if she, too, were being incarcerated.

An old rusted elevator took them to another floor. With a jangle of doors, the elevator opened into a bare room drenched in yellowish light. That room led to a larger one, where a series of partitions created small open cubicles; each contained one stool and a telephone. Behind a wall of heavy glass, inmates in blue uniforms were being marched to assigned places before their visitors. Searching urgently for her son, Amalia saw, in another section of the large room and along another row of cubicles, the woman she had spoken to first; she was sitting before a young man dressed in a prison uniform like the others, except that his was bright orange.

Amalia turned away, too overwhelmed by her own grief to deal with anything else. She saw her son. Through the glass pane, he smiled at her, his mouth moving eagerly now, forming words she could not hear through the glass. Then he picked up his telephone, and she picked up hers. How strange to be about to speak to her son through a telephone when they were sitting only inches away, how strange to see him so near and not be able to touch him, hold him, as she longed to. Even his voice had been taken away! she thought, until he spoke into the telephone and she heard on her end of the line his familiar:

"— 'Amá! 'Amita!"

"*M'ijo* —"

Then they rushed assurances that they were fine, just fine.

"Everything is going to be okay, 'Amá," he asserted. He made motions of kissing her fingers. "I promise." He converted the thumb and forefinger of his right hand into a cross, which he kissed, a holy vow.

Amalia stared at the place on his hand where the white scar had not entirely obliterated the tattoo of the burning cross. "It was an accident, *m'ijo,*" she said.

He nodded, deeply.

She was sure she had meant that the near-killing of Chuco was an accident, but she wondered — later — whether her son had been remembering the burn on his hand.

The visit was over, short minutes! The public attorney had told her she could bring a restricted amount of money to her son. She had worked an extra day to manage the maximum, $40. Before a counter in the dirty-lit room through which she had entered, she lined up again in a smaller line with others who had money for their inmates, mostly change, a dollar. She filled out a slip to indicate to whom the money would go, the amount. Behind another glass partition, the inmates had lined up.

Amalia handed her slip and the $40 to a guard. He was wearing plastic gloves! Afraid of what contamination? Amalia saw him give the bills to another guard, who dipped them in water, washing them.

"In case somebody has stuck drugs to the money," a woman explained to Amalia's startled stare.

But Amalia did not care about their reasons now because she saw her son. He was standing behind the glass pane. On a sliding metal tray the money was passed to him through a small opening. He rejected it.

No, he mimed. For *you.*

Then he kissed his fingertips and extended them to her and she kissed her own and blessed him with a sign of the cross.

From jail, Amalia received a letter from her son.

> . . . I love you with all my heart . . . I'm goin to do right — I promise in the name of the Blesst Mother you allways comend me to & love so much & who loves you . . .

Amalia had to stop reading. Each word filled her with love and hurt.

Two men appeared at her house. They were not in uniform, but she recognized them. They had an official look that was cruel even when they were attempting to be kind.

"— that your son Manuel is dead."

Amalia frowned.

"He committed suicide in his cell."

"Liars!" Amalia screamed at both men. She felt furious at their lie, the terrible accusation about her son. Sorrow would come later with the awareness of his death, and it would come in huge waves that would inundate her. Now she was enraged.

The men led her to a chair inside the house. Then they walked out.

That night it seemed to Amalia that the world itself had died. She went into her room and did not allow anyone to enter. She pushed her head into a pillow to keep herself from screaming. She lay shivering in the coldness of her own perspiration and tears, which then turned hot. Then the crying would stop. A terrifying stillness would clasp her, the stillness she knew would exist forever in her life, the stilled voice of her son. The sobbing and the tears would convulse her again until there were only sobs without tears, exhausted. She would fall into a terrifying sleep, as if she were awake within total darkness, waking suddenly, again and again, into this terrible realization: My son is dead, I'll never see him again.

She claimed her son's body and buried him. She allowed no one with her. She made Raynaldo promise to stay with Gloria and Juan. She stood over the scraped earth and said softly:

"*M'ijo.*"

And she waited, actually waited, to hear his answer:

"'Amita."

Then she walked away with a new presence in her life, the absence of her son.

"'Amá, please don't be so sad," Gloria said. Amalia glanced at her daughter. "'Amita," Juan said.

"Don't call me that!" Amalia's body had jolted. "Only my Manny called me that, that was his name for me."

Juan retreated. Gloria stood next to him.

Amalia saw the hurt on their faces. She reached out for both of her children. Their tense bodies did not entirely surrender to her. "I do want you to call me 'Amita," she said, but she knew she was pleading to her dead son.

In those days it seemed to her that she could not even "see" her two other children. Oh, it wasn't that she didn't see them, really. It was just that she wasn't clearly aware of them. She realized this when, suddenly arriving home from work — and she continued to work fiercely — she would see Gloria and catch her looking at her in a certain way she could not remember before. Or was it that something else was different about her? Not the added lipstick, the teased hair, the new fullness of her breasts. A look.

And Juan. She saw him across the street one day, idling, as he had begun to now that he no longer laughed as often — when had he stopped? — and she thought, What a handsome young man; why is he so sad? — before she realized he was her son.

Now there were the endless reports concerning Manny's death. The return of the clothes. Infernal visits to the public attorney — and she insisted to Raynaldo that she did not want *any*one with her.

This is what was claimed: In jail, Manny had threatened two guards who had come to quiet his screaming. When they tried to handcuff him, he pulled one bound hand away and lashed at the face of one of them, drawing blood. The city psychiatrist to whom he was taken ordered that he be placed in a "behavior observation module" because of "unstable comportment." Instead he was put into an isolated cell.

"So they could murder him," Amalia told the attorney. "*They* choked him with his shirt." She read him Manny's letter, portions of it. "Is that the letter of someone who's going to kill himself?" Even those words tasted ugly to her. "*They* killed him."

The attorney agreed. "It's possible, God knows it's happened before. And there were irregularities in the report. I'm asking for an investigation by —"

"No," Amalia said firmly. She had come only to assert the truth, what she knew, to have it confirmed. And it had been. "I know what happened and so do you. Those men would just keep on lying, and then there would be others who would support them, and nothing would come of it. I don't want any more lies pulling at my son's life. I don't want any more pain added to his memory."

The attorney said he would write her about any "pending matters."

"I don't want to hear about them," Amalia said.

Teresa shouted at her: "He let himself be killed rather than come back to you with all your men!"

"Liar!" Juan screamed at her.

"Liar!" Gloria cried.

Amalia slapped her mother.

Teresa staggered back. Then she began to chant loudly a prayer for the dead.

"Cruel liar!" Amalia yelled at her mother. "Listen to his letter to me." She pulled out the letter she had read from over and over. "'My dearest mamacita —'" She could read only a few more words: "'I love you with all my heart —'" before she gasped and stopped.

Throughout, Raynaldo stood by her, but she was remote. He was gone more often on overnight hauls, perhaps to honor her repeated assertion that she must be left alone. During that period, Amalia felt dazed. Everything and everyone seemed to move before her without a sound that she could understand. She heard words Juan uttered — and Gloria — of consolation, of sadness. And cries. She heard Teresa's whispered prayers.

Only later would she become aware that Juan was talking tough now — and any gang would welcome him because of the defiant glow they would attribute to his brother. She would realize, later, that boys came to see Gloria and she went out. She would deal with all that soon, when these darkest days would end, this eternal time saturated with Manny's death, a time during which he died over and over in the isolated jail cell, alone.

Sometimes — she would realize this only after it happened — Juan would suddenly hug her and Gloria would rest her head on her lap. But Amalia could find nothing to say to them that would not add to her awareness that Manny was not there.

She worked frenziedly, taking extra jobs, staying late, getting up before dawn.

And she prayed to the Blessed Mother.

At dinner she realized Juan had been hiding a plate of food. He took it out. She followed him to a dilapidated garage behind the court. He was about to pry open loose boards.

"Who's in there, Juan?"

He seemed about to turn away.

Amalia entered the dark garage. Among broken fixtures and car parts discarded there, a young man sat on a blanket spread out on the dirt. He was about seventeen, about Juan's age, Mexican, or deeply tanned.

"The dude goes to my school," Juan used his tough new voice. "He ran away." The posturing voice faded. "He was sleeping in the alley, 'Amá. I told him about this garage."

Amalia looked at the boy. Was he a runaway? — she knew young people were sleeping in parks and in the streets now. Or was he a gang member, hiding because of something he had done? On drugs? He looked frightened.

"Give him the food," Amalia said to Juan.

The young man took it, began eating.

"After he eats, he'll have to leave. I don't want any more trouble than I have," Amalia told her son.

As if used to flight, the young man gathered a few belongings scattered on the dirt.

"Go back to your mother," Amalia said to him, "I'm sure she misses you."

"He doesn't have anyone!" Juan shouted at her. "He's from El Salvador."

Then the boy wasn't from school. Amalia was startled by Juan's angered tone, his words.

The young man left the blanket on the ground. He touched Juan briefly on both shoulders. He left, glancing back once more.

"He reminded me of Manny, when *he* ran away, that time, remember?" Juan turned away from her quickly. He picked up the blanket from the ground.

Remember? How could she forget? She remembered everything about her dead son — and, yes, the Salvadoran boy had resembled him; he had the same look of bewildered innocence her son had never lost.

That night Amalia thought she had screamed, but it must have been a nightmare because nobody heard her.

A few days after — when Raynaldo was away for the night — she came home late from work and threw herself in bed, exhausted. She fell asleep immediately for the first time since Manny's death.

Teresa's coughing wakened her. Amalia screamed: "Stop it! I have to work tomorrow. Stop it!" The coughing weakened, stopped.

Amalia heard her children stirring. She walked barefoot on the cold floor, telling Gloria and Juan to go back to sleep. In the converted porch, she saw her mother propped on her pillow, the way she slept to secure her breathing, control the gasping cough. Teresa's gauzy eyes were open. Amalia went back to bed.

In the morning she found her mother in the same position, eyes still open. Teresa was dead. Now Amalia would have to make arrangements to deal with this new death. So she was glad she had managed to fall asleep again last night, to get a full night's peaceful rest at last.

5

♦   ♦

*I*N THE KTICHEN of her stucco bungalow in Hollywood on the morning that had begun when she saw the silver cross in the sky — *imagined* it — Amalia prepared her morning coffee, automatically setting another cup for Raynaldo on the table covered with red-and-white checkered linoleum. She always tried to avoid looking at the tiny mounds and streaks of gray borax that lined the edges of the room to ward off cockroaches, indomitable in summer. But her eyes could not keep from lingering over the chair Manny had claimed as his — it had one leg shorter than the others. She had removed the chair from the kitchen after his death, but its absence became more painful. It was kept, unused, against the wall.

This remained out of her sight: Teresa's La Dolorosa. Amalia had put it in the closet even before taking off the black dress she had borrowed from a neighbor for her mother's flowery funeral. "A woman should have as many flowers when she leaves the world as when she married in church — if God granted her the blessing of a white wedding," the old woman had told Amalia. Even surrounded by decorated chrysanthemums, and lying in the coppery coffin with her hands crossed over her rosary on her chest, Teresa had managed to look sternly at her daughter.

After the funeral, one day — it seemed that it had occurred in one day — the deep trance within which Amalia had existed for months, in which only Manny's death was real, lifted. She awakened one morning and felt reassured by Raynaldo's protective arms about her; they had never been withdrawn, she had merely not felt their warmth. That weekend, she agreed to go dancing with him. At dinner she laughed at some nonsense or other of his. She knew that all her life she would be haunted by memories of her dead son and that the hurt and missing would always be there; but she also realized that the course of her life — which had included death instead of the peace she had thought might occur — must now continue. The Holy Mother would be with her — was with her — as she always was. Amalia had felt a saddened peace after that.

But it was soon broken by the tension that developed — or did she just begin to notice it when she came out of the long trance? — among Raynaldo, Gloria, and Juan, the tension Raynaldo must have carried with them to El Bar & Grill last night when he stalked out angrily because that young man named Angel — she would not think of him; never again! — was admiring her. And how was that *her* fault?

Was she missing Raynaldo so soon, and even though she knew he would come back? Amalia wondered in her kitchen now. This period with him had been one of the best. Not once had a utility been disconnected. . . . Well, she *would* miss his arm about her later this morning — but he'd be back by then — when she would watch her *semanal,* her weekly television drama, "Camino al Sueño." On Saturdays, when he wasn't working and after they had their coffee, he would follow her into the living room — the beds would have been folded away — and he would share a highlight of her week, that week's installment of "The Road to a Dream."

On the kitchen table were stitched pieces of lavender material for a dress Amalia was making. She was an excellent seamstress and cut her own patterns out of newspapers. She had not decided whether this dress would be for her or for Gloria.

When they entered the kitchen, Juan was wearing his pants, no shirt, Gloria was in a thin lemony dress she often put on before she made herself up. Both were barefooted.

Amalia wanted to tell them —

How beautiful they were!

Juan kissed Amalia lightly on the cheek, as he always did in greeting. "I got something for you," he said to her.

Gloria walked to the refrigerator.

To avoid kissing me? Amalia wondered, and wanted to *order* her to kiss her.

Juan sat at the table. He held out some earrings to Amalia. They were large, with lots of glittering things, the kind she loved.

Why this gift now? Amalia was immediately suspicious. Juan had never given her anything. "Where did you get the money for them?"

Juan withdrew the earrings. "I'm working after school, man." He bounced the earrings from hand to hand.

It infuriated her when he called her "man," although she knew it was just an expression. She had begun to notice that he used the word when he was trying to disguise something, hide something, by sounding tough.

"Where are you working, Juan?" Amalia felt tense just to ask that question.

"At a video rental store."

Juan resented menial jobs. When he had worked during other times, and even before his recent moodiness, he would come home and say, "That Mickey Mouse job is shit, just shit." He had not sounded like that now. "Where is the store?" Amalia forced another question. She spoke to her children in a combination of English and Spanish, sliding from one to the other in the same sentence. They would answer her like that, except that they had no accent in English, that she could detect, except perhaps now and then. She had begun to notice that, in anger, her son and daughter would shift to English when they spoke to her. With each other they almost always talked in English, with slang words that annoyed her.

Juan looked at her in exasperation. "In Hollywood, man, where else? I told you."

"He's in the movies, Mom. A big star. He's sure good-looking enough," Gloria said, still not looking at her.

And he *was* good-looking enough, Amalia knew. But you never saw young Mexicans in American movies. "You *didn't* tell me you were working, Juan." She would have remembered.

"Yeah, Mom." Gloria faced her finally. "He did tell you, I heard him."

Mom! Again that despised word that made her feel fat and ugly. "Maybe he told *you,*" Amalia could not keep accusation out of her voice, "you talk late every night."

"We hear you and Raynaldo, too," Gloria said. She scratched one bare foot with the other. "Talking, I mean."

Amalia insisted Raynaldo keep his sex sounds low, sometimes quieting them herself by kissing him only for that purpose. She wanted to confront her daughter's insolence. What are you holding against me? What could Teresa have told them? Amalia remembered Teresa's whispers, prayers — out of that time of blackness, they had become like muffled curses.

Juan placed the earrings carefully on the table. He touched his forehead, brushing his hair over the recent bruise there.

"It's almost healed, *m'ijo*," Amalia soothed him. He had explained it only vaguely — a fight at school, he'd fallen.

"Fuckin' bastards," Gloria cursed.

Juan looked at her quickly.

A cautioning look. Amalia did not know what to react to immediately: Gloria's apparent knowledge of what had caused the bruise, Juan's signal to stop her, or to the filthy word. "Don't use that word around me, Gloria, not here or anywhere else!" she demanded.

"Fuck? That word? You never heard it before . . . Mom?"

Yes, last night! "Never!" Amalia looked down because she thought her face might be flushed with shame.

"Most people have," Gloria said. "I bet Raynaldo has."

"He's never used it in my presence," Amalia was certain.

Gloria shrugged. "You love him, Mom?"

The easy words were like shots at Amalia. "Of course I love him. He's my husband!" And even if he isn't, how do you think we manage even this well? How do you think I can keep you in school? She wanted to ask them both that, remind them of her insistence that they must finish school, make something of themselves. Instead, and to halt these moments, she explained his absence, "He's on one of his overnight hauls," and she almost believed it herself.

"He must've left late," Gloria said. "Because he came back last night. When you were still out."

Returned here? To wait for her? After she stayed in the bar and — Amalia looked at Juan for verification.

"I wasn't here," he said.

"But he left right away because I told him to get the hell out of our house," Gloria said. She touched her lips as if only now discovering she had not applied lipstick.

"Gloria—" Juan seemed about to rebuke.

"How dare you!" Amalia answered her daughter. Was it possible that she — and Juan — had pretended, all these years, to accept, yes, to like, Raynaldo? "You're lying," Amalia said, and wondered, Why? "And you remember that he's been more of a father to you than—" She stopped. She tried never to mention Gabriel; only that he "had left." Juan didn't remember him, Gloria had never seen him — and it saddened Amalia to realize that.

"Yeah, Mom?" Gloria goaded. Then she laughed. "I was just joking. What did the letter you got yesterday say?"

Amalia had come in with it when she returned from work. She had placed it on the table — and they had both been there — before she put it into her purse. "I haven't read it." Despite the abrupt question, she could answer that quickly. There was nothing more the letter from the public attorney could say to her about her son, nothing.

"Cops lie all the time," Juan said.

"Man, do they," Gloria said. "Like at school —"

"Yeah, they busted a lot of the *vatos* and said they were selling drugs," Juan finished.

Vatos! Cholo talk, gang talk. Amalia knew cops lied.

"They're real shit, Mom," Gloria extended her contempt. "Know what they did? Enrolled in school, for months, pretended they're students, right? Then they bust the guys they made friends with, say they bought drugs, sold drugs — lie, lie, lie."

"But they didn't get everyone," Juan seemed to enjoy that.

Had *he* been arrested in that raid? Or had he been one of the ones they didn't get? Was that how he was bruised? Had that happened around the time he had sheltered that Salvadoran boy in the garage? *Was* he Salvadoran? Had Juan told her that only to disorient her? Or were her son and daughter only concerned for her, about the sadness the letter from the public attorney might arouse again? Amalia welcomed a sudden tenderness toward her son, her daughter. "Give me your present, *m'ijo,*" she said.

Juan held the earrings to her.

"Put them on me."

Juan tried.

Amalia finished for him. Manny would have known how, so tenderly, the way he had placed the flower in her hair, that distant day. Softly, she thanked her suddenly shy Juan.

"They look beautiful on you," Gloria's voice softened. She touched the delicate coppery fringe on the earrings. "They glitter, just the way you like."

My little girl again! And my son! Amalia thought exultantly. Suddenly the mood of separation and closeness collided, overwhelmed her. She wished she had enough money to give her daughter a *quinceañera's* coming-out. Girls her age dressed in white, vaunting their purity, carried flowers into a dance they presided over, escorted by a handsome young man — like Juan! — wearing a suit and tie. When as a girl she had worked for a wealthy Mexican-American family in El Paso, she had watched in fascination as the fifteen-year-old daughter fluttered like a bird in her frilly white dress, and — Now Amalia frowned, the memory blurring, leaving only a terrible, cold desolation. . . . "I'm sewing this dress for you," she responded to Gloria's softened tone; she had decided, that very moment, that the dress would be for her.

Gloria held the stitched portion up to her chest. "Too big. I think you're making it for yourself, Mom."

How frail closeness could be! Amalia felt. "What was that!" Had the house trembled?

"It's not an earthquake, 'Amá," Juan laughed. "Just a truck idling."

"Well, this *is* earthquake weather, so hot and still." Amalia wanted to hear their usual denials.

"Superstitions, 'Amá," Juan reassured. "There's no such thing."

Amalia had what she had wanted: reassurance that there would be no earthquake, and being called "'Amá" by Juan.

The vibrating sound had turned into the growl of a motorcycle.

"It's Mick." Gloria had peered out the barred window. She ran out of the room.

To make herself up, Amalia knew. She was relieved that there was no earthquake, but it didn't please her that Mick was here. Why did there have to be either?

Mick walked in, swaggered in.

With shiny black pants! In this heat? He was about Juan's age. He might have been good-looking, Amalia allowed herself to think — if it weren't for that . . . costume. What else to call it? All that black, and the shirt without sleeves and slit open at the sides, and the silvery belt and that wristband with studs. And those boots! — the kind *gringo* cowboys wore in Texas when she was growing up. If that's what he was attempting, he had succeeded in looking ominous, rough, although — who could miss this? — he *was* somewhat scrawny. And that single earring! . . . Was he a Stoner? — Amalia didn't want even to wonder about that, about his being one of the new breed of Mexican-American gangs who adopt Anglo ways, their drugs, their music.

"*Ésele,*" Juan greeted him.

Ésele! — gang slang for "guy"; but, Amalia constantly reminded herself, many young Mexicans speak like that and aren't in the *cholo* gangs.

Mick nodded at Juan.

Amalia was glad to detect a tension between the two.

"Hi, Am-al-lee-ah," Mick drawled.

Amalia winced at the familiarity, and his pronunciation of her name. "Hello —" She stopped deliberately, frowning deeply, as if attempting to remember his name. "Hello —"

"Mick," he reminded her.

"Pero cual es tu nombre verdadero?" Amalia asked.

"Huh? Oh, I don't speak Mexican, never learned it." Mick emphasized his drawl.

Amalia said in English: "I said, What's your real name? Mick's no Mexican-American name."

"Huh?"

He muttered that sound constantly, as if everything baffled him — and it annoyed Amalia. "I said, Mick's no —"

"Oh, yeah, well, my dad's name was Miguel." He pronounced it Mi-goo-ell. "Is that what you mean?"

"Yes," Amalia said. "Are you ashamed of being Mexican?"

Mick glanced at Juan, as if gauging whether to contain his anger. He smiled, a crooked, rehearsed smile. "Naw, but —" Then he shrugged Amalia's question away. He said, as if repeating an explanation to himself: "All you gotta do is look around to see who's on top, and if *you* wanna get there —"

"You wanna get . . . where? — *ésele?*" Juan asked him.

Amalia laughed aloud, welcoming Juan's sarcasm, even his calling Mick "*ésele.*"

"Sure is hot," Mick shifted away. "Earthquake weather."

"That's a stupid superstition," Amalia was glad to say. "And those pants make you hotter."

"Huh?" Then Mick laughed suggestively. "I'll say they do!"

"You real hot shit — *huh?* — *ésele?*" Juan taunted. "What if —?" He stopped when he saw his sister.

Dressed now in a short, tight skirt and a blouse that left a strip of her flat stomach exposed, Gloria stood at the door, as if undecided where she belonged within the room.

Incredible to believe that both skirt and "blouse" had once been one of Amalia's ruffled dresses, converted—how?—into *this* by her daughter. Well, she wouldn't be surprised if Gloria used *only* the ruffle for a skirt!... Amalia stared at her pretty daughter, in admiration and astonishment. How could she have put on so much makeup so quickly, and how could she make her hair do all *that* in such a short time?—piled and teased about her face.

After moments, Gloria walked over to Mick. He kissed her, lazily nuzzling her face, glancing triumphantly at Juan and Amalia.

Amalia looked away. Juan stared at them.

Suddenly there was a crashing metallic sound outside.

"Fuckin' shits were following me!" Mick stood up, tense. "Probably knocked my bike over." He did not go out to see.

He looks like a terrified boy, Amalia thought. There were boys like him killing and being killed now all over the city, and so she, too, felt afraid.

Juan had run out of the kitchen, into the front room.

Gloria answered Amalia's look: "Mick thinks some dudes are following him 'cause he's going out with me."

"Just crazies." Juan was back. "They're gone."

"Motherfuckers," Mick muttered.

"Hey, man—" Juan warned him, indicating Amalia.

There was no word Amalia detested more than the one Mick had just said. Juan had used it in a rage when he was fired from an after-school job clearing tables at Denny's Restaurant on Sunset Boulevard. "Motherfucker thought I was after his girl," he'd said, "and who the hell wants her, man?" Amalia had expressed her outrage at the word; it made her cringe when she heard it tossed on the street, on buses. Juan had apologized. Imagine!—that there could *be* such a word. She could not even think it. Her anger allowed warm blood to return to her body, easing the abrupt fear the shouts had created, the tension of violence—eased, too, by the fact that Juan had "protected" her; she loved that.

"They didn't do nothing to your bike," Juan told Mick. "Just made lots of scary noises." He jangled his hands at Mick. "Just some crazies passing by—did they scare you bad, *ésele*?"

"No," Gloria answered firmly for him.

"Hell, no," he echoed.

"Just *locos*, 'Amá," Juan reassured Amalia.

So many questions to ask. Had she been so overwhelmed with

grief after Manny's death that she hadn't become aware that Gloria was involved with gang members? Were they trying now to reclaim her? Amalia knew of the bitter fights over "home girls."

"We're going riding, Mick, remember?" Gloria asserted.

He seemed reluctant. "I'm not sure —"

"I'm not either," Amalia said. She was apprehensive because of what had just occurred outside, but also because she had seen girls on the back of motorcycles, hunched over the drivers, bodies pressed.

Gloria walked toward the door, waited for Mick.

Mick moved hesitantly with her.

"Gloria —" Amalia called.

"What?"

"You don't have to go out, so early," Amalia quickly substituted new words for the ones she had been about to speak.

"I don't *have* to, Mom, but I am — and it's not so early. You just slept late."

Because — "Gloria!" Amalia called out more urgently.

"What!" Gloria waited impatiently.

"Kiss me."

Gloria stood beside her mother. Then she kissed her lightly on the cheek, and then — suddenly — firmly on the lips. "It'll be all right with Raynaldo, 'Amá, I promise." She left quickly, touching Juan in good-bye.

Amalia put her hand on the place where her daughter had kissed her; it was warm. They *did* love her. How could she doubt it? She heard the growl of the motorcycle as it faded. "Gloria *isn't* in danger from a gang," she said aloud, wanting her words to affirm it.

"I told you, man," Juan said impatiently. "Those were just clowns outside."

Those ... clowns — she had seen them clowning on the streets just like kids — could become dangerous, killers.

"Sorry, 'Ama, I didn't mean to call you 'man.'" Juan misinterpreted her silence.

She would say this for him: He relented in his defiance, especially when Gloria wasn't around.

Juan stood silently before her, as if deciding something.

"*M'ijo* —?" For a moment she thought she knew what she wanted to ask him, but in the next moment the question was lost. All she knew now was that she wanted to push that strand of his hair back so she could see it fall again to his forehead. He couldn't be in a gang, with hair that long. He didn't even wear the uniform of khaki pants, loose T-shirts. But gangs were changing.

"'Amá, I was —" Juan started.

She looked away quickly. The tone of his voice had alerted her to disturbing words — and wasn't there enough, enough? But she knew he was waiting for her to react. After moments — he still waited. She said, only quietly, hesitantly, "What?"

"Nothing!" He started to walk out of the kitchen. "I was just going to remind you not to forget to check the winning Lotto number." The angry note was gone.

"I never win anything," she told him. She bought a lottery ticket each week only because Raynaldo insisted.

At the door, Juan said to her, "Whatever that letter says, remember, cops lie."

Again that concern with the letter from the public lawyer; didn't they know nothing it said would mean anything to her now? She heard the door close. He had gone out, without a shirt, no shoes. So he would be back.

Amalia sat alone in her iron-barred kitchen crammed with artificial flowers. She didn't bother to warm her coffee. She drank it cold.

Then it was almost time for her Saturday morning serial. She went into the living room. The beds had been pushed and rolled away. On a mantel in this room there was another cherished picture, of John F. Kennedy — and another Sacred Heart of Jesus, the heart in this one bleeding beautifully. In the most prominent place, Amalia had located a small statue of the Holy Mother. She had decorated this one with paper flowers to look the way she remembered the Blessed Madonna had appeared to Bernadette — except that *she* had given her more flowers to stand on, and *hers* were colored, red and blue.

Amalia looked about this room and she felt poor. But, she thought quickly, others were much, much worse off. Today that did not alleviate her depression. It saddened her even more, that others *were* worse off. Rosario had said something like that once. Today her friend's voice was echoing more than usual.

She heard a car. She looked out the window. Juan was leaning into the shiny new car that had just driven up. From here Amalia could not see the driver. There was someone in the passenger seat. A dark young man? She had the impression that she had seen him before. No. She saw Juan take something — exchange something? Then he looked back toward the house, spoke into the car, and retreated from it. The car slipped away from Amalia's vision. It was just someone asking directions. Amalia saw Juan look at something in his hand. Money? A packet? Drugs! Who had received what? No, her suspicions were all wrong. Juan had just forgotten to return the slip of paper with the address the driver had inquired about. But why was he still waiting? For the car to park somewhere else? Now he walked out of her range. Amalia waited for him to return. He did not.

She sat down on the sofa bed, trying to force herself not to conjecture anymore. She fixed her full attention on the television. Raynaldo had bought it on credit at Circuit City, $15 a month to be paid forever. She waited through interminable commercials, refusing all the questions ganging up on her, about Juan, about Gloria. Where *was* Raynaldo? What if he had returned here last night only to verify that she hadn't left El Bar & Grill right away? What if the bartender, who was jealous because she had rebuffed him several times — what if he told Raynaldo about —?

That bastard Angel! Amalia thought — and wished her serial would hurry up. She tried not to curse aloud, only to herself. Of course, God would still hear, He heard everything, didn't He? So He must have heard Angel arouse her sympathies last night, and He would know that she responded with compassion — and Rosario would have approved, too. But first Angel had said, in his deep, oddly mournful voice:

"Eres una mujer muy linda, una verdadera mujer."

A beautiful woman, a *real* woman! She had laughed in a way that resounded strangely to her. How old was he — twenty-eight? Difficult to gauge; you keep looking twenty-five until you're past thirty. The extra beer must have already begun to take effect, because she had felt a tingling sensation — she would be the last to deny that. She was savoring the beer he had brought her, but she made a face to indicate she wasn't used to three, in case he'd noticed she had already had her two with Raynaldo. It was then that he broke her heart — God and the Holy Mother would attest to this — when he told her in a lowered, hurt murmur about being forced to flee his country — Nicaragua — dangers, confusions, dislocated loyalties, new enemies . . . Amalia had been amazed that he had been able to survive it all, that *anyone* could survive all that violence. "You have to survive, *bonita* Amalia," he told her, "there's nothing else." Her heart broke again. She agreed to take a walk with him, that's all, perhaps with her company to soothe, at least attempt to soothe, his painful memories. Of course they would leave the bar separately so that no one would misunderstand. Then, outside, at the corner, she would thank him, courteously, for the extra beer, the compliments, his shared memories. And for the beautiful flower. Then she would wish him well — and walk home, alone . . .

Damn the whole night!

And most of all, damn that extra beer! In her Hollywood bunga-low unit as she sat before the television screen, Amalia welcomed the throbby ballad about the endurance of dreams that introduced her serial. She leaned back. She forbade all worries. She surren-dered to her *semanal* — so what if Raynaldo's arm wasn't about her? She concentrated on her cherished Saturday serial:

CAMINO AL SUEÑO

Antonio Montenegro adores his beautiful wife. He's a successful architect in Mexico City — "*la capital.*" He is a loyal son and a devout Catholic — he was once honored with a private audience with the Holy Pope. His adoring servants call him "El Señor Arquitecto."

So handsome, Amalia thought, and so kind. *There* was a combi-nation. That man would never beat his wife. Nor walk out on her in an unjustified jealous fit at El Bar & Grill.

Antonio and his wife, Lucinda, of the prominent Soto-Mayor dynasty, have a perfect home, all chrome and glass and staircases.

Amalia touched the armrests of the sofa bed. The covers she had sewn slipped off every night. She felt the matted cotton underneath.

In the household of Antonio Montenegro, Lucinda has changed, becoming cold. "*Una extranjera,*" he confides to the oldest retainer, an old woman, perhaps Indian, part Indian, dark brown, as wise as she is devoted to the Montenegros. She dresses in black even in summer —

Like Mick! Amalia almost crossed herself at the irreverent thought.

— and wears a huge crucifix on her chest. She invites Antonio to sit down in her servant's quarters — "although they are much too humble for you."

"What do I care about worldly possessions when I am losing my beloved wife, Ti'ita?" He calls the old woman "little aunt" because she raised him.

Ti'ita looks sadly at her beloved Antonio. *"Tienes que ser muy fuerte,"* she exhorts, demanding his strength. "Remember that the Montenegros have a most noble heritage."

Well, the Gómezes had quite a history themselves, Amalia might have said to Raynaldo, who would have laughed appreciatively.

"I have been privileged to serve the Montenegros from before your birth," Ti'ita reminds Antonio. Her dimming eyes convey the distance of her cherished memories of devotion. "Your sainted father and mother — who now rest in the special place that God provides for such generous people in heaven — entrusted me to raise you under their just guidance. I would have given my life for them, and then for you — and now for our Lucinda."

"Why has she changed?" Antonio begs.

Not because she knew he would walk out on her — Amalia would attest to that.

Ti'ita shakes her head at the weight of the words she must speak: "Lucinda's past has caught up with her."

Antonio is baffled. "She has no past except that which belongs to us both. Our lives began when we found each other."

"That is what your love assures you." Old Ti'ita smiles. Then she turns her head in outrage: "Lucinda was forced into a vile marriage before she met you, when she was but a child."

Like me, Amalia thought.

"It's not true!" Antonio protests. "Tell me you're merely testing my strength as a Montenegro."

"If God would allow me to lie!" the wise Ti'ita laments. "Antonio, Lucinda's parents were rich — and corrupt. They squandered fortunes in ways that God forbids."

"Liquor, gambling," Antonio begins to understand.

"That — and more." Ti'ita makes a sign of the cross, indicating the enormity of unnamed trespasses.

Antonio tries to understand. "And because of their many debts —?"

Ti'ita speaks the terrible words: "Her parents *sold* Lucinda to a brutal man who shunned God and his own family."

"Sold?" Antonio cannot accept the word. "My beloved Lucinda — sold?"

The faithful Ti'ita nods. "Lucinda had no choice."

No choice, Amalia thought. None. Never.

"But she ran away," Ti'ita tells Antonio. "God in His infinite kindness led her to you, my son."

"There has been no happier life," Antonio asserts.

"But now that evil man has returned." The old woman slows painful words.

Gabriel came back, Amalia thought. So did Salvador.

"He has come to claim her as his rightful wife," the old woman finishes her terrible message. "He is her husband. God heard their vows in His holy church."

"Lucinda and I were married at the altar," Antonio reminds her. "God heard *our* vows. My beloved Lucinda wore the purest white."

And I did not, Amalia thought.

"All of that is rendered unbinding, according to the just strictures of our Holy Church," Ti'ita says firmly. "Who are we to question?" She looks down, inward. "Perhaps my just God is punishing *me* for loving you so much I kept this horrible secret —" She dabs at tears.

"God would never judge *you*, Ti'ita, never!"

"God holds us all accountable," the wise old woman replies.

"Yes," Antonio's devotion tries to accept.

But would God permit —? The question almost formed for Amalia. God *was* mysterious, even in the *semanales*.

Ti'ita sighs: "Lucinda has chosen to make you hate her because she must leave you."

"I would sooner hate my soul!" Antonio vows.

"And she loves you with all her heart," Ti'ita asserts. "But that evil man has threatened to reveal all if she does not return to him. Antonio, he threatens to destroy you and the whole dynasty of the Montenegros!"

"Destroy my proud family? How?"

Ti'ita bows her head. All must be spoken now. "It was the Montenegros who, in their infinite generosity, lent to that vile man the exact amount he paid to the corrupt Soto-Mayores for —" She gasps the rest of her words: "— for their daughter — *for Lucinda, your beloved wife!*"

"Then my own family donated to —" Antonio begins to grasp the enormous complexity of his destiny.

"They did not know!" Ti'ita sobs.

"I have a gun! I will kill that godless man!"

"*Antonio!*"

But he is gone.

The old woman speaks to her clenched crucifix:

"*O Dios, O Madre Sagrada!* Is there no way out of this nightmare, O God, O Sacred Mother?" She shakes her weary head. "None." She begins to look up. "None except —" She gazes at heaven: "Only a miracle can save us now! Give me a sign that you understand!"

6

♦   ♦

*W*HAT IF God sent a sign — by way of the Blessed Mother — and you did not believe it! Worse yet, ignored it? — not willingly, of course. Who would deliberately ignore a miraculous sign? That would be like having a winning Lotto ticket and not checking to see whether you had won — or like losing the ticket.

The lyrics of "Camino al Sueño" swelled over the supplicating face of Ti'ita. Amalia clicked off the television.

Would winning the Lotto be considered a real miracle? Those who received miraculous signs were carefully chosen; were those who won the Lotto? Rosario had announced grimly one day that a millionaire had won even more millions in the state lottery. That might have been one of God's most mysterious ways. . . . If you didn't understand the messages that precede a miracle — were there always three or only two? — would they be sent to someone else or just simply go away? How terrible.

Amalia remained sitting on the sofa bed. Her thoughts persisted: Well, there was this to make you think twice about receiving a miracle: Everyone who did ended up in a convent or a monastery, clinging to their beliefs, while everyone else disbelieved, even ridiculed — with the exception of one or at the most two priests who remained close to God because of their humble origins, like Father Ysidro in El Paso. Was he still alive? Women had to go to remote convents and live among sneering nuns in black habits. No convent for *her,* thank you.

Those odd thoughts again! Musings aroused by the *semanal,* Antonio, and Ti'ita, their impossibly complicated situation — that's all.

Look at poor Bernadette — Amalia had seen the movie again recently on television — pleading with cynical bishops. She had to make such sacrifices! — saying good-bye to her good-looking curly-haired boyfriend —

Amalia was suddenly awed: A miracle was so enormous! It altered everything around it, and not just for a day, like in "Queen for a Day." No, a miracle wasn't small, like the tiny amulets on Teresa's Mother of Sorrows. Should she take La Dolorosa out? A miracle made everyone kneel with you in astonishment at the site of the apparitions. Then *you* had to shun "worldly things." But shouldn't a miracle set things right, not make them sadder?

If Father Ysidro were here, she would ask him more about that. . . . She would ask him over for a cup of coffee, some fresh *pan de dulce* — Too hot for coffee. Well, they might sit outside in the shade . . . Where?

"Father Ysidro —"

"*M'ija?*"

"Father, what if the Blessed Mother sent me a sign?"

"What kind of sign, *m'ija?*"

He might look stern for a moment, but she wouldn't notice because she would be basking in being called "*m'ija*" by this saintly old man. "Well, Father, say a silver cross in the sky . . ."

"Then I would say it was a puff of smoke from one of those sky-writing airplanes that fly over the city."

I'm sure that's what it was, Amalia thought. Oh, she was *still* thinking about *that*! . . . She touched the earrings Juan had given her. So very pretty. They would certainly become favorites. But why this present today?

The sour taste returned to her lips. That extra beer! No, the taste was gone, the memory of it remained souring. It's not as if she hadn't been noticed before by men like Angel, years younger than she and so good-looking and dreamy-eyed. They would often make comments about her sexiness as she walked past. But she didn't think of being with them, and she hadn't thought of being with Angel, no, not even when, at El Bar & Grill, she consented, after they had finished their beers, to walk outside with him. As agreed, she said loudly enough for the bartender to hear: "And don't bother me again, *hombre.*" Angel had backed away, while smiling privately at her.

Outside, she decided to accompany him a short distance, because the way he was looking at her made her realize how pretty and young she must appear to him; and she felt that way. She made sure to keep a distance between them so that no one could assume they were together.

"Will you?"

She had realized only after moments that he was inviting her to his home, "very close by." She felt the effect of the third beer — but, then, it had warmed her. Still, she didn't answer as they walked on.

He touched the gardenia he had bought her. "*Bonita* Amalia," he sighed.

What was wrong with a brief visit? For extra assurance, she sought the cross he wore about his neck. She would make sure he lived in a place that wasn't isolated, remain outside for a few minutes, then leave — all for the purpose of allowing Raynaldo his usual few hours of sulking, after their rare spats.

Angel lived off Fountain Avenue in a large, recently painted house separated into rooms and small apartments. A few youngish men and women — new aliens — lingered outside. They would think she and Angel were *novios,* because they must look like "sweethearts." That warmed her in a way that had nothing to do with the night, which was cooling, as warm days in Los Angeles often do.

"Please —" He was inviting her in.

He seemed saddened by the prospect of being alone after all the memories of loss he had shared with her. She walked with him into the hall of the house, the door open. She would allow nothing to happen, and nothing would, because anyone could tell he was a gentle, tender man who was looking at her in a special way no one ever had before.

He opened the door to his room. She was not entirely sure, but she thought he might have bowed slightly. Now he waited for her to enter. She looked in. It was a front room, neat, with two windows, curtained, and a small kitchen. Clearly, he worked, earned proper money, had done well, considering so much hardship in his country, leaving his country. Would he be as generous a provider as Raynaldo? She didn't welcome that thought. It had been aroused only because he was making her feel like a courted girl who has not yet learned about ugliness. And then she saw it, on a wall, a small picture of Our Lady of Guadalupe! What could be more convincing that she could trust him than his reverence for the Holy Patroness of Mexico? Still, when she walked in — and this time she was sure he had bowed — she left the door pointedly open.

In her Hollywood bungalow, Amalia realized that she had been staring into the black television screen. She got up. She decided: She would go out. Perhaps have breakfast at the Carl's Jr. coffee shop nearby. If Raynaldo didn't come back — although she knew he would but why was he staying away this long? — and if harder times came, she might as well indulge herself in a meal out. Yes, and when she returned, he would be back, full of regrets. *She* might even sulk a part of the day. Had he gone on one of his overnight hauls?

She dressed in a pretty light-orange dress that had a ruffle across the shoulders, and a nice swirl to the skirt. What would the blonde wife of Mr. Lewis think of *this* dress? — Amalia often soothed that chafing memory of years ago. Touching them delicately, she left on the earrings Juan had given her. She put on her creamy sling pumps and wondered, as she often did, why so many women no longer wore high heels — *that* accounted for their slouchy walk.

She found an empty pop container, filled it with water, and placed it by the door to water the rosebush behind the court. Then she opened her purse to make sure she had Manny's letter with her. Of course she did. She never left it behind, but still she would often re-check to make sure she did have it. When sadness pulled severely, she would take it out, read his words of love: "My dearest mamacita . . . I love you with all my heart."

She looked, startled, at the harsh printed return address. She had pulled out the wrong envelope, the unopened one from the public attorney. Had Gloria and Juan glimpsed that address and thought the letter was about something else? About one of them? Saying what? She put the envelope back, banishing her suspicions.

At the door, she looked back at her living room. Would it look better without all those paper and cloth flowers? Should she add new ones? On this morning that had begun so brightly, with a lulling peace she could not remember having wakened into before, ever, Amalia forced herself not to sigh.

It was Saturday. There would be yard sales up and down the blocks, mostly junk, a bargain or two. In the several shopping centers nearby, some stores would have put up their SALE TODAY ONLY signs, although prices stayed the same. She'd go look at dresses, appliances, jewelry — she loved to look at extravagant wedding rings — and, as always, she would seek out a huge-screen television that wouldn't fit in her bungalow. She might even stop by El Bar & Grill, hear a word or two about Raynaldo. Had he gone back there looking for her last night? Who knows, she might even pay a visit to the *brujos* in the neighborhood, the old Mexican woman and her husband who gave *consultas* and claimed to have "powers" — *and* to be good Catholics. She had never been to them — she wasn't a *supersticiosa* — had gotten as far as their door once. She knew from a woman in the court that you could discuss certain troubling matters with them, though, and what was wrong with that? Nothing, especially since — she added this quickly to her itinerary — she would stop at the big church on Sunset Boulevard.

And light a candle for her dead son.

And one for Teresa, of course. . . . Before she did any of that, there was somewhere else she had to go, although the prospect frightened her. She had to know whether she had actually seen the graffiti of a new gang on the wall she had turned away from yesterday.

With the can of water she had prepared, she stood outside on what she called her "front porch," the small square of concrete at the entrance of her unit. She heard a rising siren, then another. There were always sirens screaming now. At times it seemed to her that the city itself was shrieking, protesting violence everywhere, even under the earth, stirring into earthquakes.

This early heat would scorch all the flowers, Amalia worried as she walked down the narrow cement path that separated the three units on one side from the three on the other. She stood before the despondent rosebush. Only a few feeble buds remained — how sad that they would die without opening; others had crumbled like long-dry blood. She watered the bush anyway.

A little farther into the garage area, a plant had managed to squeeze through a large crack in the cement. She had noticed it, but today it had blossoms. In the center, their petals were rolled into folds, like candles, and then they opened at the bottom; and they were white. This is not rare in Los Angeles, that flowers seem to grow overnight, perhaps from seeds scattered by wind and then surprised into premature life by sudden heat.

Amalia plucked one of the white blossoms, brushing off a dusty splintery covering on the stem. She liked facing the day with a flower in her hair. Few women did that anymore. Well, she still did. Its whiteness would look grand in her black hair.

As she walked on with the new blossom in her hair, she paused, as she always did, over tiny clusters of flowers surviving before another unit. They looked like bridal bouquets, lilac and yellow centers. Well, the music belching out of radios that had been on since early morning was *not* a wedding march.

On the sidewalk and just a few feet from her bedroom window was a sign that said TO HOLLYWOOD FREEWAY. She wished she did not live this close to the freeway. Its vibrations had come increasingly to resemble those that begin an earthquake. Garbage cans were already placed near the corner for collection. She could not move away from garbage, she often thought. She sought this out: In the narrow space between the back of the bungalow court and an Armenian grocery store were . . . deep-red gladiolas.

Oh, if only . . .

"Is there something up there, Señora Gómez?"

"What!" Amalia looked down at the little boy who had asked her that. He lived with his fat, superstitious mother and God knows how many aunts and uncles and visiting cousins in the noisy bungalow at the end of the court. "What did you say, Lalo?" she asked the eight-year-old boy.

"Is there something up there? — where you were staring." He gazed up.

She *had* been staring into the sky! Amalia realized. "There was a cross in the sky earlier." Of course she had said that only because she wanted to hear, and that way dismiss entirely, the silly words.

"I saw it, too," Lalo said. "It was over there." He pointed up.

Amalia was irritated. This boy *always* lied. "You did *not* see the cross, Lalo, because there wasn't one. And even if there was one, you wouldn't have seen it." Her anger mounted.

"I did see it." Lalo backed away from Amalia's threatening voice.

"Liar!" She reached out toward him. He dodged, almost toppling against a garbage can. "Say you didn't see the cross!"

"I did."

"If you admit you didn't, I'll —" She opened her purse.

Lalo held out his hand.

She found a nickel, some pennies. She tossed them into his skinny hand.

"I didn't see anything," Lalo said.

Amalia moved hurriedly away from him.

"Did *you* see it?" Lalo called out.

"No!" Amalia did not turn back. "It was smoke!"

"Well, did you see those *vatos locos* banging up on that motorcycle in front of your house?"

"No!" She walked on.

"Were they after John-*nee?*"

Had the altercation been aimed at Juan? Of course not! Amalia turned sharply to question the boy — and protest the mocking Anglicized inflection he had given her son's name. But Lalo had run away.

In the vacant lot across the street, a few boys had gathered, about twelve years old, no older than fourteen. Another boy, older, perhaps sixteen — all were Mexicans — was talking to them. They exchanged something. *Dios mio!* Were those children buying drugs? "Selling death to their own people," Rosario had once lamented.

Catching sight of her, the boys challenged her look openly, as if *she* were intruding. Amalia walked away with added fear of her immediate destination.

What contrasts in the neighborhood! The area around the Fox Studio, sealed off by high walls and watched over by security guards stationed at every entrance, looked like a well-tended private park. Yet on almost every block in the neighborhood were declining houses, windows smashed, shells of cars left on dirty lawns. Increasingly there appeared wires strung across porches, for drying laundry in backyards, to economize. There were, too, the stubbornly pretty houses, freshly painted, with urgent gardens and grass, but even those had harsh black iron bars protecting windows.

And everywhere, everywhere, trees and flowers splashing the neighborhood with desperate beauty!

Young men in undershirts were working on their cars already — where they got the money to paint all those flames and dragons on them, God only knew. Girls talked with them or sat on the curbs. Families were putting out their items for yard sales, or sitting on gutted sofas outside, courting a nonexistent breeze. Rock music and Mexican ballads waged battle. Amalia greeted some of the few people she knew — people these days tended to keep separate, even though this was still a predominantly Mexican-American neighborhood.

"Look, Amalia! It's you!" One of the neighbors she regularly greeted was pointing to a drawing he was putting out for sale in his yard, along with chipped dishes, shoes, old clothes, vases, painted bottles, broken lamps — and old plastic flowers. Amalia recognized that the drawing had been cut out of a calendar and framed: In resplendent "*poblana*" costumes, the dress of their village, pretty Mexican girls with thick braids and dazzling sequins sewn into patterns of flowers and butterflies on their whirling skirts danced joyously with good-looking *charros,* their wide-brimmed hats adorned with silvery swirls to match those on their short jackets, snug pants. Nearby, smiling old women washed clothes at the edge of a serene river running through their village of pretty adobe huts.

"This girl looks like you." The man was indicating one of the women in the dance.

"When you were young — perhaps," his wife amended.

Pretty poverty! Amalia thought she could hear Rosario reject the calendar drawing. "That girl looks to *me* like Maria Felix," she told the man. The image of the Mexican movie star of her girlhood had come easily into her mind. Why ? Only because she had wanted to extend the man's compliment. She dismissed any further importance to the thought, but it had left a welcome warmth inside her.

"Ah! La Maria!" the man toasted with a sigh.

"You want to buy the picture?" the woman demanded testily to Amalia.

Amalia knew why the woman was annoyed, because she, Amalia, had seen her buying some of the items in her yard from Thrifty's Drug Store, on sale — and now she was trying to resell them, for more! "No," she told the woman, "because I have that calendar — and I could have bought one of those odd lamps for less, at Thrifty's." She moved on, to her determined destination.

Amazing what people tried to sell in these yard sales! Amalia passed more of the outdoor displays, more mangy clothes, worn shoes, clumsily painted jars trying to pass as vases. "Garage sales," some people insisted on calling them, even when they had no garages, let alone cars. Of course, *those* cloth flowers were pretty, weren't they? — newer than hers. Well, later, she might stop and barter for them; they might add some needed color to the house.

Now she was passing a sight she usually avoided. All the units in this court, except one, were boarded up heavily, as if captured by rotting planks of wood. Weeds scratched at patches of dirt. Amalia had seen an old woman lurking about the one unit not yet sealed, but crumbling. There she was now.

"*Que ves?*" the old woman challenged Amalia. A crudely rolled cigarette did not leave her lips; it merely trembled there slightly.

"I'm not looking at anything," Amalia answered. Drying vines and trees arched across the units, creating a tangle of shadows. Toward the back of the desolate court, five or six boys roamed, one as young as six, the oldest perhaps sixteen. Hearing the woman's challenge of Amalia, they moved forward, still within shadows.

Amalia had a sense of menace. Perhaps the woman was a *coyote,* specializing in bringing the children of illegals across borders. Did she send them out to rob? To sell drugs?

Amalia hurried away. She glanced back once and saw the old woman push aside some boards into one of the sealed units, and she went in. The boys followed. Then all remained deserted.

Yet if Amalia proceeded only two blocks in another direction, toward Sunset, or toward Melrose Boulevard, she would encounter television studios and tourists, men and women, young people, children — always many in shorts — lined up to gain entry to their favorite shows. No matter how they tried to do their hair, wear their clothes, they still looked like tourists. . . . And around the corner a condominium had just been completed. NOW LEASING LUXURY UNITS, it said on a large banner decorated with colored balloons that wobbled against its balconies and sliding glass doors. From that height, you would have a clear view of the beautiful homes scattered over the Hollywood hills, lawns *always* green.

Think of it! This was Hollywood!

Amalia reached her destination: a corner on which a wall rose two stories high. On the upper level of the small building were rooms for rent. They were held up flimsily on stilts over a large garage. Most often, the rooms were inhabited by incongruous Anglo men and women, shaggy, in their thirties; they lived there only briefly, shady transients. Next to the garage, garbage spilled out of an open bin — left uncollected — cans, bottles, shreds of tires, gutted boxes, paper dishes with the remains of food. At times men and women would pluck out old clothes and food from the trash.

Amalia assumed those were the shadows who crept into abandoned houses for night shelter.

She faced the wall she had avoided yesterday.

LOS VATOS NUEVOS.

"The New Dudes." The name of a gang.

The fresh, bold letters were painted over older graffiti. And across the gang name had been sprayed an even fresher harsh black "X." A sign of challenge from another gang, a signal of invasion, violence. And along with that would come another invader, another gang, just as deadly: the police. Only a short time ago cops had raided and smashed houses randomly in south central Los Angeles, and amid the wreckage they created in search of unfound drugs in the neighborhood suddenly under double siege, they had spray-painted their own *placa,* their own insignia: LOS ANGELES POLICE RULE.

Amalia looked around at the familiar blocks that had suddenly altered; a threatened *barrio.* What would the "New Vatos" look like? Full-haired, shirtless? — like Juan? But the car she had seen him talking into had not looked like a gang car. Of course, there were those men — and even women now — who sold *drogas* to gangs for further street sale.

Nowhere to move to, nowhere else she could afford! And yet — Amalia held on to this, firmly — there were, increasingly, gang imitators, who merely dressed like members of gangs, even performed their superficial rites, like posting graffiti. On that wall, and for more than a year, there had been scrawled nicknames that sounded like those of a *klika*: CHICO, BLUTO, LOCO, JOKER — even BASH-FUL — children's nicknames, it always amazed Amalia to realize. But there had been no gang activity in the neighborhood. So the new name there meant nothing definite, she told herself. Still, feeling cold, she walked away from the terrorized wall.

Minutes later she was on Western Avenue.

She walked faster, past a man lying on the sidewalk, slumped over a sack overflowing with rags next to which a tattered woman sat, gazing straight ahead. A sight that was no longer exceptional on this street, becoming ordinary — and less exceptional was what was occurring nearby: A squad car had pulled aside a car with four Mexican men in it. Only *we* look suspicious to them, Amalia often thought.

She was nearing Sunset Boulevard. Before they had moved into this neighborhood, there had been many prostitutes on that strip of the street. Amalia's face had burned with embarrassment when she and Raynaldo drove past women with skirts so tiny their buttocks showed. Most of the women were black, many Mexican, a few white. Some wore skin-tight flesh-colored pants that made them look naked. Amalia could not conceive of a woman selling her body — imagine! — and so she had looked at the women with disgust. But on another Sunday evening, when she and Raynaldo were caught in tangled traffic, she saw a squad of cops mounted on horses herding the garish women along the street. They corralled them into a mass of painted flesh. Amalia detested the smirks on the faces of the cops. She felt sorry for the women. She remembered the way Immigration patrols had rounded up Mexicans crossing the Rio Grande. Under the paint, the women had suddenly looked frightened to her.

Now most of the cheap rooms that had been rented by the hour housed the new aliens from El Salvador and Guatemala and Nicaragua.

The Clive Barnes Liquor Barns Bonanza — it always astonished Amalia that Anglos often attached their names to questionable places in Mexican neighborhoods — displayed a large *L,* signaling a Lotto station. Amalia walked past it, deciding she would postpone comparing her number with the winning one. That made her feel good, for now, merely not discovering that, again, she had not won.

With a growl, a motorcycle halted at an intersection. Two women were mounted on it. Both were dressed in leather, wrist bands studded with metallic tips. One had ferociously blonde hair, the other's was inky black. One wore black leather shorts, the other pants; both wore shiny black boots. Amalia was relieved that they were not Mexicans.

The new sights of the city still accosted her. Hollywood Boulevard, just a block away from here, was the worst, at times like a graveyard for the walking dead, so many of them young, dazed, hollow-eyed —

Look over there! Across the street. That terrible place near the freeway. A giant sign proclaimed proudly: ALLAN WALLACH'S FEMALE WRESTLING EXTRAVAGANZA NIGHTLY ... AMATEUR NIGHT ON WEDNESDAYS. Incredible! Who could enjoy wrestling in mud, and who could enjoy watching it? On weekends, lines formed outside the square building.

Thank God the Pussy Cat Theater, farther on, no longer displayed those brazen posters outside. Years earlier it had. Amalia could not believe that a woman or a man would allow being photographed like that, with only those heavy black spots over their private parts. When Raynaldo informed her that those spots were not there in the actual films, Amalia gasped.

Now she stopped to look longingly at one of the many sofas in a "gypsy furniture lot." On weekends, or at night, sofas were put up for sale on the lots of closed gas stations. Red, blue, green, purple, velvety, satiny! Amalia could *see* one of these sofas in her living room — and Raynaldo had offered to buy her one soon.

A bus bench nearby had a picture of "la Marilyn." Near it — incongruously — a group of six young men and women — three were Mexicans — clustered — young, yes, but they seemed to want to look old, dressed in new yet oddly drab clothes. All held —

Bibles. Protestant Bibles!

The group was coming toward her. Amalia could not understand Mexicans who became Protestants. It was unnatural. There was one television evangelist she especially detested, a wrestler at one time. He gathered hundreds of gullible Mexicans, who sat quivering and trembling and hallelujah-ing with raised hands. Once Amalia had watched the Mexican preacher demand that an old man rise from his wheelchair and walk. The man tried — and fell. Amalia had no doubt it was God who had pushed him for being there. . . . As an intense young woman with glasses and a thick black Bible approached her, Amalia increased her interest in an electric-blue sofa.

". . . not only beautiful," the lot salesman was hawking, "but it's very durable, feel it — *real* — and so inexpensive you won't believe it, and for a small down payment I'll hold it for weeks — I'm at this location every week, and —"

The girl with glasses held her Bible inches before Amalia's face. "*La palabra de Nuestro Señor!*"

"I speak English," Amalia said. "I am a Mexican-American." She touched her pretty dress to affirm that.

A young man joined the girl with glasses. He was tall, thin. "Are you born again!" he demanded of Amalia.

A Mexican man and his wife were strolling by. They stopped. "None of your fuckin' business," the man asserted to anyone, everyone.

The woman with him shouted: "Why don't you born-agains go to a *real* church and pray for forgiveness?"

"God is everywhere!" A girl wearing a gray sweater whirled her Bible in the air.

A teenage boy and two girls ran from across the street, to join. A young man thrust Bible tracts at them.

"Get out of our neighborhood. It's a Catholic neighborhood!" yelled the teenage boy.

"You're going to hell if you don't heed the Word!"

"No, *you're* the one who's going to hell!"

"*You* are!"

"*You* are, son of a bitch!"

Amalia sought for something intelligent with which to accost these brash people with their Protestant Bibles. "You don't even believe in the Holy Mother's divine intercession." She had remembered the exact words from her catechism classes with Mother Mercedes, in El Paso. The little nun's spirit would be smiling on her for that.

"That's right, we don't, because God doesn't like intervention," another of the young men with Bibles asserted.

A girl poked his chest three times with her finger. "I was born Catholic and I'm gonna *die* Catholic!"

"Then go on believing in idols and incense —"

"Oh, you are *really* going to go to hell for that!"

"*You're* the one who's going to hell!"

Amalia could have settled it all right now. Those Protestants had one foot in hell already. Everyone knew that leaving the holy Catholic church was a mortal sin. Of course, Protestants could always return, if they repented, because God, in His infinite love, forgave everything — except blasphemy against the Holy Ghost, Amalia remembered from her holy lessons. But who would *want* to commit blasphemy against a holy ghost?

"*You're* lost, we're *found*!" "*Who's* lost?" "Let go of my hair, bitch!" "You scratched *me*, shit!" "Satan!"

When the sofa salesman started pushing the debaters from his property, and they pushed back, Amalia hurried away.

She was on Sunset, within the crazy maze of fast-food stands, malls, variety stores: Alpha Beta, Stephen Holden's Pollo Loco, Carl's Jr., Thrifty's, Maurice Zolotow's Pots, McDonald's Billion Burgers, The Colonel's Chicken, Denny's Food, Howard Kissel's Best Pies, Tommy's World Famous Burgers of Hollywood, Builders Emporium, Sal Chavez's Fashions.

Standing there, wondering where to go first, Amalia felt very angry. That Lalo! she thought. He did not see a cross in the sky this morning.

7

◆   ◆

*J*UST MIDMORNING and it was this hot! Amalia heard a brief, nervous rustle of palm fronds. Then again, the air was still. Was this the season of scouring fires in the hills? That's when hot desert winds invade and palm trees thrust dead branches on the street. The sun becomes red, and it seems as if the city of lost angels is under fierce judgment for its beauty, its ugliness.

Amalia did not think that. She sensed it as she stood on Western Avenue and Sunset Boulevard. She did not want to add anything to the worries that had followed her all morning.

SUMMER SHADES MEAL DEAL
$2.99, Plus Tax.

That enticement of free sunglasses was stretched on a banner across the long window of the Carl's Jr. fast-food restaurant. Well, she hadn't planned to spend that much money on breakfast, but perhaps she could talk them into the glasses anyway. That consideration made Amalia decide to go there instead of across the street to McDonald's, though its pretty lawn with bunches of lavender and white oleanders had beckoned. In its own way, Carl's Jr. was just as attractive; and at McDonald's there were always boisterous young people with rock music plugged into their ears — where it should stay. She *did* enjoy some Western music, secretly, when she happened to overhear it; it was not entirely unlike the Mexican ballads she loved.

Lowering the orangy ruffle across her shoulders and with the white flower in her hair, Amalia entered Carl's Jr.

Jr. Crisp Burritos.

She read the new item on the menu posted over the counter where she waited to order. Crisp burritos! Burritos were soft! What next? She placed her order for breakfast — two eggs with the yolks well cooked, and sausages. "And the free sunglasses." She smiled at the teenage Mexican girl — in a pert tan uniform — who was taking the orders.

"The glasses come only with the full meal." The girl pointed toward the lunch menu — all kinds of hamburger combinations.

"But it's not lunchtime." Amalia was indignant.

"No," the girl recited, "but we serve burgers all day and that's the only way you get the sunglasses."

Suddenly, getting the glasses was essential to Amalia. She decided to have a very early lunch and then not eat again till dinner. No one could say a pound or two less on her would make her look gaunt, and thank God for that. "I'll have the Western Burger — *very* well done — with the bacon and the cheese. And French fries," she added — to get her through to dinner and to qualify for the sunglasses. . . . She *did* enjoy a good hamburger like everyone else. Some people still thought Mexicans ate only beans and rice. Well, she *had* eaten her share, who hadn't? — but she had also come to like fried chicken, now that Gloria and Juan loved it so much, and even a sandwich with mayonnaise — but not too often.

Before she left the ordering counter, she had added a large Diet Pepsi to her lunch. When she paid, she was given a plastic tab with a number, which would identify her order when it was ready, in minutes. "My sunglasses —"

"Shades," the young man in a tan uniform corrected. He gave her a choice of frames, green or fuchsia.

Green.

Amalia chose a booth that would face the window and at the same time offer her a view of the colorful pictures on the wall to one side — bunches of shiny fruit in one, buildings and their shadows in another. She set her free sunglasses on the table, glancing at them now and then.

"Booths are for more than one. *Tables* are for people who are alone." That was said by the girl delivering orders.

Alone! Raynaldo *would* be back, was probably waiting for her at home — or out looking for her urgently. . . . Amalia adjusted the sunglasses firmly before her plastic tab, asserting her intention to remain in the booth.

"Just don't let the manager see you," the girl warned dourly. "And if he does, don't say I didn't warn you."

The same girl delivered her order a few minutes later. "This isn't a hamburger with cheese and bacon," Amalia said. "It's one egg!" And the egg looked uncooked, the yolk floated in liquidy whiteness.

The girl checked the plastic number — and yanked the plate back. "This belongs to *her.*" She pointed an accusing finger at a woman eating hurriedly nearby. "*She* got *your* order."

The woman grasped her plate and ate the elaborate hamburger more quickly. She was Anglo, shabby, but trying to retain some elegance by constantly adjusting a tilted felt hat on which a red-dyed feather quivered.

"That's not *your* order!" the girl yelled at her.

"*You* brought it to me." The woman gulped the hamburger.

Good! Amalia thought. She ate better than she had intended. "Where's my order?" she called out to the girl.

The girl stared at both women as if they had conspired against her. "You're going to have to pay for the hamburger you ate," she threatened the old woman with the feathered hat.

In a loud raspy voice, off-key and inserting words of her own, the old woman burst into a song:

I'm the yellow rose of Texas —

Only a few in the coffee shop bothered to look at her.

— the yellowest rose of Texas
that ever God made bloom —

God! Texas! And she, too, was from Texas! And there was a rose-bush in her court! — even if it was dead. All this was too much to be a coincidence! It was a *sign!* . . . Of what? Amalia questioned herself. A sign of the craziness of Hollywood, that's what, she answered herself sourly, angered that an old woman who had eaten *her* hamburger and had sung an awful song about a yellow rose — and in a terrible voice not even the compassionate Holy Mother would tolerate — could have lulled her into the memory of the beautiful silver cross she had *not* seen this morning.

With rigid dignity, the shabby old woman walked out of Carl's Jr., tilting her hat as if to a vastly appreciative audience.

Soon the girl was back icily with Amalia's replaced order. The potatoes were limp. Amalia sipped the tall cold drink. "This isn't a Diet Pepsi, and the potatoes are limp," she told the girl.

The girl plucked up a potato and broke it to show how crisp it was. It made no sound. She sniffed the Pepsi.

Amalia poked suspiciously into the hamburger. She recoiled with disgust, the beginning of fear. Blood had flowed in a red streak from the patty. "I said *very* well done."

The girl whisked the plate away again and in a few minutes replaced it with another.

Amalia felt dejected. She looked at the sunglasses. She located them at another angle, so they would catch a glint of sun. She ate, trying to savor her very early lunch, not entirely succeeding. She moved the sunglasses a half inch more, studied the green frames.

Nearby, a fat man and an even heftier woman with several chins sat with two plump, colorless children. Grandchildren. Obvious tourists. With red hair. And they were talking about —

Earthquakes! The "Earthquake Extravaganza" that Universal Studios had recently added to its attractions.

Amalia did not want to listen, but the fat woman was talking loudly, interrupting herself with tiny gasps and snorts: "Well, you know, the *real* earthquake will be much, *much* worse than what those good folk at Universal Studios simulated, bless them."

The man continued to eat, as if he had long ago stopped listening to the woman, even looking at her. The fat boy and girl waited for more details of disaster.

"Well, you know," the woman went on, "*everything* will blow up and the whole city will burn and everyone will drown in the ocean and landslides —"

Amalia glared at her. She detested that Universal Studios "attraction." Television clips and giant billboards all over the city proclaimed ominously, over scenes of fire, buildings collapsing, people running, screaming: EARTHQUAKE! SURVIVE IT ONLY AT UNIVERSAL STUDIOS! There were stupid people and there were even more stupid, *cruel* people, and those at Universal Studios were the *most* stupid, turning something as terrible as an earthquake into entertainment — and making money out of it. What next? A gang killing for tourists? ... The roll was soggy on her Western Burger. She ate around it. She took the sunglasses, glanced through them, put them down again.

The tourist woman was embellishing her picture of doom — pointing out to the suddenly frightened children that *they* would all avoid it because they were leaving Los Angeles "in five days." "Well," she regained momentum. "Lord help all those poor folk who live here, crushed, mangled, burned, and drowned." She addressed everyone at Carl's Jr.

Amalia said to the woman: "The earthquake is predicted for *today,* I heard it on the radio." The moment she said that, she wished she could draw back her words. She had wanted to frighten the woman and the children, but she had terrified herself. Would her words help to bring the earthquake on? She reminded herself she was not a *supersticiosa* — but this couldn't hurt: She crossed herself and said an urgent prayer.

The fat woman laughed, an ugly laugh that grew louder with each tiny gasp she had to take: "Well, *we're* not worried at all. Well, don't you know, we *always* avoid disaster. Well, you know, a few years back when we were visiting here we were on the freeway when there was a *huge* disaster. Well, don't you know, we weren't even scratched and everyone around us died." Wheezing, she gathered her silent husband and her fat grandchildren, and, flesh bouncing, ushered them out of the restaurant.

Amalia felt even more despondent now, more alone. Why had she come here? Of course! To reexperience a happy time — when Raynaldo had brought her and Gloria and Juan here to celebrate Gloria's fifteenth birthday. But had it really been a joyous time? No — but why not? Certainly not because Raynaldo didn't try, told them to order whatever they wanted, never mind the price. He'd even brought a surprise cake, which he presented to Gloria. "To the most beautiful girl," he'd said. No, he had called her "the most beautiful daughter," yes, and added: "Amalia is the most beautiful mother." Had Gloria even smiled? Whatever she had done, Juan had absorbed her mood instantly. What had gone wrong? And why was she thinking about that now? Trying to find pretty memories and coming up with — .

She turned the sunglasses away from her. A blade of light had flashed in her eyes. She looked out the window. A truck had parked nearby, with fresh fruit. What if she had suggested this morning that she and Juan and Gloria go somewhere by bus, to a park, and have a picnic? She couldn't even imagine either of her children on a bus. They probably would have stared at her in disbelief. Perhaps not. A picnic, with fruit afterward, with her children.

The entrenching mood — part sadness, part vague anxiety — made her consider going to confession today. She liked the feeling of closeness to God, with a priest, in the quiet of a confessional booth. She would always remind God that she was a divorced woman who saw no reason to be separated from His holy church, remind Him that Father Ysidro had spoken about that to Him that day in the church courtyard in El Paso, and —

Manny is dead!

Suddenly, with a rush of sorrow, the fact of her son's death had assaulted her mind and her whole body with such force that she wanted to scream. How strange! An entire absence would exist the rest of her life. Each time she realized that — and the realization would come at her without warning, over and over — it was as if it were the first time of discovery, that powerful, that strange, the knowledge that she would never again in this life see or touch her son.

She opened her purse and took out his letter. She read from it, the same words she had already memorized — recited them silently to herself like a personal prayer, again, ending, always, with the same words: "I love you with all my heart." She had restored her breathing. She returned the letter to her purse. She looked out the window, to thrust away her thoughts of death.

A squad car had stopped to question two young Mexican men who had been walking along the street. From the window, they looked harmless to Amalia, like other boys in the neighborhood loitering about on a Saturday morning. Two policemen got out of their car. One was — *a woman!* — blonde, hefty, her hand already on her gun. Why did women want to be as terrible as men? Amalia wondered. Then she noticed that the other cop was — *a Mexican*! She turned away in confusion, because she had also thought: What if those boys just killed someone, what if they're members of Los Vatos Nuevos? Was anything clear anymore?

"Amalia!"

Oh, my God, it was Mr. and Mrs. Huerta — were they every-where? — neighbors she constantly ran into, always bragging to her that their son was studying to be a lawyer. Now she wished she *had* taken a small table, so they couldn't plop down with her and gnaw her ears with their reports.

"What a pretty flower in your hair." Mr. Huerta was preparing to invade her table. His hand was on the back of the booth.

Amalia touched the white flower.

Mrs. Huerta, as thin as a brown skeleton, peered at it. "That's a poisonous weed!" She backed away in shock.

"What!" Amalia believed it instantly, the way she always accepted disaster as inevitable. She tore the flower from her hair, threw it on the floor. *I put a poisonous weed in my hair!* She stared at the blossom, amid scraps of food not yet swept away from an earlier meal. Depression stabbed at her.

Mr. Huerta was ready to slip into the booth. "You know, our son —"

"I'm waiting for Raynaldo," Amalia said firmly. "And I see him now across the street." She pretended to wave out the window.

Alone now — the Huertas had taken a table far from hers — she flirted with the top of her pretty dress. What would Manny have become? she wondered. So smart but with little education. And Juan —?

A man nearby was avidly looking for something in the newspaper he had been reading. Not quite middle-aged, not attractive. Why did so many men — and *so* many Mexican men — allow themselves to get a fat stomach so early? . . . Not Angel. He had a slender, flat stomach . . .

It was true that, last night, she had felt at ease in his rooms when she noticed the picture of Our Lady of Guadalupe. The benign brown face of the Virgin seemed to assure her she had done right, keeping this lonesome man company. The small apartment — a room and a kitchen — would have looked even better if he hadn't left clothes lying about.

"Because I don't have a woman," he interpreted her look. "And, Amalia, a man without a good woman is worthless."

She had reacted again to his murmury voice, his liquidy eyes. She sat on the chair he cleared for her. Oh, yes, the effect of the extra beer increased even more when he stood near her. Through the open door — he had made no move to close it — she heard the sound of a woman coaxing her child to do . . . something. It didn't matter; she merely heard ordinary voices that told her there was nothing wrong with being here.

Angel touched her shoulder, so briefly that it seemed for a moment that she had imagined it.

"I'm sorry," he said. "It's just that it looks so soft that I had to touch it, and it feels even softer than it looks."

He was admiring her the way a young man admires a young woman he is thinking of falling in love with, will romance a decent interval, marry. There was no doubt he had mistaken her for a woman much younger than she was, perhaps his age? It wasn't that she wanted to look younger; no, it was just that she wanted to recapture — No, you couldn't recapture what had never existed. It was just that she wanted to think she might experience perhaps only a hint of what she had been denied, what it would have been like to be a young girl loved . . . and, yes, desired. It was that feeling of a denied beginning, lost before it could be hoped for, that kept her there so that when —

That bastard! In Carl's Jr. Amalia pushed away the cold, ugly plate of food before her.

"I won!"

The man nearby had found what he had been looking for in the newspaper. "I won," he said in amazement to the people turning to look at him. "It's my number. Printed right here. Look. I won the Lotto!"

A girl in shorts rushed over to him to verify the impossible. A young man demanded angrily: "*You* won two million dollars, man?"

"No," the elated man said. "I just have four matching numbers."

"Oh, wow," groaned the girl disdainfully. "*Four* numbers, oh, wow."

The young man informed the man: "Well, that means you'll get —" he paused to figure it eagerly "— that means you'll get about . . . thirty-four bucks."

"Or less," the girl predicted, back in her seat.

"So what?" the man said. "I won, you didn't."

Others in the restaurant withdrew their interest.

So little, so grateful, Amalia thought. How many dollars' worth of tickets did he buy every week? Once Raynaldo had bought forty dollars' worth of tickets he couldn't afford. Would this man now buy even more? Would he ever win anything again? Amalia drank her Diet Pepsi, mostly melted ice now. Maybe she should check her own number in the newspaper. Being near someone who had won something might increase her chances. No, that didn't make sense.

Her eyes wandered out the window, onto Western, splashed with bright colors concealing gathering grime. She followed the sweep of palm trees along Sunset. Beyond, the sky was uncommonly blue.

What would constitute a miracle in her life?

That silliness again! She chastised herself for the thought that had seeped into her mind. She searched for a substitute thought, something that would make more sense, something that —

Maria Felix.

The great Mexican movie star entered Amalia's mind for the second time today. Until this morning she hadn't thought of her since . . . She couldn't even remember when. . . . La Maria was always indomitable, always triumphant. Even when she died or was killed, she was redeemed. Amalia remembered her in a variety of roles: an empress in a puffy dress keeping her kingdom together for her subjects; a peasant woman in immaculate white fighting the landowners for justice; a modern-day millionairess in a wide-shouldered black gown ministering to the poor and needy; a proud, poor woman in a flower-print dress; and —

The Virgin Mary!

Yes, she *had* played the Holy Mother, played her so marvelously that Teresa had made a sign of the cross when she appeared on the screen. Amalia remembered the movie, *El Monje Blanco,* yes, *The Monk in White,* about a handsome young carpenter and his beautiful wife, their Christlike child. Wait — Maria Felix had played the *mother* of the boy. Yes, because she had knelt before the Blessed Virgin, who had appeared to her in a dazzling radiance of miraculous light; and it was Maria who had asked the Holy Queen: "Why have you deigned to appear to a humble woman like me?"

"Because you —"

Amalia could not remember what the Blessed Queen answered; but, now, it seemed to her that Maria *had* played the Virgin Mary. Wait! She had played *both* roles, the wife *and* the Holy Mother. *Had* she? Well, she did remember this: In real life — Milagros had read this aloud from a Mexican tabloid to the others at the sewing factory — Maria Felix's son, a handsome young man who had come to Los Angeles to try to get into American movies, had been arrested, for drugs and — And —

All of this was a sudden jumble to Amalia as she sat at Carl's Jr. and realized that her meal had been a disaster. Still, she *did* have the sunglasses.

"Huccome you didn't eat?" The girl who had delivered her order was already clearing the table.

"Because I didn't like it," Amalia said.

"It's what you asked for."

That infuriated Amalia. "No, it is *not* what I asked for." She walked out. At the door she realized she had left her sunglasses behind. She returned to get them. The girl had pocketed them. "They're mine," Amalia said. The girl surrendered them as if she were being held up.

Outside, Amalia tried on the glasses. She stared at her reflection in the window of Carl's Jr. She looked like a bat with phosphorescent green eyes! She took them off and dumped them in the nearest trash container.

She stood in the large parking lot of Carl's Jr., Sav-On Drugs, Alpha Beta Groceries, Wherehouse Records, and — Roaming the lot crammed with cars were tribes of ragged people. They were everywhere. Some were sleeping on the concrete now. A few seemed still to be trying to look ... clean. They were all shadowy, even in full daylight. Across the street, before M. Zolotow's All-Week Check Cashing for New Citizens Open Weekends, a line of people waited — to be charged a huge fee from what they had managed to earn somewhere, Amalia knew. In the distance — she saw — a glossy building was going up — another one! If everything was going to collapse in a giant earthquake, why did they keep building those tall things?

Noisy honking! A wedding. Amalia saw a white veil swirling out of an open car window. She felt a brushing sadness. Last night, with Angel, she had thought, Oh, how pretty I must look to him with the gardenia he gave me —

A few feet away three tough-looking Mexican girls sat in an open car ... drinking beer! One had a large tattoo on her arm. They were Gloria's age. *Dios mio!* Was it possible? Girl gangs? Would Gloria —? No, as Raynaldo had often commented, Gloria was not only beautiful but she had a good head on her shoulders. She would never —

Such strange laughter! Walking toward her, fluttering, was a flurry of young men. Two were blond, bleached blond, another was Mexican, the fourth was black — all wore makeup. *Maricones!* Amalia thought. Some young men whistled derisively at them from a passing car. The effeminate young men exaggerated the movements of their hips. Amalia turned away from them.

"There he comes!" one of the young men had called excitedly.

"Johnny!" another welcomed.

"He's more gorgeous every day!"

"Those eyelashes!"

"Who's looking at his *eyelashes*? That *body* — and he *never* wears a shirt."

Amalia froze on the hot sidewalk. She saw the young man the effeminate boys were waiting for. He was crossing the lot toward them and he had not yet seen her. It was her son, her Juan. Of course she should have known. Of course she *had* known —

The shirtless young man joined the eager group.

It was not her son. Of *course* not. It was another good-looking young man, tanned, not even Mexican, holding his shirt slung over his shoulder. How ridiculous that she had thought even for a second — she hadn't *really* — that it was her son, that her son was —

Just what did she suspect her children of?

Nothing! Everything!

A man was rushing at her. She had not even seen him emerge out of the maze of parked and circling cars in the vast lot. Tall, thin, his skin darkened by years of exposure, hair and beard matted, he was a presence so terrifying that everyone nearby dodged away, except Amalia. She could not move. Before her, the man raised his arms, fists ready to strike down on her. Fear coiled about her body. All she could do was wait for the inevitable.

The man's hands unclasped. Then one hand scratched slowly at the air in a tangled benediction. "It's all ended, all of it, isn't it?" he gasped.

Now that she knew she was no longer confronted by violence, Amalia's challenging anger rose: "How dare —!"

"All ended?" the man pled out of the depths of some private hell.

His eyes were so full of hurt insanity that instead of raging at him, Amalia shook her head. "No," she told him — and then she moved past him.

8

♦   ♦

*A*MALIA STOOD at the corner of Sunset and Western, out of the parking lot that had turned into a pit of madness. When she looked back at it now, it was again only a crowded lot on a busy Saturday. It had *felt* like a pit of madness.

What if the Divine Mother sent a sign you misunderstood? Wasn't the world full of strange occurrences, like the encounter just now with that madman? How could you tell one of *those* from a divine sign? If you thought about it, it wouldn't be difficult, would it? The earlier encounter was a sign of only one thing, these terrible times. Divine signs were wondrous: A spring flowed out of a rock, a tree grew in the desert, warm snow fell in summer.

"Amalia, I want a chapel built right here."

Amalia laughed aloud, caught herself, wondered whether that thought required only a sign of the cross or a prayer; how irreverent had it been? She had imagined that the Blessed Mother had asked her to tell the priests that a chapel must be built on this lot, to replace Carl's Jr., M. Zolotow's All-Week Check Cashing, McDonald's, Tommy's Famous, El Pollo Loco . . . Hadn't Father Ysidro told her that Our Lady had once demanded a chapel in a swamp, on quicksand?

"Merciful Mother, you really mean exactly here, in the middle of all *this*?"

"Yes."

"But —"

"Amalia! Don't you understand me? Must I send my messages through someone else?"

Well, *now* she must say a prayer. Her thoughts had spilled too far. Who would question Our Blessed Lady's demands? — no matter how impossible they sounded. God and she always had a reason, a good one. Still, Amalia wished she had asked Father Ysidro whether the chapel in the swamp was ever finished and how many people were swallowed into the sand.

"I understand, Blessed Mother. The chapel must be right here, in this shopping center."

"Yes."

"I'll tell them."

But try to convince the *owners* of the businesses!

Amalia tried to take control of her thoughts. But —

"Amalia Gómez has had a visitation, Your Holiness."

That is what the local priest would finally tell the Pope.

"Are you sure it wasn't smoke from a sky-writing airplane?"

Well, there were *always* initial doubts.

AMALIA GÓMEZ OF EL PASO HAS VISITATION!

She revised the tabloid headline. She had to allow for unbelievers.

AMALIA GÓMEZ OF HOLLYWOOD CLAIMS
VISITATION BY THE HOLY MOTHER!

A miracle. . . .

Amalia sighed.

When the headline appeared in all the supermarket papers, the women at the sewing sweatshop would say, "Why, she's my very best friend." Milagros would claim to have expected it all along. The people whose homes she worked in would wish they had been much more generous to her. And her husbands — and some of the other men she had known — would be *terrified*. They would say: "God help me!"

Enough! Amalia decided where she would go now: to have her blood pressure checked at the other end of the huge lot. Every two months or so the Red Cross trailer stationed itself there for that purpose. The service was free. She hadn't been to the county clinic downtown for longer than she liked — for "woman things." The free clinic wasn't exactly free. She wasn't poor enough for that; she paid what they determined she could. She worried because she had overheard some women on the bus say that the governor was going to shut down many of those *clinicas*. Where would the women go? Thank God she and her children were healthy. Perhaps the Blessed Mother would ask for a clinic instead of a chapel.

Rosario might have said *that,* but *she* had gone too far in thinking it. She might have to confess it. The Blessed Mother *always* asked for a chapel. Who was she to question eternal mysteries?

Instead of crossing the lot full of craziness in order to reach the Red Cross trailer, Amalia decided to walk along Sunset Boulevard.

Suddenly a car painted over with spitting flames zigzagged to intercept another on the street. Other cars swerved, braked. Pedestrians dodged. Amalia pulled away as far as she could on the sidewalk. The two cars halted. Out of them, several young Mexican men rushed at each other. Amalia heard a shouted gang name: "Los Locos!" Then she saw clubs and — The battle was over in seconds. Both cars screeched away.

She did not look to see whether there was blood on the street. Not those savages in my neighborhood! she thought. And where had those policemen been just now? Two squad cars were racing in the opposite direction. Hadn't they seen what had occurred? — someone on the sidewalk had been hurt. "They'll turn away as long as our own are killing each other, *corazón*," Rosario's voice continued to pursue her.

Amalia walked faster along the street. Well, nobody had to tell *her* that the police were just another uniformed gang. Hadn't they turned on the people who were enraged by their indifference when a seven-year-old girl was struck by a stray bullet in another brutal gang shooting? — beating her family brutally. And in a poor neighborhood where they hadn't found the weapons they claimed were there, hadn't they crushed whole homes with sledgehammers? And hadn't two dozen of them only watched as four of them — savages — kicked and clubbed a black man more than fifty times while he lay helpless on the dirt? Nobody had to tell *her* that the jailers of her son were as vicious as the pillaging *gangas*.

Amalia stopped at an outdoor stand, to get a frothy orange drink. It would cool her in this unbudging heat, and calm her anger.

When she reached the Red Cross trailer, a few people were waiting in line, others milled about, undecided. Inside the van, a man and a woman — "*el doctor y su enfermera*," everyone called them, whether or not they were a doctor and his nurse — were earnestly checking an old man's blood pressure. "Is it high? Is it high?" he kept asking as the two continued to stare at the gauge. In the line there were only two Anglos, a young man and a woman who looked to Amalia suspiciously like born-agains. If they said anything about hell —

"Last time I was here," a hefty woman was informing everyone in Spanish, "a woman went into labor." She found that hugely funny. She repeated the story to everyone who joined the line, her laughter increasing each time. "Oh, I forgot to tell you," she added suddenly, "that her name was Concepción."

Now *that* was funny, Amalia admitted. It never failed to amaze her how many Mexicans had religious names, like Concepción. There were also Asunción, Incarnación, Milagros. Milagros — Miracles. That struck her now as the oddest; the name sounded different today. Quickly, she checked in her purse to see whether she still had the address Milagros had written down for her the day she'd learned that Rosario had "disappeared." It seemed now to Amalia that Milagros had definitely indicated she knew more about what had really happened to Rosario. She longed to see her friend from the sewing factory, talk with her again — today! She found the worn paper with the address on it. Perhaps she would visit Milagros — not far away — to find out what she knew. The prospect of locating Rosario brightened her.

The hefty woman in line before the Red Cross trailer was repeating her story about the woman named Concepción who had gone into labor, "right here."

Gloria, Amalia added to her list of religious names. Of course Rosario — rosary. And Consuelo — hope; Dolores — pain. But those weren't necessarily religious, were they? And Salvador —

And Angel —

His eyes had been on hers, last night in his room, as if to be granted permission to do what he did. Did she nod? Perhaps, but only slightly. He bent to kiss her mouth. She closed her lips, to render the kiss innocent, as it must be. Then he did this, so softly, so soundlessly that she was not jarred, not frightened: He closed the door that had remained open. He stood before her then and slowly, very slowly — yes, ready to stop if she forbade it — he drew the dress from her shoulders and kissed them gently.

Yes, and she let him. Because — Because —

Because he had done it with such caring and tenderness, the way it had never been done before, not clumsily, not angrily, no, but the way it must be, the way he was now removing her dress, her clothes, so lovingly, the way it should be, the way it should have been, the way it would be now — and then she realized he had removed his own clothes, realized it only when she glimpsed his body — briefly, because she had never seen a man look so naked, so — Yes, she had felt embarrassment, wanted to cover herself — but that was natural, clean embarrassment. He stared at her breasts as if in awe, studied them, so closely that she felt his eyelashes brush her nipples. "*Linda, linda* Amalia," he breathed the words. Oh, was it possible this was a first time for him? — and it felt as if it were for her, as if she were returning to a time that had gone wrong, was being righted now, cleansed, clean desire . . .

"— went into labor, right here." The hefty woman was telling her story to a prim old man and old woman who had just extended the line. "And do you know what her name was?" The laughing woman stopped her story abruptly.

Amalia felt a slight trembling of the earth.

The old man and the old woman grabbed each other and would have fallen if the Anglo young man had not caught them.

"Is it —?" Amalia could hardly speak.

"It's *not* an earthquake," the "doctor" called out to them from the Red Cross trailer.

"Our motor has to be generated every so often," the "nurse" explained the continuing vibration. "Everyone's so jittery about earthquakes," she laughed. "They've been with us since the beginning of time."

Nevertheless — Amalia hoped the subject would end there.

"When the Big One comes —" The prim old man shook his head.

"It won't come for thirty years," the woman who had witnessed Concepción going into labor dismissed.

Amalia was always encouraged when she heard that repeated estimate. Still, within thirty years included tomorrow . . . or today. "There isn't going to be an earthquake," she said assertively. Faith was forceful, wasn't it? And if faith could move mountains — She backed away from that thought, not appropriate now.

"Yes, there *is* going to be, a huge one, it's going to be an eight-point-five," the old man said. His wife clenched her purse, as if the earthquake would threaten it first.

You couldn't get away from this talk! Amalia thought testily. This old man probably figured he'd die before anything else could happen, and that accounted for his pleasure. "Maybe — if there is one — something heavy will fall on *you,*" she told him, to shut him up.

"Not on me," the man said with assurance. "Maybe on *her.*" He indicated his wife. He seemed delighted at the prospect of an enormous disaster that would leave him as sole survivor. "*I'm* prepared with bottles of water. You should be prepared, too," he directed at Amalia. "You can't rely on miracles."

Amalia looked at the sky.

The young woman who looked like a born-again said, "There's no such thing as miracles."

"Just catastrophes," her companion laughed.

Well, they weren't born-agains, Amalia reached for small consolations.

"Yes, miracles *have* ended," the old man announced. "You want me to tell you why? Because God thought —" He deepened his voice into the authoritative voice of God: "Why should I give them my miracles when they've changed everything?" In his own voice, he said, "Look at what people used to do to prove their love of God."

"Yeah," said the young man, "slicing up lambs —"

"— and offering children for slaughter," said the young woman.

"I'm not talking about *that,*" the old man dismissed. "I'm talking about weddings. They used to be beautiful. That's why people stayed together. I've been with *her*" — he gave a stern nod in his wife's direction — "fifty-four years." He went on to describe his wedding that had honored God with days of singing and lots of crying.

Like Teresa's — days of celebrating in her white dress, with its full skirt, yards of material, all white, all pure, Amalia thought. *She* had never even felt married, ever. She had never felt courted until —

Last night. With Angel . . .

She had felt his hands lightly on her breasts. He didn't crush them, didn't squeeze them. He cupped them as if they were precious — and they were, the way a girl's full breasts are precious, and beautiful. "Sweet, sweet," he sighed. Her body quivered, a warm quivering that spread. This was how it was supposed to feel, she knew, now, with this man, this young man, this Angel — who still wore his holy amulet about his neck. She was aware of a new excitement, the excitement of first exploration, an excitement that should have occurred before rape and accusations and anger and deaths. She glanced to one side, to a chair. She imagined that a white veil that had swirled in a breeze rested there. . . .

Bastard, bastard, *bastard*! Amalia banished Angel — again — from her thoughts.

"And if they won't have beautiful weddings with music, I'll give them earthquakes!" The old man had deepened his voice into God's again.

Enough! By now her pressure would have soared beyond the instrument's ability to record. Amalia left the line. . . . It wasn't true, what those people had said. Miracles did happen, several a week, according to that tabloid at the grocery store. Of course, most of them didn't sound right — like the story about those teenagers in Europe, six boys and girls, who claimed the Blessed Mother visited them regularly and insisted they wear expensive clothes so the "youths of the world" would look up to them, and that if —

"'Amá!"

She thought she heard her son calling to her, just as he had when he was alive. That's how powerfully she imagined it when it occurred, as it had now, at unexpected times. She might be at work or at home — or talking or even laughing — and she would hear his familiar: "'Amá, 'Amita!" and she would answer in her mind: *M'ijo!* All she could do then was to clasp her hands in order to control the pummeling sadness that followed, and then — increasingly now — there would often seep into that sadness an additional sorrow, for Juan, for Gloria, and all she could do was sigh.

Amalia sighed now.

She hurried briskly along Sunset Boulevard, away from her memories. She saw a Mexican bakery with the large *L* that proclaimed the sale of Lotto tickets. She went in, to buy one, to occupy her mind. She would still not check last week's drawing.

"How many tickets?" the large Mexican man asked her.

"Just one is all it takes to win." That's what Raynaldo always said when he bought his, although he'd end up buying several — "and one more for the road," he would add if there were others there to laugh. She remembered that fondly now. . . . She chose her lottery numbers carefully, a combination of her age, the year she arrived in Los Angeles, the year of Manny's birth.

"If you win, that'll keep you off welfare — at least for a while."

"What did you say to me?" Amalia clenched the ticket the man had just sold her.

"A joke. I tell that to all my Hispanic customers."

His careless remark had thrust her into the memory of the time the welfare woman had come to investigate whether she was living with a man, right after Manny was born. "You are despicable," she told the man.

"It's a joke I tell all my Hispanic —"

"*Coyote!*" She yelled back at him the harshest name she could think of, that of the men who prey on their own people.

Outside, she paused, saddened and angered, on the hot street, wondering where to go next. Oh, if only she had thought of something insulting to say to Angel last night.

Last night —

She had lain back in his bed, last night, and he leaned over her, his head just slightly bowed. As if honoring her initiation into clean desire, she had thought. Then with his hands he touched her body slowly, all of it, desiring it, not assaulting it, touching every part of it, lingeringly, as if he wanted to ensure she was feeling all these wondrous sensations — sensations which had been killed by Salvador and had remained dead with the others; bringing her body back to life.

In the muted light he had left on — "so I can see all of you, pretty Amalia" — she saw her body as if for the first time, saw her breasts, lush, yes, hued a deeper brown in this light, the nipples just darker, saw her hips, sensual in their fullness, allowed herself to see the abrupt velvet-darkness between her thighs, which extended the sinuous line of her hips. All of this — and his body, beautiful, too, taut, just lightly brushed with a film of hair — was right in its nudity, not dirty for abuse, but clean for desire and love.

She slid her hand over her breasts, down her stomach, to her thighs, to assert that this responding flesh was hers. She let the same hand glide over Angel's shoulder, to affirm that he was with her — and now he had become for her a knowledgeable initiating groom, who had realized that it was — truly — a first time, the way it should have been. She reached up to touch the gardenia in her hair. Even if it had begun to wilt, it would appear fresh, in this light, lustrous.

He held her hands and raised his face to her lips, which he brushed, just brushed this time, with his. Then his mouth moved over her breasts. His tongue circled them, narrowing on her nipples. He sucked them lightly, paused, studied them, sighed, resumed licking them. He laid one of his hands, softly, between her thighs, so softly she was aware of her own sensation before she was aware of his hand. She touched that hand, and — She felt an intrusive anxiety, the sharp edge of fear inherited from the past. She rejected it, with the memory of Salvador, yes, and of the others who had only taken her body, the way Raynaldo took it, grasping. . . .

Angel kissed her stomach. He parted his lips slightly so that as they slid down, down, they left on her flesh a moist warmth, a warmth that radiated from his lips and over her body, into her body — there — warmly, warmly, and she felt his aroused member pressed against her, not yet entering, not shoving, not demanding, not forcing. She was aware of a stirring she welcomed, did not welcome, welcomed — yes, welcomed as her whole body awakened. . . . That disturbed her — no, it excited her — no, it — Yes. Her body trembled, and she sighed. Gratefully, she looked at Angel as he knelt before her.

There was a twisted smile on his face. She heard his voice, a stranger's harsh voice:

"Yes, like that, pretend it's your first time, play it real good for me."

Pretend! The dim light in the room exploded into ugly brightness, exposing her utterly naked body in a stranger's room. She turned away from this man, not only from his naked body but from his naked eyes — and from the holy amulet on his chest, which in that moment had glinted like the edge of a knife. "Don't," she was able to whisper.

"Don't what?" He held her thighs and his mouth pushed roughly between her legs. Then he looked up at her, still holding her thighs. "Say it. Say, 'Don't eat my cunt, don't fuck me.' I want to hear you tell me not to. Act like it's your first time." He spoke in English so that the words sounded coarser to her, and there was a new drawl in his voice.

As if he was pretending to be a *gringo*! Amalia wanted to pull back — from him, from Salvador, from memories even fouler now. But she could not because his hands clasped her more tightly. You made me feel clean! she wanted to scream at him, but all she could say to protest the violent change was: "Where did you learn such ugly words?" She was trying to remind him of all he had told her, of his recent arrival in this country, the dangers that had aroused her pity.

"From a good *puta,* a bitch," he said.

"*Puta!*" The most despised word a woman can be called. Worse than just "whore." "I am not a whore!" Her voice was hardly audible to her. In a moment she would not be able even to speak. Fear was crawling over every inch of her being.

"But that's what I want — to turn you into a *puta* while you pretend it's your first time." He waited for moments, kneeling before her, holding her thighs. Then he released her, shrugged, stood up.

That was what allowed her to grasp for her clothes. She lifted them from the floor, pressed them against her body, to cover the sudden nudity.

Glaringly naked now, he stood before her in the light that seemed to flood the room. "Relax. I'm not going to force you." He spoke in Spanish. "That's not what I wanted."

She understood — he had wanted another humiliation, not physical violence; and so she was able to put on her clothes, each intimate item pulling her into a new awareness of how naked she had been. She realized only now that, for the first time ever, she had been unfaithful to a man she lived with. She had been unfaithful to Raynaldo. She twisted into her dress, put on her stockings, shoes.

Angel went to a small refrigerator, brought out a beer, flipped it open, drank from it. He leaned back, watching her. "I thought it's what you wanted, too. I was going to give you a good time."

His words deepened her shame. Fully dressed, she stood up. She saw the withered gardenia on the floor. She stepped on it. Then she walked to the door, opened it, ready to leave this despised room.

He aimed his most deadly words at her. He said, "A woman like you . . ."

On Sunset Boulevard — not yet noon and so hot! — Amalia refused to allow the rest of Angel's words from last night to enter her mind. She needed a distraction, right away, anything! She saw, ahead, a small boy, about ten, black, waving a long strip of bright-yellow plastic paper along the street. She caught up with him.

"What's that?" she asked cheerfully. She needed to hear something happy; that he had been to a birthday party decorated with paper ribbons; that he had —

"Police tape," the boy said. Pants much too large for him drooped over ragged tennis shoes. He brought the plastic paper to his mouth. He held it there for moments.

"What?" And what was he doing alone on Sunset Boulevard? Amalia wished now she had chosen someone else to talk to.

"My sister was shot last week, right on our porch. Killed. I was with her, seen it all. Cops roped off the porch with tape to keep other people away. I kept this piece to remember her. She was nice." He eyed Amalia with enormous brown eyes, as if baffled that she would have to ask.

"I'm — " Before she could finish, try to console him — she had wanted to hold him, he seemed so lost — the boy disappeared along the street, waving the police tape, which didn't flutter in the still air, just dragged behind him on the hot pavement.

Who had killed her? A gang? The police? . . . Feeling sadder, with something more to push away from her thoughts, Amalia decided she would go to El Bar & Grill, to find out about Raynaldo.

One of several such places in the area — they evolve into "neighborhood bars" — El Bar & Grill was once Elmer's Bar & Grill, frequented by movie stuntmen. The last letters of Elmer's name blurred. The clientele changed to Mexican. The bar became El Bar & Grill, although the grill had long been gone. Now, at night and on weekends, when it opened early, a woman from East Los Angeles delivered delicious homemade tamales, kept hot throughout the day.

Before she could change her mind, Amalia entered the bar. All bars look harsh in daylight, and El Bar & Grill certainly needed a good painting.

Raynaldo was not there.

But Andy, last night's bartender, was. He eyed Amalia as he always did. Three other men sat at the bar, drinking beer.

Amalia went to a table, one of only two in the immediate bar area; the others were in the "family section." Avoiding the droopy look he fixed on her — which he apparently considered attractive — Amalia told Andy, before he could reach her table, that she wanted two tamales. After all, she hadn't really eaten that hamburger earlier — and she didn't want to plunge carelessly into her reason for being here.

"Chicken or pork?" Andy was now hovering over her.

"One chicken, one sweet." She would have preferred pork instead of chicken, but she had to think of her health. She waited tensely at the table. When Andy placed the steaming tamales before her, she began to eat quickly, to banish him. Hmmm, delicious.

American food just couldn't compete, no matter how they kept trying.

"That man you were talking to last night after Raynaldo left is a *coyote.*" Andy had leaned over and said that to her.

A coyote! With renewed horror, Amalia remembered hearing recently about two *coyotes* in Texas who, in danger, fled from their trailer, leaving a dozen men and women locked inside; three old people had died from the heat. And *that* was the breed of man she had been with last night! "Are you sure?"

"Ask Elidio when you see him. He was the one who told me after you left. He was too scared to say anything earlier."

Amalia wanted to believe that Andy was lying to her because of the old rejection. But it all fitted now, from last night. "Why is Elidio frightened?"

"*Coyotes* are dangerous."

"I'm not in danger from him," Amalia said, because she felt suddenly afraid.

"Why should you be?" Andy looked at her slyly.

"Besides," Amalia said, and wished it had been true, "I knew he was a *coyote.* I knew he wasn't from Nicaragua." Thinking she might have revealed too much, she added, "That's why I walked out right after he approached me."

She left, without eating any more. Her stomach had wrenched in disgust at what Andy had just told her. Angel had preyed on her as he did on his own people. His sorrowing eyes, his sad story about danger and loss — lies to arouse her sympathy! . . . Outside, she realized she had not even asked about Raynaldo. . . . *She had been with a* coyote *last night!* If only she could talk to Rosario, who would help her know what to think about all this. . . . Milagros! Yes, she would go visit Milagros. She *had* urged her to contact her — and it *had* been about Rosario. She was sure of it now, and she *would* go see Milagros. The gossipy woman would think nothing about her just turning up — that's how visiting occurs among people without telephones.

From years of riding buses, Amalia was an expert in maneuvering throughout Los Angeles. She knew the bus system, its connections, even some of its schedules, the way others in the city know the maze of freeways . . . She had to wait only a short time for the bus, and so she reached the MacArthur Park area in minutes.

Years ago, she had come to this park with a possible "boyfriend."

They had looked at the glistening lake at night. Romantic couples huddled in rowboats floating on the water crowded with water lilies.

Now the park looked like a ravaged battlefield.

The most destitute — the wasted bodies of men and women, flesh on bones — congregated in one corner of the park, separated by tangles of rusted wire. The grass had died. Black people, brown people, white people, men, women — many young, a few with children — staggered about. Others sat on the rubble of spilled garbage, against oxidized cans, sat as immobile as still-living allows. Some lay on rags, on newspapers, on weeds. Others wandered with carts stuffed with debris. In the periphery of stirring corpses, shabby men and women sold drugs.

Others extended their selling into an area of the park still shaded by pretty trees heavy with flowers. A car would pause for a purchase and then speed away. In that same area there were swings and slides, and children played on them, watched anxiously by their mothers.

If a shooting occurred, would one of those children —? Amalia rushed away from the park.

On the streets, there was the buzz of an outdoor fiesta, this early Saturday afternoon. Men and women from across the various borders lavished the blocks with life, spontaneous conversations, even an occasional song, the strumming of a guitar. They walked or lingered along blocks cluttered with outdoor shops — bright clothes resplendent in the sun, colored glass jewelry nestling among ribbons and toys in improvised trays, second-hand stores promising unheard-of bargains. From small food stands everywhere, vendors offered exotic delicacies — a drink of fermented corn, cheese turnovers, the food of the new aliens — and vied with the sellers of tamales and tacos. The air was flushed with spicy scents. Sitting on a milk crate, a woman sold her proud creations, huge mangoes peeled into flower shapes, dabbed with lemon.

So many pretty young women in the area! Amalia noticed with pleasure; they were so new in Los Angeles that they wore little makeup, if any, dark shiny hair loose or braided, and they were still so shy, avoiding, with hidden smiles, the young men who praised them. Would the Anglo people who drove around these blocks in search of cheaply hired maids ever see how lovely these girls were? Amalia wondered. . . . Voices were lowered now, movement slowed — a sudden tension captured the blocks. In a slow squad car two policemen surveyed the street, as if choosing whom to question and for what. A few drugged bodies that had managed to straggle beyond the park shuffled away, that instinct still alive.

Amalia crossed the street, to another block.

The building whose address Milagros had given her had probably once been a stylish hotel. Its facade held on to colorful fragments of a tiled mosaic. Now, near its entrance, addicts, drunks, dealers, desolate men and women loitered. Pedestrians passed by, no longer even noticing them. For a few minutes, Amalia hesitated to enter — because she saw that it was made of bricks. All over the city brick buildings were being torn down or reinforced to resist the shaking of earthquakes. Amalia had grown used to noticing the giant bolts that indicated a building had been "anchored." She did not see any on this building. And so it was being abandoned, to decay or to an earthquake. Did Milagros know that?

The building's lobby, too, hinted of another existence. It had graceful arcs, layers of paint now chipped away in violent scratches. The man who oversaw the building sat behind a barred cubicle, like a cell. When the door opened, he reached automatically for something to one side of him. When he saw Amalia, the hand withdrew. He continued to scrutinize her carefully.

Amalia made her way past an open iron-webbed gate, up stairs cluttered with trash. Children played in dark hallways. The stench of Black Flag roach killer saturated the air despite paneless windows along the corridors. On the third floor, the door to Milagros's room was open.

"Amalia!" Milagros welcomed her, happily, into one room, a small room. "I'd given up hoping you'd come. It's been so long —"

On a bed were two children — one, about ten years old, a boy, played with a stick; the other, younger, a girl, slept. Milagros explained a window Amalia was looking at. It was partially covered with crisscrossed boards, loosely nailed: "*Ay, mujer,* it's to keep the children from falling out — and the bullets from coming in — or shattering the glass — what's left of it! — on me while I'm asleep." She laughed. "There're shootings every night." She laughed more forcefully. "I never go out at night anymore." The laughter stopped.

She invited Amalia to sit down, clearing a place on the bed. "It's more comfortable than those chairs." She offered her some *orchata,* a delicious, cool, milky drink made from sun-dried canta-loupe seeds. Amalia savored it.

A long piece of flowered cloth, darkened with grime and hanging over a stick, converted a corner of the room into a "kitchen." There was a hot plate; a small sink intended as a hand basin. There were paper flowers everywhere — and rat traps ready to spring. On a table were a framed picture of the Holy Mother, a coppery crucifix, and a small television. Through flimsy walls — Amalia noticed the ominous cracks — the constant cries of children, the blare of radios, and occasional shouts assaulted the room. The day's heat was accu-mulating here, entrenched. Milagros gave Amalia a pretty cardboard fan, to cool herself. Then she blurted: "Amalia, I'm terrified. My oldest son — he's on probation now — he's a *tecato.* He stole my week's pay."

A heroin addict. Like Salvador. Was Milagros's son one of those dazed young men she had seen wandering the park? Amalia let Milagros sob — what else was there to do?

"Every time I hear a shot, I think he's been killed, or that he killed someone. What am I going to do, tell me, *mujer!* And my other son, Amalia, he's only fifteen, and he drinks!" The sleeping girl woke, crying. Milagros held her, kissing her softly. "Amalia, I'm not even legal. My papers are fake. Every time *la migra* comes around, I want to die. That's why I make even less money than the others, because I'm not legal and Lewis knows it."

Amalia studied Milagros. In her forties — weary beyond her years, permanent shadows about her eyes. Had she been pretty not long ago? And this was the woman who at the sewing sweatshop kept everyone entertained with her gossip.

"I've been trying to bring my mother over, to help me with the children so I can take another job. I paid a *coyote,* but I haven't heard anything more about her. I don't even know where she is."

A *coyote.* Like Angel. "Things will get better," Amalia tried to console.

"But how?" Milagros pleaded.

Yes, how? Amalia wondered. Like living with a gun pressed against your head — that's how Rosario had described this ex-istence.

Milagros wiped her face. "*Ay, mujer,* you didn't come here to listen to my miseries. We all have them."

"Yes," Amalia said. "We all have them."

Milagros announced with sudden excitement: "You haven't been around, and so I haven't told you what's happened in 'Arco Iris al Cielo.' It's my favorite television serial now. Well! Imagine! Esteban has been deeply in love with Clara for years, from when they were both young and used to visit the local bishop — but now that Hector, Clara's stepfather, has miraculously come out of a coma, and —"

Amalia listened attentively, caught in the web of romantic anguish.

"And *that's* where the last installment of 'Rainbow to Heaven' ended. Can you believe they would leave us in such suspense?" Milagros finished.

"Always at the worst place," Amalia commiserated.

"Always." Milagros shook her head.

Soon she would ask about Rosario. Milagros had seemed so destitute that she had not wanted to reveal her reason for being here, that it was not to visit her. "In 'Camino al Sueño' —" Now Amalia went on to share with Milagros the details of her *semanal,* which, Milagros rued, she could not watch because she worked Saturday mornings cleaning the building's office in return for lowered rent.

"*Dios mío, mujer!* What can Ti'ita possibly do to save the marriage of Antonio and Lucinda, especially since God is so clear in his strictures about matrimony, *mujer,* and, after all, the evil man *did,* under God's eyes, marry Lucinda first!"

Amalia shook her head despondently at the complexities of the besieged Montenegro dynasty. Then she was quiet for a few minutes while Milagros tried to cool her little girl with a moistened towel. Finally, she said, "Milagros, do you know where Rosario is? I would like to find her."

"I've told you everything I know." Milagros looked away from Amalia. "*La migra* would also like to know where she is. They came asking about her again. They won't say why. But we keep hearing those rumors that she's hiding Jorge and that he killed a *coyote.*" She faced Amalia. "The way the *migra* keeps coming around, *I* believe he killed one of *them.* They wouldn't care about a *coyote,* no one does."

"No, no one does," Amalia agreed. In that moment she was sure Milagros was in touch with Rosario — to inform the older woman about what she heard at the factory. But Rosario had considered Milagros only a gossipy woman — or had she, too, come to know more about her, about her life beyond her serials? Amalia dug in her purse for some coins. "Just in case you do know where she is —"

"I told you I don't." Milagros's lips tightened.

"— or if you do hear from her —"

Milagros accepted the change.

"— then you can call me." She wrote down her telephone number on a piece of paper and gave it to Milagros. Then she reminded: "Rosario and I were such good friends."

"You have a telephone!"

Amalia was slightly embarrassed. "Yes." Besides, she might not have a telephone much longer if — But Raynaldo would be home by the time she returned.

"You're so lucky," Milagros said.

Amalia promised she would visit her again soon. Then she walked along the darkened corridor pocked with smashed light bulbs, past a dark bathroom reeking of urine, down unswept stairs, past the iron-webbed gate now drawn closed in the lobby. For a short time — in the miseries of Milagros — and of Esteban and Clara and Hector and Lucinda and Antonio and Ti'ita — she had managed to lose herself.

On the sidewalk a man was being handcuffed by two white cops. Now even more men, some women, idled outside. The stench of beer was assertive in the heat. There were angered voices. Sobs? Or was it laughter she heard? Increasingly she noticed desperate brown men like these, bewildered, all about the city. Now as she passed them on the street, she thought she heard a long, long sigh of loss.

A shot!

Threatened, Amalia halted. Then she realized the shot had not occurred near her. Quickly she looked up toward the third floor of the building she had just left.

She saw Milagros leaning out through the suddenly parted boards at her window, staring down into the streets where the gunshot had erupted.

Amalia hurried away from the shriek of sirens, as abrupt as if the street had screamed.

She walked two extra blocks to another bus stop, to avoid MacArthur Park. When she boarded the bus, she looked closely at the few scattered riders before she sat down — not long ago there had been a man who had suddenly begun shooting at passengers. There was danger everywhere. Like living with a gun pressed to your head. Rosario's words had followed her. If the gun was pressed there, it intended to shoot. That meant there was nothing you could do — and there never was, was there? Just the image of a gun, pressing, filled her with such fear that the day's heat felt only pasted to her suddenly cold body.

Now that she had found nothing more about Rosario, her need to talk to someone became urgent. Confession! She would go to confession. Thank God there was always confession, even when you didn't really have anything to confess.

She got off on Sunset and walked past stores with perennial SALE TODAY signs, past glossy buildings shoving them aside, another shopping center, another, and banks facing banks. She was so eager to reach the large church on Sunset that when she barely saw it, still in the distance, she made a sign of the cross. When she was there, she was immediately grateful for the green leafy welcome of its lawn, trees cluttered with huge blossoms like pale orchids.

The church was desert-yellow. Above three elaborately carved doors at the top of two sweeps of steps were statues of two saints, a man and a woman, welcoming. To one side, three palm trees vied for attention.

Amalia took out a lacy handkerchief. She always carried one in her purse for just this purpose. She covered her head — as Teresa had insisted must be done. She waited for the perspiration to cool, cherishing the anticipation of surcease the church would bring from this disturbing day that had begun with exhilaration. Then she was aware that a few pedestrians on the street were reacting in shock to . . . something . . . to someone . . . to —

An old Mexican woman, seventy, older, draped in a heavy black shawl, dressed entirely in black, had dropped to her knees on the sidewalk outside the church. Her face was so pale it merely looked stained brown. Dark circles rendered her eyes hollow. She proceeded to walk, on her knees, toward the steps of the church. She had lowered her black stockings just enough to expose her flesh more harshly to the chafing, hot concrete. She clutched a black rosary in her twisted hands. In a chant that rose and fell she prayed aloud in Spanish:

"*Así como El Señor Jesús subió al Calvario, así ofrezco* . . . Just as Our Lord Jesus climbed Calvary for my sins, I offer up my pain and sorrow to your glory, O God!"

A young man with a turban had been sitting on the sidewalk playing a flute. He looked startled at the strange, dark apparition and he moved away from the wall of the church. Other pedestrians stopped to watch. Some cars on the busy boulevard slowed down.

Amalia had seen *beatas* like this performing their promised pilgrimages to the altars of churches. She had seen them in South El Paso, more in Juárez, some prostrate, crawling on hands and knees for the last few steps of their journey. Here in Hollywood, today, on this street, the mournful figure looked like something carried over dead from the past.

The old woman draped in black had reached the first step. She raised one knee with deliberate slowness onto the first landing, and she began her ascent. Her face contorted in pain, she ground one knee and then the other on the rough surface. She clutched her rosary in a fist, and she pounded it against her chest.

Her firm voice rose: "*En complemento de mi promesa* . . . In fulfillment of my promise made for your mercy on me, I offer this, and my prayers. . . . *Santa Maria, Madre de Dios* . . ."

What possible mercy had been granted for her to remain this destitute, perhaps ill, a cadaver in black, so terrifying in her display of sorrow and pain? Amalia wanted to look away from her, but she could not.

"*Dios te salve, reina y madre* . . ."

The old woman climbed more steps, her voice rising in incantation:

"*Madre de misericordia* . . . O merciful Mother!"

Still on her knees, she reached the top of the steps. Her withered body wrenched in agony as she pulled the heavy door open —

"*Bendita tu eres entre todas las mujeres* . . . Blessed among women!"

— and she entered the church to continue her ritual to the foot of the altar.

Smears of blood tainted the steps behind her.

Amalia flung her eyes up, to the top of the church, the cross there, impassive against the blue, still sky.

9

♦   ♦

*A*MALIA STOOD under the knot of shade created by the three palm trees to one side of the church. Even there, she felt little respite from the heat. She still stared at the door behind which the veiled cadaver had disappeared. Was that what God expected, that ritual of pain, more pain? She thought of Milagros. Add *this* to all her miseries? Milagros yearned for less pain. She thought of Teresa's almost-blind friend in El Paso, longing to be crowned queen for one day. Was the old woman in veils courting something more with her crawling on bloodied knees — a miracle — by displaying her endurance for greater misery?

Miracles did seem to add pain to those who witnessed them. Amalia knew that miraculous visitations did not bring much good to the one who perceived them, not much practical good, she amended quickly — because, of course, there was the spiritual good, the rewards in heaven. But why no happiness in life? Why not less pain? Why more sadness? Wasn't there enough? Times *had* changed, though. Priests admitted that — and adjusted to it. Look at the Mass sung with music by mariachis in the church near Echo Park on lower Sunset Boulevard. Look at the clothes nuns wore now. Wasn't it possible that miracles, too, had changed? God's mysterious ways were not predictable, anyone could see that.

Amalia was baffled by her thoughts, but they provided a welcome comfort in her heart and she wanted to extend that. She considered this: Perhaps *new* miracles would make life better for the witness, set things right? Of course — and she would be the first to uphold the justice of this — the witness to a miracle would have to share its beneficence — mainly, of course, with those who were poorest; she adjusted that to conform to God's thinking, and also to Rosario's. . . . Oh, where was her friend, with her strange ideas?

Amalia blew coolness into the top of her dress, and then she perked up the ruffle there. Why did those chosen as witnesses have to look so drab? Poor Bernadette would have been pretty without all those heavy, odd clothes. Of course those teenagers in Europe who were claiming regular visitations were *too* expensively dressed, and *that* was suspicious, very suspicious. Still, Amalia did not like drab clothes. After Manny's funeral, she had refused to wear mourning, in defiance of his death. Why should she honor such terrible pain? She had worn mourning in her heart, where it was still draped.

She went into the church quickly.

A priest was rushing to intercept the old woman, who had almost reached the altar on her ragged knees. He raised her and guided her hurriedly out a side door, perhaps to minister to her in the sacristy. Soon, a church worker, a woman who looked like a secretary, out of place on her knees, was wiping away the stains of blood on the floor.

Amalia dipped her fingers in holy water from a font overseen by two angels, and she crossed herself.

The church glowed amber, tinged with gold from lighted candles throughout. Reflections from tall stained-glass windows smeared pastels on the floor. There were several confessional booths; and recessed partitions formed small shrines to various saints, one to the Blessed Mother, located just before the church narrowed and rose into the altar. On the walls were the stations of the cross. The figures were beautiful in their brightly painted agony; and Amalia would always look at each, going slowly from one to the other, reciting a slow prayer. The faces that remained serene in pain and sorrow soothed her.

A few people knelt or sat about the large church.

As always, Amalia went to say a prayer before the holy painting of Our Lady of Guadalupe, which was next to the elevated pulpit. The face was brown, but that was all about her that looked Mexican, Amalia always noticed; the features were like those of all the other saints and angels throughout the church. Manny had once asked her if all the saints, angels, Jesus, and God were *gabachos*. Amalia, too, wondered why they all looked like Anglos.

Now she knelt before the altar. Light flowing from one side of the church carved shadows on the body of Christ nailed to a large crucifix, his loincloth revealing carved sinews over his groin. Amalia began an urgent Our Father when she remembered Angel's body, last night, so naked it shocked her even in memory. Well, there was nothing holy about *that* man, that *coyote,* despite his name.

She moved into the shrine dedicated to the Virgin Mother. There was only one other person here now, an old man, head bowed, praying. All the candles were lit. Once Amalia had seen a priest carefully blowing out those that had not burned too long. Certainly to make more available to others, Amalia had explained it, rejecting her initial suspicion that he was soliciting more quarters. Since then, she did not hesitate, when all candles were lit, to blow one out and relight it as her own. The initial prayer would have reached heaven by then — if it was going to at all; so what was wrong with adding her own? She did that now, relit a candle.

"For my murdered son," she whispered aloud.

She held her hand over the lit candle, feeling its warmth just before it turned into heat, a hint of what her son must have felt that day of the terrible accident, the tattooed burning cross of the gangs — of Salvador — singed over the flame of her stove. She pulled her hand away. The hurt inside was enough.

She put the necessary coins in the slot.

The statue of the Holy Mother was separated by several wooden pews from the tiers of candles, which were located at the back of the shrine.

Amalia knelt before the Blessed Mother.

The statue was arranged against a glittering mosaic of variously blue stones. Overhead, a hidden light showered it with a silvery radiance. Within that dazzling radiance, the Queen of Heaven reigned in an alabaster gown, her crown golden, her graceful cape a deep blue.

How beautiful and pure! Amalia always thought, in awe and love and devotion. And trust.

Kneeling before the Holy Mother now, she closed her eyes. Then she rubbed them fiercely — and looked up quickly at her. . . . What was she doing, rubbing her eyes like that? Trying to recreate the impression of the silver cross she had *not* seen this morning — Ridiculous! She bowed her head and prayed her usual reverential Hail Marys, in Spanish and English.

She heard the hushed sounds that occur in church when confessions are about to begin, the whispering of priest's cassocks, the nervous shuffling of those confessing as they gather near the enclosed booths. One of two priests had remained kneeling before the altar. He could have been Mexican or American — now that this diocese was mainly "Hispanic," every priest heard confessions in English and Spanish. Had this priest glanced at her just now as he passed her? — in judgment of last night? Amalia often attributed to priests a powerful added sense about everything on her mind. Perhaps that glance signaled sympathy? Oh, the priest had glanced only toward the shrine of the Sacred Mother, soliciting added understanding from her to extend to the penitents. He was about her own age, Amalia figured, perhaps a few years older. She would confess to him.

In El Paso, Amalia had sometimes listened to the confessions of others, just fragments and, really, not deliberately. She might hear a word or two and instead of moving away, move closer. That allowed her to compare sins. If she heard something very modest — "I lied once" — she would not follow that person, supposing her own sins might seem weightier, although there was nothing extraordinary about them. In this church, with its much more enclosed and private booths — like small rooms — listening was not possible. What she would do here was follow into the confessional someone who looked ... well, not quite innocent — and never an old woman wearing a dark shawl.... The first penitent today, a bland middle-aged woman, moved without trepidation into the confessional. Amalia would not follow her, especially because this time she wanted — would she be able? — to speak about ... Angel. She needed to thrust all that away from her.

Nearby, a young man knelt, rehearsing his confession in a whisper. He looked extremely worried. He kept dropping his hands to his lap — and raising them up in guilty surprise. She heard his soft words: "... morning, when I'm about to wake up, my hands just —" She might follow him. She sat nearby.

She, too, rehearsed her confession. That was important in how she would be perceived. There were ordinary sins everyone mentions — lies, impatience, anger. The ones you had to be careful in telling were the more specific ones — and when she felt the need to tilt certain details in her confession, for a clearer understanding only, of course, she always made sure to add a few prayers to the penance she received, to adjust to what God might have inferred.

What — exactly — was there to confess?

Her odd thoughts from the time she woke and saw — thought she saw — a silver cross? Was that sinful? No. She dismissed that for now. Still, about that, she did have a question or two she wanted to ask. . . . Well, she would have to confess about —

Last night. It was true she needed to *talk* about that. But confess? Wasn't the memory punishing enough? What was the exact sin she had committed? That she had been unfaithful to Raynaldo? She hadn't, technically, since the act of infidelity hadn't really happened, had it? Well, perhaps that was an area left to speak for itself. More importantly, she and Raynaldo weren't married; so — Confess that she had gone to a man's room? No sin in that. That Angel had taken off her clothes? . . . The problem was how to state it all so the priest would see that Angel — and that extra beer — were responsible for what happened. She would tell him Angel's name, a powerful reason for her having gone with him. She might insinuate that there was a picture of Our Lady in his room. No, that might work against her, as might the fact that he had worn a crucifix on a small chain about his neck.

The beautiful gardenia he had given her . . .

The priest would not understand that. Only she could. She rehearsed: Father, last night, after my husband ran out on me at El Bar & — Raynaldo was not her husband, and it wouldn't be good to mention a bar so quickly. . . . She tried again: Father, last night a terrible *coyote* who — The *coyote* part she would definitely use. Even priests must detest *coyotes*. . . . Father, he took off my clothes — She would *not* be able to say that!

She would just let the priest infer most of it, while she kept reminding the Holy Mother of her reasons. Would the priest allow her to tell him about feeling like a girl last night — yes, a bride — and about the hurt when it all changed? No, priests never asked for reasons, just what and how many times, *always* how many times.

Of course Amalia never doubted what the correct outcome of her confession should be — and God would easily approve it: The priest would say: "It is that despicable *coyote* who dares call himself Angel and to wear a holy crucifix and even have a picture of Our Lady in his room — it is *he* who should be kneeling here in the confessional pleading for forgiveness — which God in His infinite mercy *may* grant *but I will not!* — for deceiving you into what you saw as an act of purification. You had no choice."

She didn't really need to confess at all, Amalia concluded, just talk about several matters. Perhaps she might find a way to bring those up *as if* they contained something sinful on her part. What she needed to talk about was the festering humiliation of Angel's last words to her when she was already at the door. Could she even repeat them? No! . . . And she needed to talk about Gloria and Juan, explore what they could possibly be holding against her — and what they were withholding from her. How could she connect them into her confession? Where could she interject anything sinful, on her part, into that? . . . And to talk about Raynaldo. New complications had delayed his divorce — she never disbelieved him, and he had shown her letters — but soon it would be final and they would be married. Now there was the tension among him and her children. How to discuss that in confession, when she was not a part of it? . . . And how to speak about the stifling pain she felt over Manny's death? Impossible even to *force* anything sinful into *that*!

The bland middle-aged woman emerged from the confessional with the beatific look of someone who has been given a very light penance. Let the young man go in after *her*. Amalia bowed her head as if she was not aware of the waiting confessional. The young man did not stir. Well, she would outlast him. She began a slow Our Father. . . . Teresa. Why had *she* intruded on her thoughts now? She'd given her the expensive funeral she'd demanded. And if there was any sin there, it belonged to — Amalia said a quick Hail Mary. It was not good to question the dead. Still, it seemed to her now that often confessions were about people who should themselves be doing the confessing.

The nervous young man had not budged, trying to outlast *her. He* didn't want to follow the smug woman. Now a man in his thirties, who kept twisting a gold band on his finger, paused before the confessional — and then went in. After a short time he came out — crying. The young man got up — but Amalia seized what she saw as the best time to enter the confessional — now. She bowed her head reverently, said, "Excuse me," to the young man, and went in ahead of him.

Inside, she felt soothed, close to a holy man, who was close to God, close to the surcease she needed to find within this troubling day. Kneeling, she made her usual quiet declaration to God: I am a divorced woman, but I do not want to be separated from your church. Father Ysidro may be reminding you about this now in heaven if he is already there. She waited in the hushed booth.

The small window in the partition that separates the priest from the penitent's sight slid open. Amalia saw only the silhouette of the priest's head behind the shaded screen.

"Bless me, Father, for I have sinned," she began.

He recited whispers.

"These are my sins . . . Last night . . ." She could not speak about that yet. She revised: "Father, I've been thinking about miracles."

The voice was puzzled. "How is that a sin?"

"Why don't they occur anymore?" Amalia rushed that so he might answer.

"They do. Each day God allows us breath is a miracle."

Just that? Amalia did not ask.

"And there's the constant miracle of faith. Have you had doubts about your faith?" the priest asked.

"Certainly not!" she said emphatically. "I have faith in all of God's works, even the most mysterious. And in His forgiveness," she added pointedly.

"One may not transgress counting on Our Lord's infinite forgiveness," the priest warned. "What is your confession?" The voice was already impatient.

Amalia felt a sudden desolation. "Last night —"

"Yes? Last night —"

"Last night, I —" She still could not give the harsh memory words.

"I must hear your confession, or —" the priest was firm.

"Last night, when my . . . husband . . . walked out on me at a bar — a *family* bar," she amended, "there was a man there, and he invited me to where he lived and I went."

"You went to his home? Alone?" the priest asked.

He was already accusing her. "Yes."

"And what happened there?"

"Father, he was a *coyote,* one of those people who exploit their own, they —"

"And how is that your sin?" the priest asked.

She took a deep breath. She wanted to skip the earlier parts, move on to what Angel had said to her just before she left, the words that bruised even more today. "In his room —" She shifted quickly: "There was a picture of Our Lady of Guadalupe."

"That is *commendable,*" the priest told her.

She had done it, shifted sympathy toward Angel. "But what he *did* there —" She stopped.

The priest cleared his throat. "When you went alone to his home with him, did he attempt something sinful?"

"Yes." She was very grateful for his help.

"Nothing more, only an attempt?"

"Not exactly."

"Confession must be truthful."

"It wasn't really . . . completed."

"Did he disrobe you?"

Amalia was even more grateful for his directness, because now she did not have to speak those words. She knew it was necessary for priests to locate precise sins, and to do so in exact words, no matter how mortifying to the one confessing. After all, she reminded herself, these holy men must have heard everything. They were themselves, in their purity, separated from certain aspects of life; but that only made them more attuned to those who turned to them. They were here to provide an immediate substitute for salvation, which you earned fully at the end of your life. Every Catholic understood all that. "Yes."

"Even your intimate items?"

Amalia closed her eyes. "Yes, Father."

"And —?"

She waited for his further help.

"I cannot hear you."

"I didn't say anything, Father."

"I cannot grant you absolution unless — Did he touch you?"

He was becoming angry at her already, she could tell. "Yes," she whispered.

"When he had already removed your intimate clothes?"

"Yes!" The violent sense of last night's betrayal with Angel grew.

"How many times did he touch you?"

"Twice . . . three times." Now that she had been able to answer what she knew he had to ask, she would move on, tell him that when she was at the door — and fully dressed —

"Where did he touch you intimately, the first time?"

"I can't tell you." She could not.

"What! I am your *confessor*!"

"I can't tell you, Father."

"You are confessing!"

"He touched my . . . breasts." That was enough. She would say no more. It was bringing it all back to her.

"After he had removed your intimate clothes, he touched you there, the first time?"

Amalia burned with shame, as she had last night, and disgust. She considered running out of the confessional. But she needed surcease even more now.

"What did you say!"

"I didn't say anything," Amalia said.

"The second time, where did he touch you?"

"I can't tell you."

"Where!"

He was reacting with so much indignation that now she considered rushing this part: "Between my —" But she could hardly gasp those two words.

"Where!"

"Between my —" She could not say it.

"Between your legs? When you were disrobed?"

She was making him even angrier by her avoidance. "Yes!" She added silently, Keep in mind, God, that it was no longer the way it had been when I went with him, the way I thought. It had been pure, and then it was dirty beyond my choice.

"Where did he touch your disrobed body, the third time?"

She remembered those moments now with renewed outrage that Angel had put her in this position, to have to speak these things to this priest, whose indignation was mounting. "The same place but with his —" She tried to answer, would not, could not.

"Not with his hands that time? Then how?"

She spat out the words, to end this: "With his mouth!"

"*Ahh!*" A gasp, a sigh. Then the priest was silent.

So appalled that he was speechless? Amalia waited — and she wondered whether it was sinful to despise Angel even more after her confession, because she did.

"Bless you." The small door slid closed abruptly.

Amalia still waited, kneeling in the booth. She made a sign of the cross. She waited longer. Nothing more? No penance? She left the confessional.

Had it really happened?

In the large church, she felt bewildered, lost, adrift, desolate. She had wanted to speak about the silver cross — *it had been smoke!*— her sadness, all that Angel's words had stirred, were stirring, and instead —

Had it really happened? Had the priest dared to use her confession to —

She went to the shrine of Our Lady. She knelt, said some prayers, in a penance of her own, to confirm to herself that, whatever had occurred in that booth, she *had* confessed. Her feelings tangled into a choking knot of indignation, outrage, new anger.

"Please —"

She startled herself. She had spoken that word aloud to the Miraculous Mother. But what had she been about to say?

She walked out of the church.

Outside, she looked at the stains of blood the old woman had left on the concrete steps. The blood had caked brown, flecking into dusty dirt. Amalia looked away, and her eyes moved up, into the sky. Streaks of clouds had appeared, very thin, wisps, only that, and only in one distant edge of the sky, just there.

Amalia touched her heart. Somewhere in her being there was a hidden pain. Had she felt it before? Yes, but she had never tried to locate it, had not needed to locate it. Now —

Suddenly she became aware of a new stillness within the day, as if everything had stopped. All seemed about to become clear to her!

The moment passed. Perhaps it had not existed. What was there to be clarified? The sensation had occurred only because she had been so pensive that she had momentarily not noticed even the loud sounds of Saturday-afternoon traffic in Hollywood.

10

◆   ◆

*L*AST NIGHT, when she had stood, fully clothed and about to leave, stood at the door of Angel's room — that *coyote,* that doubly despised man! — he had aimed lazily spoken words at her as he leaned — still glaringly naked — against the refrigerator, with the beer he had just opened. "A woman like you —"

Why had she stopped? *Why* hadn't she rushed out? *Why* had she asked him: "What do you mean, a woman like me?" . . . As she paused outside the church on Sunset Boulevard now, Amalia asked herself that. The incident in the confessional — *had the priest dared to use her humiliation?* — was forcing out the avoided memory of what had occurred at the end of last night's encounter with Angel.

"A woman like you —"

"What do you mean, a woman like me?"

"I mean an old woman, a *vieja* like you," he said. "A *vieja* like you should be grateful that a man like me even looks at her."

Amalia had to lean for support against the door. She felt as if she had been struck, not because she was sensitive about her age — she wasn't — and not only because she had felt just moments earlier like a young girl — no, it was that single word, "grateful," that took her breath away then. It echoed back into every moment of her life — she knew that only now as she walked down the steps of the church, where the *beata*'s bloody prints were disappearing into the concrete. *Grateful! For humiliation?*

That remembered word was so disturbing that she momentarily welcomed two distractions occurring simultaneously: A new dark blue car had just driven up before the church to let out a well-dressed blonde woman with a boy and a girl; and across the street, with the no longer surprising suddenness of such now daily scenes, a squad car's bullhorn was demanding that an old, large car halt and that the occupants get out with their hands over their heads.

At the same time that Amalia thought she recognized the blonde woman and her children, she saw, across the street, that the two cops, one black, had already flanked two mustached Mexican men, who had exited from the large car, loudly protesting being stopped "for no reason . . . not speeding . . . doing nothing."

Nearer her, Amalia heard the driver of the paused navy blue car tell the blonde woman that he would go park and then join her. Now Amalia recognized the family, from television news. He was a *político,* a powerful city politician who constantly proclaimed his "Chicano heritage" and wept openly on American holidays while holding his hand over his heart. Whether his wife was Mexican or not, her hair was bleached, and their children were chattering in English. *My* children learned Spanish *and* English, I saw to it, Amalia thought — and she looked across the street.

One of the two mustached Mexican men tried to run. He was shoved to the ground by the white cop, who drew his gun as he pressed his knee against the man's back.

Gathering her noisy children, the *político's* wife retreated to the top of the steps. She waited near the church door, adjusting a lacy scarf over her head. Then she grasped her fidgeting children, firmly, one with each hand.

Across the street the second mustached man had thrown up his hands in surrender, still shouting his protests for having been stopped "for no reason . . . nothing, nothing." The indignation was so forceful that Amalia prepared to feel outrage at yet another violent, senseless encounter between Mexicans and cops. At the same time, she was aware of the *político* walking toward the church, a dapper, well-dressed man with an unfocused smile on his face. He nodded at her without seeing her.

She looked away from him, across the street.

The man pushed to the ground was being handcuffed. Ordered to, the other opened the trunk of the old car.

The *político* looked across the street to the altercation occurring. He frowned. From the church door, his wife called out to him: "Hurry up, *please!*"

The cop shouted loud words into the open trunk of the car. Out of it, cramped from painful hiding, a pregnant woman and a man emerged. They were very dark brown. The woman was sobbing, rubbing her stomach. The man rushed loud, urgent words at the cops: "— *nuestra familia está aquí, en* Fresno, *les pagamos mucho*

dinero a estos hombres para que nos trajeran aquí, a Fresno —"
From his pocket he took out a crumpled piece of paper. "*A esta dirección. Miren, miren, aquí en* Fresno."

They had paid the two Mexican men a lot of money to unite them with their family, at the address on the piece of paper, "here in Fresno," the man kept repeating. The two men had told them they would be there in fifteen minutes. Was this Fresno? Was this Fresno? The man kept looking about as if expecting his family to appear.

Amalia's anger shifted in confusion. Two Mexican men she had felt sympathy for had taken the money of the illegal man and woman. They had intended to abandon them in the midst of the huge city they told them was Fresno, which was hours away. . . . Amalia turned away to see the *político* walk quickly up the steps of the church.

On the street an unmarked car joined the squad car. Two tall men in plain suits handcuffed the pregnant woman and the man — suddenly terrified, trapped. The two new men pushed the man and woman and the two Mexican men — together — into the back of the unmarked car, separated from the front by a black screen of thick mesh wire.

With his wife and children, the *político* entered the church.

The unmarked car drove away. The squad car made a sudden U-turn on the street.

Amalia walked away from the church, along the blocks, past tall palm trees unbudging in the static afternoon. She would no longer avoid going back home to face Raynaldo, she decided suddenly — and he would be back, don't doubt it; it was Saturday, and on Saturdays she often cooked his favorite *chiles rellenos,* fat with cheese and spicy batter. Had she been avoiding going back home? Confront Raynaldo about what exactly? Whatever! She would confront Gloria about her lies. What lies? And Juan about —? No matter! She would go home.

Near one of the hundreds of minimalls that pock Los Angeles with chromy colors, an aggressively plain woman in her thirties broke away from a small group of men and women like her, and she advanced purposefully on Amalia. Another born-again!— Amalia was about to dodge. The woman intercepted her, holding a long pad of paper clipped to a board. Amalia heard others in the group asking passersby if they were qualified to vote.

"— sign a petition for cleaning up the air?"

"What?" Amalia asked the woman who held the pad before her.

"A petition to require cars —"

"I don't have a car."

"For clean air," the woman persisted. "Chemicals in —"

"What?"

"Clean air." The woman took three deep breaths, gasped, simulating a coughing fit, which she terminated abruptly. "*Aire lampio* —" she tried in Spanish.

"I understand English," Amalia said. "I am a Mexican-American. And you mean '*limpio*,' not '*lampio*.'"

"Oh, well. Do you realize that automobile exhausts account for —?"

"Feed the hungry," Amalia told her. Rosario's voice had tried to order her confusion at what the woman wanted done. Who didn't want clean air?

The woman turned to one of her male companions, who was about to accost a Mexican man waving him impatiently away. "Didn't I tell you they don't understand their own oppression?"

"It's the same in India," the man said.

Amalia turned into one of the prettier side streets off Sunset. Increasingly, she chose routes that had fewer blights, the most flowers; when she was in a hurry and had to consider only distance, she would try not to notice certain sights, like the graffiti-smirched wall she had sought out earlier and would avoid now.

CONSULTAS

Solve All Your Problems! Learn What

You Need to Know! Hear What You Need to Hear!

Expert Spiritual and Worldly Guidance!

No Appointment Needed!

WE ARE OF YOUR FAITH!

Amalia halted before the small house on which that sign was lettered on a board pressed against the window. Like others in the neighborhood, this house was holding on, huddling from the nearing contamination that begins with weeds. It, too, was caged within iron bars. Amalia often paused before the house of this old man and woman, sometimes kept one of the leaflets they periodically left in mailboxes. Some people in the neighborhood — especially the younger ones — called them *brujos*. Others referred to them more respectfully as "*espiritualistas*" or "*curanderos.*" There were almost always some of these "spiritualists with healing powers" in "Hispanic" neighborhoods. They provided "*limpias,*" spiritual cleansings, thwarted "*el mal de ojo,*" the evil eye — but some extended their "powers" into more mundane matters, offering "*consultas*" on a range of problems.

Although this old man and woman proclaimed being of "your faith" — and in this neighborhood that *had* to mean Catholics or liars — the latter consideration had kept Amalia away, because she most certainly was *not* a *supersticiosa,* although only God could tell you why not, considering that Teresa had consulted *curanderos* almost as often as she went to Mass. Yes, and once she claimed a spirit had come to her in a dream to inform her that treasure was buried under their tenement apartment. That was when she summoned an ancient old man, who squeezed under the crawl space, chanting prayers, and then emerged asserting that, yes, there *was* treasure buried there, guarded by one benign spirit, whom they must pray to, and an evil one, whom they must watch out for. Teresa and her husband dug into the moist dirt and found only more garbage.

As Amalia stood pondering the sign that promised to tell her everything she needed to hear, a car neared her; but she did not start because she had heard happy voices. She turned, and she saw a convertible with four teenagers, two girls, two boys, all Anglos, all sparkling, so *right* in that certain way she had come to recognize from the grown children of well-off families she had worked for. Of course they would all be wearing shorts, they always did, the moment the weather turned slightly warm.

"Do you know where Mariposa Street is, please, ma'am?" one of the girls asked her. The car had stopped by the curb.

Amalia knew where that street was. But she did not answer. She merely looked at them in their car.

One of the young men repeated, "Ma'am, would you please tell us where —?"

Amalia turned her back to them.

"She doesn't want to speak to us," the girl said in surprise.

The car drove away.

Why had she done that? — they had been so courteous. She knew the answer. When she had seen them, she had tried to place Gloria among them, but she had not been able to fit her there. No, they would not have welcomed her daughter, with her heavy makeup and teased hair, her shiny boots. Amalia touched the ruffle on her own dress. Well, she *did* know this: None of them could have held a candle to her beautiful Gloria.

She walked up the two steps to the door of the house of *consultas*. She needed to talk. She would have preferred Rosario or a priest, who wouldn't? But where was Rosario? And the priest had — She felt a resurgence of indignation. She rang the bell. Immediately she wondered: What do I need advice about? The whole day.

A small peep-door opened. An eye looked out.

If they're clairvoyant, can't they see —? Amalia stopped her readied skepticism. After all, everything had conventions. The door opened.

There stood Ti'ita! "Ti'ita!" Amalia said aloud.

Of course it wasn't really the wise old woman from "Camino al Sueño." It was only that the woman before her looked so much like her, tiny, old, gnarled, with an all-knowing faint smile that glowed even out of the wrinkles of her aged face — troubled and caring and loving, all at the same time. Of course she would be wise, looking like that, with ancient and new wisdom. She wore a plain gray dress and a large gleamy crucifix about her neck. Just like Ti'ita.

The benign old face was capable of a slight frown. "What did you call me?" the woman asked Amalia.

"A name of someone I trusted a long time ago, very wise. I turned to her when a man out of my past threatened to return." Amalia found a suitable adjustment.

"Ghosts," the old woman muttered wisely, "are not always dead." Amalia understood that.

"I am Esmeralda Morales — Donã Esmeralda. And this is Rogelio Morales. — Don Rogelio." The old woman was introducing an old man who had materialized out of the dusky light of the house.

Her husband? Her brother? Amalia wondered.

He was almost as tiny, a male version of Doña Esmeralda. He, too, wore a huge crucifix. He had grayish-blue cataracts, so that he seemed to be looking everywhere at once.

"I'm Amalia Gómez, I live nearby —"

"We know."

"We *know*."

Well, there was no problem with knowing that, anyone could

know that. Amalia peered into the small living room. Within the murkiness, she saw a small altar, with two crucifixes and what might be several holy amulets hanging over them, and — this relieved her anxieties about being here — a gloriously colored picture of the Blessed Mother, her cape sprinkled with silver beads.

"Please . . . come into our humble home," Don Rogelio said.

In an oddly deep voice for such a tiny old man, Amalia thought. She walked in.

Near the altar, votive candles glowed in red and yellow jars. The scent of incense, sweet, just like in church during Mass, wafted through the air.

The house of devout Catholics, Amalia was sure — but what was that over there? Jars that looked like those from the *botanas,* the charm-and-magical-herb stores in East Los Angeles. . . . And those strange feathers on the wall? That clay face under them? An Aztec God? And . . . my *God!* . . . was that a chicken claw? . . . Well, what was wrong with a little decoration?

Still, Amalia thought she should announce quickly: "I am a Catholic, a *good* Catholic."

Doña Esmeralda's eyes misted over with hurt. She bowed her head. So did the old man. Then the old woman touched Amalia's hand, instantly forgiving, extending boundless understanding. "We are of *your* faith," she affirmed. "Tell her, Padre Rogelio."

"But what else, *m'ija?*" The old man touched his crucifix.

Padre? Reverend father? The old woman hadn't called him that until now, had she? Nothing serious. There were retired priests. But he had better be her brother. . . . Had she only now noticed it or had he just put it on when her eyes had returned to the chicken claw? — the man was now wearing a white collar about his neck, a frayed white collar. "I didn't mean to offend," Amalia allowed an apology, because as always she was pleased to be called "*m'ija.*"

"Come into the cooler part of the room," Doña Esmeralda invited. "The shade of a serene tree blesses our humble home with coolness."

"And it's a particular blessing on this uncommonly hot day," finished Don Rogelio — Padre Rogelio.

If they mentioned earthquake weather — Amalia thought it opportune to say: "I am not a *supersticiosa,* like the women at a sewing place I used to work in. When someone made a prediction of an earthquake, they ran out." Just in case they could read her thoughts through her eyes, she looked down. "I did not run out, nor did my friend Rosario."

Padre Rogelio shook his head. "False prophets abound. Our Lord and His Holy Church warn us."

The old woman nodded sagely for a long time.

Amalia saw on a wall a picture of Our Lord in festive robes. But she also saw that a twisted jar under it was filled with colored water.

Curtains almost completely drawn created the room's duskiness. The branches of the sheltering tree just outside filtered out the bright afternoon light.

They sat on three chairs about a small table covered with a colorful serape — Amalia welcomed that. Now she waited nervously while two pairs of aged eyes focused on her.

Then the man rose, stood behind her. She felt him fanning the air. "What is he doing?" she asked the woman.

"Cleansing the air of intrusive elements, *m'ija,*" Doña Esmeralda said tolerantly. "So that we may see into your problems clearly." With that she, too, rose, and reached for a goblet. She poured a little of the dyed liquid from the jar and brought it to Amalia.

Amalia jerked back from it.

"Rain from God's heaven. A few drops will further cleanse the air."

Amalia still backed away.

"It was blessed by a priest from your church," Doña Esmeralda informed.

Oh.

The woman spattered a few drops of liquid about them all.

Amalia smelled pepper.

Padre Rogelio was brushing her lightly with a branch with shiny leaves.

"What is *that*?"

"The branch of a pepper tree," Doña Esmeralda instructed. "Our Lord's crucifix was made of such wood." She made a very slow sign of the cross.

Fine. But if the old man tried to touch her with the chicken claw — A hollow sound made Amalia jump. The old man had blown into her ear with a conch shell.

"The *limpia* is over," Doña Esmeralda announced the end of the cleansing.

"The air is purified for God!" the old man proclaimed, breathing it deeply.

With his careful help, Doña Esmeralda managed to kneel. Then the old man, too, struggled to his knees. Cautiously, Amalia knelt also. After all, what was wrong with kneeling before an altar, Our Lord, and his Holy Mother?

"*Dios te salve, Maria* —" Doña Esmeralda chanted. Her clasped hands — suddenly — held a rosary.

Where had she been keeping it before? — Padre Rogelio, too, was now clutching reverential beads. Well — whatever — Amalia could certainly relax with a Hail Mary and two rosaries. "—*El Señor es con tigo,*" she prayed especially loudly, for God to hear and know she was not a *supersticiosa.* Who could be, and still honor the Blessed Mother?

Again they sat about the table. Amalia waited. Four cloudy eyes were on her again. Silence extended. Amalia brought one hand to her lips and leaned to one side, to emphasize that she would wait for them to speak first.

"A prayer for guidance out of the silence of distrust," Padre Rogelio proffered.

They all knelt again. "Our Father, Who art in heaven —"

They sat. Silence stretched further, further —

"Your fee!" The thought occurred to Amalia only now, and with a start.

"Reasonable, very reasonable," Doña Esmeralda's voice was brisk.

Padre Rogelio clarified: "A generous donation to the sacred altar."

"And to the Holy Mother," the old woman added. The benign smile fluttered like a tic on her old lips.

"What is important is to tend to your needs, *m'ija,*" Padre Rogelio said.

Fine. "I am here for a *consulta,*" Amalia allowed herself only to say the obvious, and only so it would be up to them to speak or do something next.

The old woman went to a bowl near the altar. She lit some incense. A thin plume of smoke curled into the air. In the semidarkened room, Amalia saw how much the man and woman looked like frail, disappearing birds.

Padre Rogelio held a white sheet of paper before Amalia, and

Doña Esmeralda extended the smoking bowl to her. "Please, *m'ija,*" the man said, "extinguish the incense with the paper now."

Amalia did. God would be sure to know she was merely tolerating all this.

Padre Rogelio took the sheet and studied the outline made by the smoke. He smiled triumphantly. He handed the paper to Doña Esmeralda, who mirrored his smile. "Extraordinary!" she announced. She brought the paper to Amalia.

An ashy smudge. Amalia preferred not to say that.

"A sign of something extraordinary!" Doña Esmeralda interpreted. Her eyes glistened even more.

"Something miraculous!" Padre Rogelio exulted.

The silver cross in the sky! Amalia looked excitedly down at the smudge on the paper. It had not changed, still just a smudge. Wait. It looked like — A gun? Smoke from a gun. Amalia shivered.

The man and the woman faced her intently, like two *ti'itas.* Both touched their foreheads for seconds, as if locating the point of greatest concern and concentration. After moments Padre Rogelio sighed, "Someone is missing."

Manny. Amalia inhaled. "My son was murdered by jail guards." She looked, tensely, at the old man and woman.

They gazed at her. Then they nodded, yes.

Amalia felt suddenly confident about her purpose for being here.

"Signs and messages are everywhere." Doña Esmeralda seemed suddenly delighted.

"Messages abound." Padre Rogelio seemed to be bombarded by them — he turned his head every which way, as if dodging some.

"Why are signs so mysterious?" Amalia asked.

"God's ways." Doña Esmeralda shrugged her thin shoulders at the obvious. The smile was untiring on her lips. Then her brow furrowed — but the smile survived, radiant. "There are conflicts to resolve."

"Complications to unravel," Padre Rogelio extended.

That's why she was here, to talk about her problems. So why shouldn't she be direct? She said, "My son Juan is in trouble, suddenly he has money, he's keeping something from me, it may involve drugs, it may involve a boy who was hiding in the garage and someone who drove up to the house today." She listened carefully to her own words. "My son's afraid. It may all have to do with a new gang in the area, or perhaps —"

"A *ganga*? In our neighborhood!" The old woman snapped out of her trance.

"*Dios nos guarde!* Those savage gangs!" The old man, too, lost his concentration.

Amalia did not hear them. "And there's a serious conflict between my daughter and my husband—he's not really my husband and he's not her father, but he loves her like a father." She stopped. She felt a wave of nausea invade her. The nausea swept into violent anger.

"*Cálmate, m'ija,*" Padre Rogelio was saying.

"Would you like some water?" Doña Esmeralda was asking her.

When she heard their words, Amalia realized she had stood up, was trembling with rage, at the same time that she felt very tired. She saw the old man and woman staring at her. Suddenly she had to wipe away all her previous thoughts about Gloria, Raynaldo— She said: "Last night—" Yes! She would spew all that out, like bad beer—that damned extra beer festering in her stomach like poison—vomit it all out before this old man and woman who would tell her she had had no choice. She would purge it all, finally.

The gray heads of Doña Esmeralda and Padre Rogelio resumed their bowed concentration.

"Last night I went with a man who turned out to be a *coyote,*" Amalia said.

Doña Esmeralda looked up. Her voice was touched with a new sadness: "We have *consultas* often with families trying to locate their members, lost somewhere along the borders. *Ay,* such sorrows—"

"We guide them with the *stars.*" Padre Rogelio steered firmly away from the harsh matter. "The stars see everywhere."

"Even into the vehicles of the *coyotes!*" Doña Esmeralda added in her new voice.

"Esmeralda—!" Padre Rogelio started testily.

Doña Esmeralda slumped deeply into her former trance.

Amalia continued: "This *coyote* tricked me. He started doing all kinds of things." Yes, thrust away the false fantasies she had attached to it all—and do it harshly, vomit it all out: "He put his mouth between my legs and—"

The old woman's fingers collapsed from her forehead. Her eyes shot open. "*Que dices, mujer?*" she demanded in a harsh, loud voice. "He did *what?*" She stood up, almost upsetting the table. "Did you slap the pervert, push him away, show your disgust, kick him in the source of his perversion? Disgusting!" she screamed. A vile man. *"Es un demonio!"*

Yes! Amalia welcomed the tirade against Angel. "Then he told me to be grateful!" *Grateful!* The word still assaulted her.

"Filthy, evil, perverted!" Doña Esmeralda was extending her initial outrage.

Padre Rogelio tried to calm her down. She pushed him away. She bit a fingernail, spat it out fiercely. Then she looked at her hand as if in surprise. She seemed to be struggling to regain her composure. She grasped for her chair, sat down, ordered herself.

Amalia felt triumphant at the woman's harsh judgment of Angel. She remained standing. In a firm voice she said to the old man and woman: "Your sign on the window says you'll tell me everything I need to hear. Well, then," her voice was firmer, "I want you to tell me that there will be only happiness in my life now. For my children and for me."

Doña Esmeralda peered up at her.

Padre Rogelio glanced questioningly at the old woman beside him.

Amalia crossed her arms. "I won't pay you if you don't tell me what you promise on your sign."

"There will be only happiness!" the old woman snapped.

"Of course!" the old man agreed.

"I want you to tell me that everything in my life will be in order when I return home."

"The smoke from the incense indicated that," the old woman hissed.

"It formed the dove of harmony," the man said testily.

Amalia placed some money on the table. But she kept her hand there. She inhaled. "And one thing more. I want you to tell me that —"

The old man and the woman gaped at her.

Amalia closed her eyes. "I want you to tell me that miracles exist." And that I saw a silver cross this morning; she did not say the last.

"Who can doubt miracles!" Doña Esmeralda shouted at Amalia.

"No one!" Padre Rogelio's voice was even louder.

"You're liars," Amalia said. "I don't believe anything you've told me. I just needed to hear those words."

Outside, she felt exhilarated. Well, there were some triumphs in life after all — and this was one of them! She walked briskly now. Whatever happened this day, there was that!

But very soon, the exhilaration drained into a new frustration as she walked toward her house. What had occurred? She had extorted words — just words — from the *brujos*. She had not even demanded to hear anything possible, only impossible things that couldn't —

She stopped abruptly on the street. She listened, tensely. She looked up at the palm trees. Was a breeze stirring? She thought she had felt it, cooling the perspiration of this long afternoon. No. Yes! — a slight breeze? Enough to push a filmy cloud across the sky, twist it a little here and there? — and return the illusion that had allowed her a feeling of peace for the first moments of the morning? . . . Look! There *was* a smear of a cloud, a wisp abandoned in the blue of a rare clear day. Amalia squinted. The shred of a cloud *had* twisted into . . . a finger! Yes, a long finger! Well, not exactly a finger because where was the hand? Still, no one could deny the finger was pointing to — Directly at —!

The HOLLYWOOD sign in the hills.

Try to make something of *that*! Amalia's ruminations about a second holy sign ended.

Impulsively, she stepped into a liquor store, finally to check the winning Lotto ticket against hers. . . . Not one single number matched! Now *that* deserved a prize, didn't it? She laughed aloud.

Grateful!

The word returned to her from last night, insinuating itself into this day, like the residue of fierce pain, as she returned home.

Along the blocks in her neighborhood, some people were already gathering their mended clothes and old furniture, ending that afternoon's attempts at a yard sale. From an old man — she did this very quickly, before she could decide not to — she bought some old-fashioned plastic flowers that still had some of their original waxy sheen.

In the yard of the junior high school that Gloria went to, just blocks away from her house, some young men were playing basketball. Amalia welcomed the sounds of young life. She paused on the sidewalk. Through the wire fence that enclosed the yard, she faced the concrete basketball court surrounded by grass that wasn't green but wasn't yellow either.

There were six young men playing, about Juan's age. One had

removed his shirt, the others wore their white undershirts. The boys arched their bodies as they played, bouncing the ball away from each other, tossing it.

Amalia imagined Juan among them, that he was that good-looking young man without a shirt, his body gleaming with healthy sweat. Look how expertly he dodged the others. Now he was bouncing the basketball — tap, tap, tap. Then, with a graceful twist, his brown body shot up into the air, reaching up to the net and —

Ping!

A gunshot!

Blood erupted from the boy's chest.

The basketball, poised on the rim for seconds, dropped into the net.

The boy fell to the concrete.

On the court the others flung themselves to the ground.

Only later would Amalia realize that she had seen a car screech away, had seen, in a flash, swirls of colored fire painted on its side, had heard a young voice yell out the name of the gang that had fired: "From the Vatos of Seventh Street!"

Not able to move yet, clutching the plastic flowers she had just bought, now Amalia could only stare at the playground where the shirtless young man lay sprawled in a growing blossom of blood.

11

♦　　　♦

*A*MALIA WAS NOT sure how long she stood near the playground. But she knew she heard police sirens, and then those of an ambulance. She knew she saw the boy carried away on a stretcher, his face covered. She felt surrounded by waiting violence. There was a gang in the area and with it would come constant fear. Tonight on television she might hear the name of the dead young man, another death among those summed up daily now. What would the mother of the dead boy be doing right now, as somber officials approached to tell her her son was dead? Returning from work perhaps, and certainly tired.

And what of the mother of the boy who had murdered —?

That intruded sharply into Amalia's thoughts. She remembered Chuco's mother for the first time since she had seen her outside the courtroom where Manny was being tried. Had Chuco died? If so, then Manny —

She had to push all that away — and the vision of the bloodied boy. Even so, as she rushed away from where more people were gathering near the boy's blood in the playground, her thoughts were saturated with sadness, on this day that seemed even stiller as she crossed the street toward her house. She would have welcomed even a breath of the terrible Sant' Anas, just to stir something, push away this waiting stillness.

"'Amá . . . 'Amita!"

"*M'ijo!*" She answered, as always, the recurring impression that her dead son was calling out to her with the cherished endearment. But this time it was as if he were exhorting her to — She opened her purse. She held the sealed envelope from the public attorney. Then she pushed it back.

She had reached her stucco bungalow. Released from the filtering shadows of morning, it looked harsh. Yes, the units were crumbling, only vagrant flowers survived, dirt was smothering the dying grass. Even the sidewalk was cracking toward the back of the court. Her eyes followed the ominous split along the concrete, toward the plant from which she had plucked the poisoned flower she had put in her hair earlier. Was it really a weed? Had Mrs. Huerta lied?

She went to check, past her unit, to the back of the court. She was astonished. She did not even bother with the dubious plant because the rosebush nearby had produced —

A blossom!

Was it possible she had missed it this morning, perhaps because it had just begun to open? She stared at it. It was small, with only a few petals — but it was alive!

The second sign!

Hope sprang — strange, foreign to her — as powerful and asser- tive as, once, when — A memory had brushed her mind, a time when she had hoped — For what? The memory was gliding away. What had she ever really hoped? Of course she had sometimes wished the Texas dust storms would stop, things like that, but really hoped? — for something that would permit her some choice that would alter the dogged line of her life? No. . . . Still, the memory which had already fled had left some warmth inside her heart, a warmth quickly chilled.

By another memory? What memory? What memories? Why was she remembering the time she had dressed Manny as an angel to march in the Posadas, the same time she knew she would have made a much more beautiful Sacred Mother than the woman cho- sen to play her? Certainly that chilly night had contained no hope. Amalia's memories moved back: Was it this one? Christmas Eve, and Teresa placed the Holy Child in the manger, a beautiful doll-child, the Holy Mother impeccable beside him. . . . She searched through vagrant memories for one. Then all vanished.

Amalia touched the new rose, to restore her first reaction of joy. Hadn't Bernadette, in that movie, been picking flowers when the Blessed Mother stepped forward? Amalia looked around. Every- thing was so hushed! She waited a few more seconds.

When she entered her house, everything looked shabbier than when she had left it. Especially the artificial flowers. She stared down at the ones she had just bought. How could they have lost their sheen so quickly? A feeble rose had managed to push its way into life on a dying bush outside — that was all that had changed. She abandoned the plastic flowers on the table where Teresa's La Dolorosa had once stood.

With his back to her, and still shirtless, the way he had gone out, Juan sat watching a movie on television, a silly comedy in which people were falling all around. But he was not laughing. So sad, my handsome son is so sad, Amalia thought. Aware of her, he turned. He's a man now, Amalia knew, again, in wonder. "Has —?" she started.

"Yeah, Raynaldo's been back — twice." Juan understood quickly. "Don't worry, he said he'd be back in a while."

Amalia was annoyed by a vaguely accusing tone. "I was going to ask if your sister's back," she revised.

"No." Juan never liked to be questioned about his sister. "But a woman called —"

Milagros! She did know where Rosario was. No, it would just be one of the people she worked for, wanting her to work on a different day. "Did she speak in English or Spanish?" she asked anyway.

"Spanish."

It had to be Milagros. But, then, two of her employers did speak Spanish, mangled Spanish —

Juan had turned off the television. Standing, he faced Amalia. "Have you opened that letter?"

His bluntness made her answer, "Yes," because now she was sure he thought the letter from the public attorney was about him, or Gloria.

"I told the cops I didn't have no mother," Juan said angrily.

"What!" She felt attacked, accused.

Juan let his words stand. Then he added: "So they wouldn't contact you. I knew they would, they're pigs. So now you know."

"Yes. That you're in trouble for drugs," Amalia said. In the raid at school that he had told her about, and a gang would be involved.

"You lied!" Juan was enraged. "You haven't read the damn letter — or it's not about me."

Only now, when his face flushed with anger, did she notice that the bruise on his forehead would leave a small scar. She wished she could shut the trap she had set for him because now she had to ask words she didn't want to ask. "What are you in trouble for, Juan?"

"I'm not."

When the telephone rang, Juan turned away as if to leave the house.

At the same time that she picked up the telephone, Amalia commanded her son, "Don't leave, I have more to say."

"I got things to tell *you* ... Mom," Juan challenged back. He moved toward the converted back porch, where Manny had slept.

"Amalia —"

"Rosario!" Even over the telephone, even with only one word having been spoken — her name — Amalia recognized her friend's voice.

"Milagros left a message that you'd come looking for me. Have they contacted you about Jorge or me?"

Then she *was* in trouble. Amalia felt cheated — she had wanted to turn to her friend for help. "No. I just wanted to see you, I miss our talks —"

"I miss you, too, *corazón.*" The tension in Rosario's voice eased. "I have to hurry, I'm in a booth, Milagros leaves messages for me at this store —"

"I'll call you there —"

"I just want to say good-bye."

"But it's *Jorge* who's in trouble." Amalia allowed herself to assert only that.

"Then you *have* heard something." The urgency returned.

"Only that the women at the factory think he killed a *coyote.*" Amalia thought of Angel.

"Jorge killed a *migra,*" Rosario said quietly. Then her words burst out in anger: "The bastard deserved to die. Jorge paid a *coyote* to bring his youngest son with his wife across the border, and —" Her voice stumbled with rage. "They had to take the dangerous route across the hills because the *migra* now patrol with horses, flood the border with lights." She rushed more words, as if that way to thrust the ugly spectacle away, find relief from it. "Hundreds of people from San Diego drive there each night to add their car lights, shout their support, while desperate people are netted rushing the border — and now snipers wait for them. Yesterday a twelve-year-old boy was killed —"

With a shudder, Amalia remembered the men and women she had seen trapped by uniformed men of the border patrol in the blackened Rio Grande, remembered the drowned girl. But that was years ago. Things had to have changed.

Rosario had paused, regained control of her voice: "Jorge's son made it across the border with his wife and some others, and then the *coyote* surrendered them to a *migra* agent who paid him for them, bragged about how many people he captured." She had gasped the last words. Then her voice slowed with weariness. "Jorge couldn't find out what became of his son, the wife — probably separated, in some detention camp." Her voice was hardly audible: "You take so much and then you explode and say, *no más* — no more — and Jorge did. He stalked that savage *migra,* in San Ysidro, and Jorge made him kneel the way they had forced him to do at the factory, and then Jorge executed him."

"And you've sheltered Jorge, that's all. But *you* didn't —"

"I was with him all along," Rosario said quietly. "And when one of their own is killed, they become even more savage." She sighed. "Jorge's gone, he had to disappear — somewhere. Now I have to become invisible, too, *corazón.*" Rosario laughed: "That's not hard when they've never really seen us."

"I'll ask God and the Holy Mother to make it possible for you to return to the sewing factory, and then we can visit again." At that moment, Amalia wanted only to restore what had been.

"Amalia, *corazón,* you ask for so little of your powerful God."

"Don't *you* believe, Rosario?" Amalia had to ask. She had to hear her answer, yes, and then God —

"No."

"But without the intervention of the Holy Mother —"

"— you're left to find your own strength, *corazón,*" Rosario said softly, "you don't accept that you *must* be a victim."

"There are miracles —" What Rosario had just said had disoriented Amalia powerfully.

"Those happen only in *fábulas,*" Rosario said. "And we have too many fables."

"But nothing is possible without the help of the Holy Mother, she's the only one who can give us strength. Without her help —" She knew that without the Holy Mother's help she could do nothing.

"Good-bye, *corazón,*" Rosario said.

"I'll pray for you," Amalia insisted, to feel that she would lend holy protection to Rosario, and to try to dissipate the disturbed feelings Rosario's words were arousing.

Silence. Then: "Yes, pray for me. And Jorge," Rosario said.

Amalia hung up, slowly, not wanting to sever the connection yet. This day, this strange day that had seemed to promise ... so much ... was instead exposing only sadness and anger ... this strange day during which she had expected ... so much! Where would it lead, finally?

The thought frightened Amalia and she shivered.

Then she saw Juan leaning against the door, staring at her, waiting, showing her he had not run away from her.

She fired at him: "Are you in trouble for stealing?" Like Salvador! Like Manny! Do I want to know? she wondered.

"I already told you, I'm working, I don't have to steal."

Amalia welcomed the roar of the motorcycle outside. It had stopped what she would have had to ask. There was the sound of agitated voices approaching. Then Gloria was there, looking from Juan to her mother, detecting tension. His long hair tied now into a ponytail, Mick stood behind Gloria.

My daughter is so sexual, Amalia thought. Yes, her breasts will be as lush as mine. She looks like a movie star, yes, like Ava Gardner — no, like Maria Felix. ... Amalia needed urgently to release the tension of the unfinished confrontation with Juan, and there was a strain between Gloria and Mick — she could tell that by the way they stood apart, their raised voices earlier; and so she felt secure in saying to Mick: "*Pues es Mi-goo-ell!*" She mimicked his pronunciation of his father's Mexican name.

"I told you, I'm *Mick* and I don't speak Messican." He slurred the last word, deliberately taunting.

Gloria had smiled at Amalia's mimicking. Good! Amalia needed to spill more anger. "You're ashamed of being Mexican," she confronted Mick from this morning. She watched Gloria carefully, asserting her approval.

"I think he's just ashamed of being himself," Gloria said. She was teasing her hair with a comb. Her dark hair gleamed like a black halo. "Or maybe he just doesn't know what he is — but *I* do." She said to Juan: "You know what Mi-goo-ell is?" She took up her mother's mocking pronunciation. "He's a chickenshit."

"That right, dude? You chickenshit?" Juan taunted Mick.

Amalia did not welcome this language, no; and if she had been alone with her children, she would have protested; but, more, she cherished that she and her children were allied against the hateful young man with his silly earring — and she was glad that Juan was welcoming the split between his sister and Mick. Yes, she felt good, doubly so because her children had never been ashamed of being Mexicans; she had taught them correctly, they were Mexican-Americans, like her. Amalia wanted to assert this allegiance with her son and daughter. "And what do you say to *that* . . . Blondie?" Mick had the darkest hair she had ever seen.

Juan and Gloria doubled over with laughter. "Blondie! El Blondie!" Gloria kept gasping. "Mick is el Blondie!"

"Hey, 'Amá, you got it just right," Juan approved. He placed his arm about Amalia's shoulders.

She had pleased them! Amalia covered her son's hand with hers. With a surge of warmth, she received this sudden closeness between her and her children, the closeness of a good mother and her children — and if God knew anything about her, it was that she was a good mother. These cherished moments would make whatever would follow easier, because her mind kept reminding, My Juan is in trouble with the police. . . . But perhaps, after this close allegiance, Juan would inform her that he had just been reacting in anger to her trap about the letter, suspecting a trap, just that — of course, that was it! — and she would accept it. . . . Exulting in their approval of her, Amalia goaded Mick: "*Oye,* Blondie —" She waited, smiling, to allow Juan's and Gloria's new burst of appreciative laughter. "*Oye,* I bet you don't know that a Mexican — Colón — discovered America — and I bet you don't even know who Juan Diego is."

She waited for Juan and Gloria to volunteer the answers. When they didn't — they were still laughing — she offered for them: "My Juan and my Gloria do." She had told them often enough about Columbus being Mexican — well, Spanish, and not *really* Spanish, she knew, but close enough; and she had told them even more often about the Indian peasant to whom Our Lady of Guadalupe appeared . . . "I bet you're not even Catholic. *Oye,* Blondie," she said, delighting in the fact that Gloria and Juan were now waiting eagerly for her next words, "*eres un* born-again?"

"Huh?"

"You got it right again, 'Amá!" Juan managed to say between roars of laughter.

"How'd you figure it out so quick that Mick's a born-again chicken, 'Amá?" Gloria said.

'Amá! Gloria never called her that anymore. Amalia stopped laughing. This moment was too beautiful. . . . 'Amá. . . . She saw her son and daughter doubled over with laughter, like children, her children. She had made them laugh with her!

"Everyone who drove by the born-again chickenshit today," Gloria was saying between peals of laughter, "Mick thought was after him because he's going out with me and I used to go out with *real* Chicano guys. I told him don't worry, *I'd* straighten it all out." She bent over, searching for something in her boot. "I even walked up to this guy and asked him was he after Mick, and the guy says, 'Who the hell's Mick?' — and you know what Mick said when I told him no one was after him, that he could cool it now?" She stopped laughing for a few moments, shook her head, resumed her laughter.

Was her daughter as tough as she talked? What was she fishing for in her boot? Not a knife, please, not a knife like those she had heard even girls were carrying in the schools. Whatever it was, Gloria now clasped it firmly in her hand.

Juan had waited for his sister to finish. When she didn't, he said in pretended amazement, "Mick can't be *that* chicken. He's a tough dude with his little black shirt and his big bad bike."

"Hell, man, your sister's not worth no hassle." Mick hooked his thumbs into his silver-studded belt, but he backed away from Juan.

Amalia quickly looked at her daughter. Gloria had winced.

But when she spoke, her voice was instantly sure. "You heard the tough dude. That's what he told me earlier."

"You should be proud that my beautiful daughter even glances at you," Amalia said. And she touched Gloria's luscious hair.

"Say that again about my sister, chicken —" Juan advanced toward Mick.

"Don't bother with the chicken," Gloria told Juan, "*he's* not worth the hassle."

"No one who's ashamed of what he is is worth *un centavo,* and that means not worth a penny, Blondie." Amalia basked in Gloria's and Juan's renewed approval.

"Ashamed?" Mick challenged Amalia. "If you mean about all that heritage stuff, yeah!" He waved his hand toward Amalia's Sacred Heart of Jesus, the brightly bleeding Christ. "All that conquered warrior stuff, victim stuff? I get enough of it from my old lady. It's not for me."

Amalia winced. She remembered her own repugnance at the old *beata* draped in veils, crawling on her knees up the church steps on Sunset; remembered Teresa's La Dolorosa, and she remembered — and she felt a sudden sadness — the beautiful mural in East Los Angeles, the proud Indians about to be ambushed by invaders. What had happened to the revolutionaries in muslin? — they had looked just as proud, those men the Indians had been gazing toward. And where were the women? That question, pushed away a distant day, returned. Did they find courage?

"Where's all that pride bullshit got you?" Mick was still aiming at Amalia. "What are you? Just another fuckin' Mexican maid."

"Don't say another goddamn word about our mother, bastard!" Gloria reached out as if to force Mick to face her.

"You fucking chicken. Say one more word about our mother and I'll —" Juan moved toward Mick.

Juan and Gloria were defending her! Amalia felt overwhelmed. Had they ever defended her like this before? Had anyone? Yes, Manny . . . They love me, she thought. How can I have doubted it? — and they know how much I love them. She wished she could hold this moment, stop it, at least make it pause.

Juan's fist struck the side of Mick's face. His hand pulled back, prepared to hit him again.

Fear knotted tightly in Amalia's stomach, and she said, "Leave him alone now, Juan, he's not worth your touching him even with your fist."

Mick felt his bleeding cheek. Startled, he backed away from Juan. At the door he yelled at Amalia, "At least *I* wasn't busted for being a fag, like your son!" Then he ran out.

Her son, a *maricón*? Amalia waited for Juan's denial.

"You told him," Juan accused Gloria quietly.

"I trusted him," Gloria said as softly.

The closeness shattered for Amalia into a million cutting fragments.

For seconds there was only the sound of Mick's motorcycle dying over and over, and then it gasped, started, sped away.

What Gloria had held in her hand had fallen to the floor. Amalia saw it only now. A small pocketknife.

Openly, Gloria picked it up. "Just a file, see?" she answered Amalia's stare. She began filing her long lacquered nails. "Besides, you never know when you're gonna need protection." She said that even more quietly.

Amalia would deal with that later. Now she had to ask Juan, "What did Mick mean . . . about you, Juan?"

Juan turned his back.

"Tell her, Juan," Gloria stood near her brother. "I think she really wants to know."

"Yes, I want you to tell me now that you are not a *maricón*." Amalia closed her eyes. "Tell me that now."

Juan tossed the words at her with sudden defiance. "I was busted for hustling on Santa Monica Boulevard."

"What?" The shirtless young men she had seen on that street, the men in cars picking them up. "What?" Amalia repeated.

"Yeah — I was busted for going with guys for money," Juan answered her look of disbelief.

Amalia stared at the stranger before her. "You're telling me you're a *maricón*." Now he would deny it.

Gloria stood before her mother. "Don't call my brother a queer. That's what those cowards from the Valley called him when they jumped him on the street."

Her son, beaten up by those ugly young men she had seen attacking with bats that night with Raynaldo? She had never allowed any of the men she had lived with even to yell at her children — and Juan had been beaten by strangers? The bruise on his forehead — She felt indignant, but then a wave of new anger, at him, washed over that. "Isn't that what he's telling me?" she asked her daughter. Had they really been so close just moments earlier? "Deny it!" she yelled at Juan.

"No! Whatever you call it, yeah, I am," Juan said.

Amalia needed time. "Get out, Gloria, I don't want you to hear any of this." But she covered her own ears.

"I know all about it . . . Mom. He had to turn to someone, he couldn't turn to you."

Amalia had to sort this all out, draw some reprieve from all that was ganging up on her. But she could find none. "That boy in the garage — that Salvadoran boy —"

"Paco, his name is Paco. I met him in *jail*, he was busted for hustling, too."

"You told me you were working —"

"I am. Listen, that shit you hear on TV? About guys making so much money hustling the streets? Well, it's just cop bullshit so they can keep up their fuckin' roundups. You pick up some extra bucks, get by, that's all." His eyes leveled on hers, aiming his words. "But it's not as bad as what Paco was making hustling Lafayette Park, 'cause Salvadorans and Guatemalans make less because they're more desperate!"

She did not want to hear, she did not want to hear such terrible things! Amalia turned away from Juan. His words pursued her:

"That's why I brought him to the garage, 'cause he didn't have no place. Then you came sneaking up on us and you sent him away," he accused her.

"You're not involved with him!" She faced her son.

"Yeah, I am. We —"

Amalia stopped him. "That was him in the car this morning —"

"Yeah, man — and you know who the driver was?" Juan was shooting his words at her now. "He's a john I know, the guy I called when I was busted. He bailed us out."

"You called a *stranger*."

"If I had called you, you might've just left me there."

He wanted to hurt her. "You are not a *joto*. No son of mine could be."

Gloria laughed bitterly. "Aren't you going to ask him if he's in bad trouble? He'll have to go to court, you know."

To court. The Hall of Justice. When she had visited Manny. The woman who had gotten into the separated line. The young man in the orange uniform in jail. . . . Amalia pushed all that away.

"I'll be okay, first offense," Juan assured himself. "It's a misdemeanor, first time. My friend'll pay the fine for me and Paco, he told us, he's a good guy."

"What are you and Paco going to have to do for his generosity?" The words were harsher than she intended.

"What do you think?" Juan challenged. "You're not so damn innocent."

"It's a sin! Our church and God forbid it!"

"Jesuschrist! What the hell do they teach about divorce?" Gloria demanded.

Amalia frowned. God understood that!

"Dammit, do you ever face anything?" Gloria's words rushed out with renewed rage. "Nothing at all?"

"I don't face lies!" Amalia shouted back.

Gloria shook her head. "You don't even see what's happening right under your eyes with Raynaldo —" She stopped.

Juan looked in surprise at his sister. "What —?"

What had she been about to say? . . . That elusive memory again! It had touched Amalia briefly — that memory of hope. Why now, in these terrible moments? Why did she remember herself as a girl, Gloria's age, a time when there was another girl, the same age, dressed in white . . . ? "You're going to lie to me, Gloria, you've been wanting to do that for some time," Amalia said. She scanned the house Raynaldo had made possible.

"What were you going to say, Gloria?" Juan asked his sister tensely.

Gloria pressed her lips.

"Gloria?" Juan prodded.

"I wasn't going to say nothing," Gloria said.

The evasive memory soothed Amalia during these taut moments: She had been standing by the door in the house she worked in, for rich Mexicans in El Paso, and the girl, her age, dressed in white, held a bouquet; she was a *quinceañera,* a fifteen year old, making her coming-out. But Amalia often remembered *that.* What else did the memory contain? Oh, yes, the girl's mother had been there, and she said —

Juan's voice had become steely: "What about Raynaldo, Gloria?"

Why is Juan staring at me? Amalia wondered. . . . Then the insistent memory mixed with the darkness of a filthy corridor, where Salvador thrust her onto the floor and — How did that connect to the memory of the *quinceañera*? — and to even a tinge of hope!

"I told you. Nothing," Gloria answered Juan. She adjusted her tiny blouse over the bared middle. She returned the knife to her boot.

"What the hell were you about to say, Gloria!" Juan demanded.

Gloria's head snapped back. "Raynaldo's been coming on to me —! Just touching me," she added quickly.

"I'll kill that motherfucker!" Juan said.

"You won't have to, 'cause if he ever again —" Gloria looked at her hand as if she still held the penknife.

Amalia felt her heart had been stifled. At the same time that she wanted to hold her daughter, to protect her — from everything, everything! — she wanted to slap her, for lying, for begrudging her . . . some peace. . . . Then, out of the still-wafting memory, she remembered that the *quinceañera's* bouquet had been white-and-pink carnations. Then a dark memory inundated that one, and she remembered the rancid flowers in the garbage near the door of the dank corridor where Salvador had pushed himself into her. . . . "I don't believe you, Gloria," Amalia said. How could she believe that — about the man who was going to marry her, lighten her worries permanently? — a man who cared for her, yes, loved her, was kind to her, the only one who had never even threatened to strike her, a good provider — *and who loved her children*. . . . The rent would be overdue, the bills unpaid, she would lie awake trying to figure out what to do — *and they needed a father*! . . . "He probably just tried to hug you, didn't he? — and you misunderstood, didn't you? He's an affectionate man, I know that. He loves you like a father." She felt a sudden resurgence of the nausea she had felt earlier, with the *brujos.* "He just tried to hug you, like a father, didn't he, Gloria?"

Gloria said, "Yeah, that's all. That's how it was."

Juan held his eyes on Amalia.

Puzzled, Amalia looked at her two children. She must force herself to stay in control. She had to thwart their stares at her. "I've tried to make the house pretty," she said. "I've tried to make a good life for you."

"Yeah," Gloria said, "it's fucking beautiful here."

Juan laughed harshly.

Could all the closeness have evaporated, just like that? Had it even existed? Amalia's brief composure broke. "Maybe it's not beautiful, but it's a *home*! — and Raynaldo made it possible. My husband has made it possible, remember that!"

"Your lover!" Juan yelled at her. "And what do your church and God think of that?"

"My husband," Amalia asserted.

"You honestly think we believe that crap about you and Raynaldo suddenly getting married, don't you?" Juan said.

"We did get married!"

"Jesuschrist! You think we've never heard you talk about when his divorce is final? — it's a small house, remember?" Gloria said.

"You defended me when Teresa said I wasn't married," Amalia

◆ 185 ◆

reminded them of their loyalty then. And just minutes earlier? Had she misinterpreted that?

"We grew up!" Gloria thrust at her.

"Goddamn it, Mother, can't you face anything? Nothing?" Juan seemed to plead. "Can't you see you were trying to force me to lie about myself? — and that you did force Gloria to lie?"

"She did lie." Amalia stood very straight.

"Jesuschrist, Jesuschrist," Juan shook his head.

"And I want you to tell me that you lied, too, when you said you were a —"

"Fuck off!"

"How dare you speak that language to me?" She raised her hand before her son. She had never slapped her children, never.

His own hand shot up.

She stared at it in shock.

Juan looked startled at his raised hand. "I was just going to stop you from hitting me," he said softly.

"I have never hit you."

His face darkened. He turned his hand over, palm up, toward her. "You want to burn my hand, *Mom,* like you did Manny's?"

Amalia did not know whether she would ever be able to breathe normally again. "It was an accident," she said.

"You held his hand over the burner." Juan's eyes seemed black. "Manny told me and Gloria."

"Never! My son never said one word against me!"

"Just once, 'Amá." Juan's voice was subdued now. "After he ran away, the morning he came back."

Amalia remembered that morning, barely morning, dawn. Manny had sat in the kitchen, his words a dazed whisper, telling her those strange stories. Now, for several moments, an eternity of despair, she could not speak. When she did, her voice was hushed, strange even to her. She faced Juan. "He was on drugs that morning," she said in an even tone. "He didn't know what he was saying." Automatically she had reached for her purse, had already brought out the letter in which Manny expressed his love. "Listen to what your brother wrote to me in his last letter: 'My dearest mamacita — I love you with all my heart —"

"Why don't you read the whole damn letter, why do you just read words from it?" Juan said.

"I've read it all to you." She could hardly hear her own words.

"No, you haven't." Gloria stood with her brother.

Amalia looked at her son and daughter accusing her. "You went through my purse."

"Yes," Juan said.

"To steal from me." That was preferable to believing they had wanted to verify the words she had read.

"No. To read Manny's letter."

"And we did," Gloria said quietly.

Amalia sighed, just sighed.

Then Juan said softly, almost as if he were pleading now, "'Ama . . . 'Amita . . . are you ever going to face that Manny —?" He stopped, as if waiting for her reaction.

Amalia's body had turned rigid. Juan was about to make a monstrous accusation. She knew it, even knew what it would be. She had to stop it, no matter how. *"Puto!"* she shouted at her son.

He reeled back.

"What the hell did you call him?" Gloria demanded.

Amalia could not repeat the despised word. She had never used it before, never even thought it, a word even more demeaning than "queer," much harsher.

"You're the *puta,* mother!" Gloria shouted at her. "You're the fucking bitch-whore."

Amalia lashed her hand ferociously across her daughter's face.

Gloria almost fell back. Quickly she recovered. She slapped Amalia with all her force — and then again.

Juan grabbed his sister. "Gloria!"

Stunned, Amalia touched her face in surprise. But why did the palm of her hand hurt much more than her cheek? She looked at Gloria and Juan as if they would answer that question.

Gloria pulled away from her brother. She screamed at Amalia: "You left our father and you were with one of your men when you burned Manny's hand!"

Teresa had told them that, discovered it somehow, somehow — it couldn't have been her son, not her beloved Manny, Amalia *knew* that. And should she tell Gloria that her father had walked out because her brother was about to be born and that he didn't even know she existed? No, she would never speak that. "I've been a good mother," she heard herself say.

"No, you haven't!" Gloria screamed at her. "You have *not* been a good mother!"

Amalia's heart died. My daughter and my son hate me, she thought. They know nothing about me, nothing about the tenements, freezing rooms, garbage, beatings, the rape, more beatings. And they remember nothing, not about how I took them with me when I went looking for work; they don't remember they were never hungry because I saw to it, and that I was always protecting them. They know nothing about me, she thought in surprise; and she could not tell them anything because it was impossible to speak.

She looked away from her son and her daughter and she stared at a crack in the wall. It looked like a scar, white, jagged. She heard sounds of traffic from outside. There was loud music. She looked back at Juan and Gloria, still facing her. Yes, they hate me. Haven't they ever understood that I've always wanted a father for them? — more than anything else.

The look of rage faded, and Gloria took a step toward her mother. "'Amá, I'm —" Then she ran crying out of the house.

Juan stood before Amalia. He extended his hand toward her. "'Amá," he said softly. "'Amita," he started again, and then, pausing for long moments, he walked slowly away after his sister.

Amalia could hear their voices outside. She heard Gloria's sobs. Then the voices and the sobs faded, moving away.

Amalia sat on the patched couch. The world is coming apart, she thought. I am coming apart.

And then the full memory that had eluded her entered her mind: That distant afternoon, the *quinceañera*'s mother had said to her, "My daughter is fifteen, your age, Amalia, the most beautiful age for a pure girl, the beginning of adulthood, she'll be pure for her husband, she'll wear my own wedding dress." She put her hand tenderly on Amalia: "You should have a *quinceañera* celebration, too. Look how pretty you are, tell your mother that I'll help her out so you can have one." Amalia exulted: I *will* be a *quinceañera,* and then I can have a white wedding, like Teresa's, I'll wear the dress she saved for me. It was then that Amalia decided she would pull out of her body the hideous impurity that Salvador had forced into her. She went home and she threw herself on the floor over and over until she felt the terrible moisture flowing from her legs with blood. Even as she moaned with pain, she knew, I'm pure again, now I can have a white wedding. As she passed out, the pain dissolved and she was the happiest that she had ever been.

"Amalia —" Raynaldo had walked into the stucco bungalow.

Amalia looked at him, this heavyset man with a full mustache pricked with white hairs. She stood up.

Raynaldo put his hands on her shoulders, his fingers inching toward her breasts. He kissed her. "I've missed you, my beautiful Amalia, I'm sorry about last night, it was nothing. I love my Amalia, my lush Amalia," he said.

She pulled away from him. "*Lárgate, desgraciado,*" she said. "Get out of my house, you bastard."

"Your house? *I* pay most of the rent."

"You won't anymore," she said. "Get out. Don't ever even dare to look at my daughter again." She waited for him to demand an explanation, to protest.

Without a word, he walked past her, into the bedroom. She heard him gathering his clothes.

So it was true. She had wanted it not to be. But it was. Would Gloria have used her knife on him? If she herself had had one in that rancid hallway would she have been able to use it on Salvador — or would she still have frozen with terror?

"Amalia?" Raynaldo paused with his clothes.

There were tears in his eyes — the first time she had seen him cry. "*Lárgate, desgraciado.* Don't ever come back," she ordered.

He sighed a long sigh of loss.

And the only man she was sure had ever loved her was gone.

Amalia sat down again. After she had flushed out the child conceived near garbage in a rotten hallway, she lay in a rumpled bed, and she saw Teresa, who stood before her dressed in black. For a feverish moment Amalia thought she was the Mother of Sorrows.

"I'm clean again, 'Amita," Amalia managed to say. "I can wear your wedding dress."

Teresa shook her head solemnly. "You're doubly filthy. You allowed that man to enter your body and you killed your own child." She held a rosary, and her lips quivered.

In her stifling bungalow unit in Hollywood, Amalia remembered Teresa's next words: "Never ask God for anything. Be grateful that He's even permitted you to live."

12

◆   ◆

ALLOWED ONLY NOW into her mind but always there like a dark weight since they had first been spoken, Teresa's words stagnated in the dull heat of Hollywood as Amalia sat on her couch. They stayed like a curse, those words, and so did the ghostly black-veiled image of Teresa, which had faded, that day, into that of the Mother of Sorrows. Now Amalia did what she had done that distant day, what she had done instinctively throughout the years — but she recognized this only now — whenever a sense of the hopelessness she accepted as part of her life threatened to crush her. She closed her eyes to blot out the dark image and evoke another of the cherished Blessed Mother with hands outstretched, not clenched in grief. That always reassured her that however dismal her life became, she was being watched over.

But on this day she was not soothed. The pain of Teresa's words stayed, powerful, entrenched, suffocating.

Only a miracle can save us now.

Those words flowed into Amalia's mind. Where had she heard that? Oh, Ti'ita had said it at the end of this morning's installment of "Camino al Sueño." On her couch, Amalia felt the beginning of a new weariness. Had it ever been possible to find a real father for her children? That question remained on the surface of her mind, as if its answer might resolve everything.

Did God understand why she had never asked for anything since she had hoped for the impossible? She had always assumed His total understanding of her. Could it be that He had not understood? The thought shocked her. Even so, the Holy Mother would have explained to Him. Had the Holy Mother mistaken her not asking as a lack of faith? Did *she* wait to be asked? . . . What would I ask for? That my children come back so I can hold them, she thought. But something that natural — and the Miraculous Mother would know its naturalness — should not require a miracle.

The shattered day taunted Amalia with its early promise, which continued to stir strange longings. *Only a miracle can save us now.* From what? From today, she answered herself. *From my life.*

She ordered her thoughts to halt. But others flowed over them with added sadness. *You are not a good mother!* Gloria's words resounded in her mind. In protest, Amalia tried to resurrect the moments when her children had defended her with such passion.... Had she misunderstood all that? Had it all been anger at Mick, not support of her? That added to her sadness.... *You are not a good mother....* She had slapped her daughter, for the first time. It didn't diminish her regret to remember that her daughter had slapped her.

She *had* to go out! Leave this house echoing with anger. She would go ... Just out!

Pausing only to pick up her purse, she left the stucco bungalow.

Darkening shadows would soon surrender to dusk. On this hot day the sun would loiter on the horizon, phosphorescent orange, strange behind the gathering evening.

Amalia walked familiar blocks. Yard sales had ended, unsold items left outside to become new garbage. She walked past walls scarred with graffiti. She passed the playground where the boy had been killed earlier. She tried not to glance at the crumbling, darkened courtyard where the old woman had confronted her this morning among boys lingering in the shadows of rotting trees.

Days ago, in a periodic city ritual, men mounted on mechanical ladders had sawed off shaggy dead under-leaves of palm trees that lined the streets. The trees looked renewed — Amalia searched for signs of resurrection anywhere — but they also looked even more indifferent to her, with their trimmed branches held so high. No trees in the world should appear to be ignoring you.

A slight vibration —

Holding her breath, Amalia stopped abruptly. Was it an —? That was how earthquakes began, with a slight tremor, a smothered rumbling, and then followed eternal sounds during which the muffled roar stopped or exploded. Amalia looked about the street. Nothing was shaking. Perhaps there had been only a small earthquake. It reassured her when she heard that those small stirrings might relieve some of the pressure under the earth, but it frightened her to hear that they might also augur a much greater one soon after.

She wandered back onto Sunset Boulevard, to see life, other lives she didn't have to worry about. Weekend traffic would soon clog the boulevard. She sat on a bus bench.

Gloria and Juan did not know she had sent Raynaldo away!

That would prove her love to them! The thought acted like a balm on her. Of course, and when they knew that she had sent Raynaldo away, for them, they would realize what a good mother she had been, and was — She was sure they would realize that. And then instantly she wasn't. Only a miracle could give her the strength to understand all that had occurred today, and to face — What!

She opened her purse. She brought out Manny's letter. When she saw the beautifully shaped letters that were almost delicate — how smart her son had been, with hardly any formal education! — she almost gasped with the always-fresh realization of his death, always, always like a first time. She was about to put the letter away, but she held it, and then she read it slowly, all of it, not just the parts she had read over and over, memorized; she read it all for the first time since she had learned her son was dead.

My dearest mamacita —

I love you with all my heart — I'm sorry I cause you pain — your sad because I'm in troble agan but this time I'm goin to do right — I promise in the name of the Blesst Mother you allways comend me to & love so much & who loves you just as much — I'm goin back to school & not make troble & make lots of money to buy you a butiful house — you & me & Gloria & Juan — you wont have to work & everthin will be butiful — Mamita, it was my fault the day of the tatoo & the burn — remember that — Amita, if I thot I would only come out & hurt you again like I have befor I would take myself away — thats how much I love you with all my heart — allways belive that —

Your son who loves you —
Your Manny

Amalia let the letter rest on her lap. She had allowed herself to see what she had always let her eyes glide over, Manny had blotted out some words, and written over them. "*I would take myself away*" instead of — No! Amalia took out the envelope from the public attorney and opened it angrily.

Dear Mrs. Gómez:

I am sorry to relate that ample evidence exists to indicate that your son, Manuel Gómez, did, in all probability, take his own life by tying —

No! Amalia tore up the letter from the public attorney. The heated air was so still that the falling pieces of paper did not even flutter.

She closed her eyes. In that second she heard a car screech and stop, idling on the curb. She pushed herself against the bench. She saw a carload of ugly young men with shaved heads. Had she seen them before? Their faces twisted in angry laughter. She felt her face struck by something moist, stringy, the oily remains of gnawed chicken. The garbage flung at her streaked her face, a piece of skin slipped down her chest. With a cry, she thrust it away but it had already stained the ruffle across her shoulders. She wiped her face. The car raced away. Out of it, words exploded within laughter:

"*Fuckin' Mexican bitch!*"

Anger consumed her.

She felt herself walking, hurrying, running to a sudden destination.

Amalia faced the Blessed Mother in the alcove of the church she had been in earlier on Sunset Boulevard.

When she had rushed in moments before, she had not even paused to cover her head, had not moistened her fingers in holy water to perform a sign of the cross. She had walked directly to the shrine.

Now she stood before the Holy Mother.

Within the silver sheen of the mosaic shell behind her, the statue was bathed in an even greater radiance, now that glimmering church lights were being turned on. Shadows draping the back part of the alcove intensified the glow of candles. Flames flickered reflections on the statue's face. Stained-glass windows shone with the last of this day's light, barely illuminating one side of the face. Saturday evening Mass was over, and only a few people remained scattered about the vast church. But Amalia had not noticed them.

Standing very straight before the Holy Mother, she said aloud:

"*I*—!"

Only that word broke the trance of rage that had propelled her back to the church. Her body lost its rigidity. It sagged under a terrible weight. She bowed her head. She lowered herself to her knees. She adjusted the top of her dress higher over her chest. She searched her purse for her lacy handkerchief. With it, she covered her head, tucking her hair behind her ears, subduing the lush mass. She made a slow sign of the cross, and then another, to compensate for the one she had not made when she first entered. Then she began her favored prayer, honoring Mary, blessed among women:

> *Dios te salve, reina y madre,*
> *madre de misericordia,*
> *vida y dulzura,*
> *esperanza nuestra . . .*

The prayer would soothe her, quell the recurring surges of anger aroused in the street by the tossed garbage; it would help her regain her natural breathing. Full of reverence and trust, the prayer would still the shaking of her body. That's why she had turned to Mary, the Holiest of Queens, Mother of Mercy. And Mary would—

The Blessed Mother was not even looking at her!

Amalia had glanced up and had had the impression that the glassy eyes of the Madonna had glided beyond her to the back of the alcove, toward the candles lit in her honor. Bewildered by that sense of avoidance, Amalia stared intently at the statue until it seemed—yes, in a split second during which a candle blinked— that the Madonna had looked at her—

> *Vuelve a nosotros esos tus ojos . . .*

—and quickly away!

Amalia lowered her head again and closed her eyes, to stop the false impression. Of course the Blessed Mother was looking at her—who could doubt it? She always looked at the devoted. The prayer just uttered asserted that she would turn her eyes full of mercy toward—Amalia glanced up to ascertain that.

The Blessed Mother's stare remained distant.

Amalia closed her eyes even more tightly. She started another prayer:

> *. . . bendita tu eres entre todas las mujeres . . .*

And who could question that Our Lady *was* the most blessed among women? Amalia reiterated to herself. Just look at the dazzling white radiance within which she stood in this sacred alcove. Amalia's eyes had shot open onto the full spectacle of the Queen of Heaven's shrine. And why shouldn't the Holy Mother bask in such resplendent glory? She was, after all, the Immaculate Conception.

The Immaculate Conception! *And* the Virgin Mother!

In awe of that enormity, Amalia bowed her head lower, and prayed, "*Bendito es el fruto de tu purísimo vientre . . .*" The Sacred Mother's womb was pure —

Not sullied by rape in a dark hallway near garbage!

At the same moment the thought invaded her mind, Amalia had stared up again at the Virgin Mother. Impassive! Amalia placed her hands on her forehead, pressing her palms over her eyes, resuming her prayers, words out of sequence now: "*O clemente, O piadosa, O dulce siempre Virgen Maria —*"

You're a woman, like me!

In reaction against that assaulting thought, Amalia reached for the top of her dress, to raise it still farther. But she didn't — her fingers had brushed her full breasts. She allowed her eyes to flow back to the statue.

Your woman's body is always hidden in the folds of your beautiful dress.

The Blessed Mother had turned away from her. No, the weaving light of candles had created that impression. No, there *had* been a frown on the face, and then the Madonna had looked away. . . . Amalia crushed her thoughts with holy words: "*Dios te salve Maria, llena eres de gracia . . . muéstranos a Jesús . . .*"

I lost a son, too!

> *Santa Maria, Madre de Dios,*
> *Santa Maria, Madre de Dios,*
> *Santa —*

Blessed Mary, Mother of God, Blessed — Amalia repeated those words over and over to control her thoughts. Apprehensive, she forced herself not to look up at the Holy Mother's face. Her eyes swept along the panels of the stations of the cross on the walls and stopped on the station she often prayed before: The Virgin Mother knelt weeping before her martyred son, and she was dressed in white, embraced by light that blazed on a golden halo; her face was bright with tears.

Your tears are too beautiful!

Ruega por nosotros . . .

My tears hurt when my Manny was born and even more when he died and nothing that hurts that much can be beautiful. . . . Amalia clasped her hands against her forehead, blocking her persistent thoughts:

> *Dios te salve Maria . . . reina y madre . . .*
> *esperanza nuestra . . . reina y madre . . .*
> *Virgen Maria —*

Queen and mother! Virgin Mary! Amalia raised her head and tried to meet the vacant stare of the statue.

You don't look pained!

> *—y después de este destierro muéstranos*
> *a Jesús . . .*

But you *are* a mother, and so you *had* to hurt when your child wrenched from inside you, you had to scream when flesh was ripped from you —

> *Bendita tu eres entre todas las mujeres . . .*
> *tu purísimo vientre . . .*

Or didn't you feel pain because you conceived purely? — a Virgin mother, your womb always untainted, unhurting. . . . *Then how can you be blessed among women!*

The head of the Holy Mother tilted as the light of fading candles wove shadows over her face. She seemed to be —

Waiting.

For what? You want something from me, Amalia was certain at that moment. What? Proof of my devotion? How can I give more evidence of that than that I'm here, now, before you, kneeling, on this terrifying day? You want me to assert my belief even more? I have never doubted, not you, nor God, nor your Holy Son. What do you want me to say? I've confessed everything, to you. Everything. . . .

Amalia looked down into her hands. *What do you want me to*

say? That I knew my mother was dead when she stopped coughing and I went into her room? . . . That memory entered her mind easily, without hurt. I was tired from all those days of my Manny's death. Certainly there was no sin in wanting to rest before I tended to another death. Amalia inhaled. And Teresa was cruel, she added quietly.

In a fleeting glance, Amalia thought she saw on the Madonna's face . . . understanding. No, the face had remained the same, still waiting.

That isn't what you want me to say. Amalia bowed her head. I sent away that boy Juan brought to live in the garage. I saw his sad young eyes. I knew what I was doing was cruel. But I also knew what was really involved between him and my son. . . .

The Madonna's face had not changed, expressionless in the veiled light.

But how can you accuse me for that when your Holy Church forbids it all so harshly? She screamed that silently because she had remembered why she had thought that she might have seen the men who had flung trash at her — it had not been them, no, but men like them — on Santa Monica Boulevard beating up the loitering young men on the street, young men like her Juan — and they would call him the filthy names she had called him. The realization struck her with such force that she gasped. And even as she imagined herself among the women in the separated line outside the Hall of Justice, she thought: I won't turn against my son. I won't turn against him no matter what!

> *O clemente, O piadosa, O dulce*
> *siempre Virgen Maria. . . .*

She realized she had raised her head to the statue. The face had . . . softened. Then why did it still wait? . . . Would you have wanted me to stay with Salvador, keep a child born from the filth he pushed into me? Sinful to divorce that despised man who beat me daily? Sinful to try to find someone else for my children? And for me, for me, too. Is *that* sinful?

Amalia's eyes strained to intercept any new expression on the statue's face. But the glow of expiring candles was diminishing and a dark translucence masked the face. Still, she thought she could feel the eyes becoming —

I knew Raynaldo was coming to desire Gloria, but only that, and I knew she sensed it, but I didn't want to hear about any of it because I never suspected anything more — *I swear that!* — and I was sure it would pass and I wouldn't have to give up the little we have, because it's so hard without help, for all of us — and that's why I tried to force her to say it wasn't true, to force it not to be true, but when I knew today there was more, I sent him away. And that doesn't mean I don't want to find another man, a good man who will love my children. And me. . . .

Against the silver mosaic shell, the statue had become a waiting outline.

Amalia cupped her face in her hands. I burned my Manny's hand. . . . Her body sagged lower with the enormous weight of the years-long horror of that day. She huddled against herself, to warm her body, which had suddenly turned cold, cold. . . . I burned my Manny's hand that day I was with a man and he walked in on me. All I saw was his gang tattoo, like Salvador's, I *saw* Salvador while I held my son's wrist over the burner, and then I screamed when I realized what I was doing. And I licked his burn to soothe it. *You heard him say it wasn't my fault and he even wrote it to me in his last letter!* . . . But it was my fault. . . . In the church now, Amalia heard her son's words from that day: ". . . 'Ama, 'Amita, if I thought I would hurt you again, I would kill myself" — and those were the words he had blotted out in his letter, masking them from jailers.

My son killed himself.

Amalia felt a gasp knot in her throat. She tried to stifle it, but it came, a long, long, deep moan. Then she closed her eyes. She said silently to the memory of her dead son, But I know you loved me, just as I know you never doubted how much I love you.

When she looked up, the face of the Madonna seemed . . . kind. But why was it withdrawing into the candlelit mistiness?

Don't turn away! You saw it all! — the ugliness, the humiliations, you saw my father, and you saw Salvador discard me against the trash, you heard Teresa accuse and hate me and you just listened, and I raised my children the only way I knew — and didn't you see Gabriel and the others walk out on me as if I was nothing? — and that man last night said I should be grateful! Grateful for what?

For the garbage flung at me?

The Madonna's eyes seemed about to pull away.

Face me!

The Madonna glanced down.

You gave me no choice!

More candles flickered dead and a shroud of darkness veiled the statue's face.

Amalia's fingers clenched into fists. She stood up. The covering on her head fell to the floor. Suddenly dizzy, she grasped the back of a pew in order to remain standing.

The features on the statue cleared.

I have not lost my faith! It has grown stronger, strong enough for me to speak to you like this.

The Blessed Mother faced her.

Amalia inhaled.

That is why I am finally able to plead with you — pray for — supplicate — ask for — I am hoping for — I beg — I ask — I need —

She yanked her hand away from the supporting pew.

I demand a miracle!

It zigzagged with bolts of red-and-blue neon lightning, a purplish blocks-long structure held together by a network of chromy escalators that floated within plastic tunnels lit ice-blue.

After she had left the church, Amalia stood on Sunset Boulevard before a bench with a picture of Marilyn Monroe. She stepped into a bus that stopped there, and it took her to the huge shopping complex at the edge of Beverly Hills.

During a time when she had worked nearby, she had seen the giant mall from the windows of the bus she rode, had seen the flow of well-dressed people gliding on its many escalators to its various levels.

Today, she got off at the far corner, across from a hotel that proclaimed its name over uniformed attendants waiting on decorated guests:

MA MAISON SOFITEL

Night remained as still and hot as the day. As she crossed the street toward the shopping center, Amalia noticed for the first time that over a restaurant situated at one corner was what looked like the rear half of a car, inclined, as if it had crashed intact through the roof. Clusters of pretty young people — so many wore shorts, she always marveled about Anglos — waited on iron-grilled benches to enter the restaurant:

THE HARD ROCK CAFÉ

Through open gold-painted doors, rock music burst out. Amalia glanced inside. The front portion of the car mounted on top of the roof outside penetrated the ceiling into the restaurant to assert the impression that it had crashed through. What an odd decoration, Amalia thought, where everything was so peaceful. Just look: Along the block, newspaper racks, not toppled over, not broken into, lined the sidewalk neatly.

She floated up an escalator. From it she looked away through its clear enclosing tunnel, and she saw the vista of the vast city of angels. From this distance, it was all cleansed by night, turned lustrous by thousands of lights. Many people — young, old, men, women, children, teenagers — roamed the complex. They all seemed to be laughing or about to laugh, talking spiritedly as they spilled from the various escalators onto the various floors. Even several young Mexicans here looked prosperous and untroubled in this enclosed world of chrome.

She walked into the first level of the great complex. She looked about, at stores with names that were impressive, no matter what they meant. Black letters engraved on white, scrawly letters carving their own designs, letters intertwined through swirls of colors:

EPISODE . . . LAURA ASHLEY . . . LENZO OF PARIS

Shops opened into the promenade, no need for barred gates here. Amalia paused before a store that sold only leather clothes, black leather dresses and skirts. Imagine that. And they were all ugly, who'd want them? Next to that store and in a window that was almost invisible, fur-draped mannequins exhibited underclothes. Well, she was no prude, anyone could tell that, but *that* was . . . Nearby, a young man hungrily kissed a girl — probably aroused by the display, Amalia thought. . . . She turned away when the boy looked at her, said something to the girl, and she looked, too. . . . A round jewelry store in the middle of the mall was filled with glittering things. A toy shop over there displayed stuffed animals so large they wouldn't fit in her kitchen. She was shocked, and then delighted, to see that expensive sunglasses in a wall-less store looked exactly like the free ones she had thrown away this morning — and they *were* probably the same.

EDDIE BAUER ... ABERCROMBIE & FITCH ... PRIVILEGE

She continued along the promenade. She idled before shops. Now, *that* dress would look beautiful on her Gloria, with her hazel eyes that at times had a tinge of green like her mother's — and for Juan, that fringed jacket!

Amalia looked at the real plants and exotic flowers — lavender-pink with gold specks on the petals — that grew in encircled areas at regular intervals on the floor. Large, round declines carved into the promenade were outlined by upholstered benches, where people sat casually, surrounded by cascades of flowering vines.

Amalia noticed three Oriental men with cameras eyeing her. Because ... Well, obviously because she looked good among so many ordinary women, no matter how well dressed they were; why else? If the men had asked, she might have considered posing for a picture. As she walked on, she wished she had one of those pink flowers to put in her hair. A group of girls breezed by, so pretty, so sweet, so unworried. She heard a burst of giggling when they passed her. So free of cares! Oh, she wished Gloria had been one of them; but in that same moment, she saw again — a sharp intrusion in her mind now — the knife her daughter had dropped.

She walked on hurriedly. Within a huge circular plastic column, an elevator rose, people seemed suspended within it. Amalia stared up, at the arched ceiling of the mall. It had a translucent brightness like that of an eternally perfect day. Over the railings on upper floors, shoppers peered down onto the spill of shops. For a moment, she felt dizzy, dazed. Then she saw a sturdy middle-aged man looking at her. Of course — here among all these skinny women a lush woman would naturally stand out. She walked past the man, to indulge the warmth of his admiration; and why shouldn't she? But he quickly turned away.

She sat on one of the comfortable benches. She imagined she had come here to shop, was exhausted from all she had purchased, would soon resume her buying —

If I can dredge up the energy!

— and she would have everything delivered. . . . What would Rosario say about this place? . . .

Think, Amalia!

Why did she remember that? — what Rosario had exhorted her to do, that day at the sewing factory when the older woman had been so troubled. Think about what? She thought of Milagros in the building that an earthquake might shrug off indifferently. What an odd thought. Why that now? . . . But Rosario had said more, in her urgent call today . . .

Quickly, Amalia went to the window of another dress shop. *Finally,* a dress pretty enough for her! She could duplicate it. She studied it closely. Why, she might even have sewn a part of it at the sewing factory! Of course, for her, she'd make it puffier, give it a ruffle, lower the bosom, who wouldn't? In rehearsal, she adjusted the top of her own dress.

After this interlude what?

LLADRO JEWELERS . . . BELGRACIA . . . MIGNON

Controlling her breath — why was she becoming breathless? — she walked to a large tree in one of the cultivated enclosures. She was sure this one would be artificial, its leaves were much too glossy to be real.

I have to decide —

She touched the leaves of the tree. They *were* real, and not a single one was browning. What care they took with these trees in this clean, marvelous place!

CONTEMPO . . . ATMOSPHERE . . . THE LIMITED

Find your own strength. Why were Rosario's words still disturbing her? No, not those, others. *You don't accept that you must —*

She hurried to a jewelry store. She was admiring a display of wedding rings when she noticed that there was a guard there. He had a gun in a holster by his side. Even idle, that prop of violence chilled her, and she moved away from it and from his stare, to a shop that contained only crystal — think of it, only crystal! — graceful forms that transformed every speck of light into a buried jewel. With new, beautiful silk flowers, that vase would — A well-dressed woman was studying her. Well, certainly because —

Because I look out of place. That's why that boy and those men looked at me, why those girls laughed, why that guard stared. She looked down at her dress. It was wrinkled, sweaty. The oily smear had become an ugly dark stain. . . . Suddenly she felt so exhausted she leaned against a window — and pulled away instantly, afraid she might dirty it. Her body ached. *From the intense moments in the church before the Holy Mother when she had* — She must not remember that! Hurriedly she smoothed her dress, brushed her fingers through the dark fullness of her hair.

She stood in the middle of the mall, aware of herself in this glistening palace. So many people . . . Did they see her? Yes, they saw a woman who looked out of place, tired, perspiring. But did they see her? She felt invisible — *Rosario had used that word* — as if her life had been lived unseen and in silence filled with unheard cries. She let her head rest against a wall. *I have to think.* She realized, only when her blurred vision opened onto smears of bright colors, that for a moment she had shut her eyes.

After this interlude what?

She breathed deeply, deeply, to gather some energy so she could walk on. *I have to fight this weariness — to face — to cope with — What? Tomorrow, and the next day . . . if I can find the strength to move!* At that same moment, she felt the paralyzing fatigue she recognized so well, which came with fear and then surrender. Why now, when there was no discernible threat — just these strange thoughts? *If I can push this tiredness away, thrust away this* — But a feeling of defeat was invading her.

Overcome by exhaustion, she sat down on one of the smaller benches scattered about the mall. Could she ever move again? *She had to.* Would she ever again be able to make more than the outline of movements? She *must* because — *Manny is dead, Gloria and Juan are alive, and they've been suffering also, through the death of their brother and so much more, but I haven't seen that, haven't even seen them at times, nor that they've been suffering for me, too, because they do love me, and that's why they defended me, and they need me, because without my help they can't survive, I have to teach them how to survive — if I can find how to myself —*

If I can find the strength.

Blessed Mother, give me the necessary strength. Did she speak that or only think it? She knew she hadn't really prayed it; it was just the faintest lingering echo, all that was left of her impossible demand in the church. She knew that because even as she had thought it or whispered it, she had felt her body lean sideways on

the bench, and her weariness grew. She would just close her eyes —
they were already closed — just recline on this bench —

Decide . . .

She pushed herself awake, forcing her eyes to stay open. She
tried to sit up, but she couldn't. She propped her hands on the
bench and she made herself stand. She walked back to the escalator.
Near the landing, huddled against a corner wall painted red and
purple, an old woman slept on rags.

Amalia realized now that she had taken the escalator to the
ground level — because she was standing, just standing on the
street, near where a fleet of taxis waited for shoppers. Among them
a man straddled a motorcycle. His face was concealed by a dark
helmet. Amalia turned back to the ascending steps. Go up again? —
just float? Or she might go home. Or she might —

She heard aroused voices, loud running footsteps, a sharp cracking sound, then a scream, another! Suddenly people pushed back
against the railings of the escalators, against walls. Then everything
was in jagged motion, a whorl of faces and bodies and colors.

An earthquake!

Amalia wondered where to move and could not. Now there
would be the angered growl of the earth, the huge mall would collapse, and screaming people would —

But the ground under her was not moving. It was some other
violence that was occurring. Had she heard a gunshot?

Hands grabbed her. A man was pulling her against him. His arm
locked under her neck. He pressed a gun against her temple. He
pushed her with him toward the curb, toward the motorcycle, its
engine suddenly roaring.

"Put your gun down, I'll shoot her!" Those words exploded in
Amalia's ear. The man holding her had shouted them up at an
armed guard who had appeared at the top of the escalator. In a rush
of awareness, Amalia knew that this man with crazed eyes — she
saw them now or remembered them — had robbed a store, perhaps killed someone, and he might kill her, but if she did not move,
did not breathe, did not protest —

At the top of the escalator, the guard lowered his gun to his side.
"Stay back!" he yelled at horrified faces, excited faces, startled faces.

Everyone pulled back, and then there was a sudden clearing
within which Amalia stood alone with the man holding a gun to her
head. She was aware of moisture on her face, her arms, her chest.

His perspiration? Hers? She thought she heard or felt the beating of the man's heart. Her own? No, it was not hers because her body had been clamped by fear, frozen.

Police sirens erupted. Squad cars halted with a shriek. The man waiting on the motorcycle started to flee, the machine spun, he fell. A policeman held a gun over him. Two other uniformed men crouched by the side of their black car.

"Put your fucking guns down!" the man holding her ordered. "I'll shoot her, I swear it!"

Amalia felt the cold iron pressed harder against her head. Within a strange, long, loud silence, she heard a tiny click at her ear and she knew that a bullet had slid into position to kill her. She would succumb, yes, finally, to the weariness of this long, terrible day that contained the weight of her whole life, she would surrender —

"*No more!*" she screamed.

And she thrust the man away from her with ferocious strength and she flung her body on the concrete.

The man fell back against the escalator. The gun he had held against Amalia's head recoiled. A bullet ripped out of its chamber, and then there was another shot, this one from behind the black cars. Blood exploded from the man's chest. Another shot hurled out of his gun, and Amalia saw a beautiful spatter of blue shards that glinted and gleamed like shooting stars as they fell on splotches of red like huge blossoms, red roses. For a second she stared in wonder.

The wounded man dropped a bag he had been clutching, and he crumpled on the stairs moving up. Then his body slid back down onto the sidewalk. He staggered two steps and collapsed so close to Amalia that she felt the convulsions of his body as he strained toward her and she saw that he was young.

"Bless . . . me."

Amalia sat up. Had he whispered that to her? Had she imagined it? Had someone nearby spoken it? Her hand rose. Angrily, she stopped her movement. But her hand remained raised. Bless a man who had wanted to kill her? Her hand sliced away in an angry jerk. And then in compressed seconds she knew with startling clarity that by blessing this dying man she would be blessing away something in her whose death she welcomed. Her hand finished its slow benediction.

The man's head fell onto her lap.

More sirens. An ambulance. More police cars. Several men in uniforms carrying stretchers. . . . A man with a television camera, another man following with a glaring light —

Amalia was aware of people staring at her — in surprise that she was alive, she knew. And she was, she *was* alive. Suddenly she was crying for the first time since her son had died.

Men moved cautiously toward the bleeding man's body.

Amalia stared up at the sky.

A bright light smashed at her. A television light? — She was aware of men crouching, kneeling, lifting the body beside her, and someone was asking her something. There was another burst of light — A camera? — She was about to close her eyes against the flashing lights but she didn't because before her she saw a dazzling white radiance enclosed in a gleam of blue and within it on a gathering of red roses stood —

Within it stood —

The Blessed Mother, with her arms outstretched to her.

Amalia held her breath and closed her eyes in awe. The Miraculous Mother *was* there.

When she opened her eyes again, a medic was leaning over her and asking, "Are you all right, lady, are you sure you're all right?"

The Miraculous Mother had appeared to her. Suddenly with all her heart Amalia knew that, and she would never doubt it, because a surge of energy was sweeping away all her fear and she felt resurrected with new life.

Triumphant, she stood up. "Yes!" she said exultantly, "I am sure!"